D0722411

DATE DUE

JA 29'90	OC 28'90	
AP 23		
NO 26'90	NY 27'97	
DE 7'90 MR 27'07		
MY 13'94		
MR 17'95		
AO 3'95		
OC 21'95		
DE 23'95		
NO 18'97		

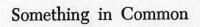

Something in Common

Other fiction by Langston Hughes:

Not Without Laughter
The Ways of White Folks
Laughing to Keep from Crying
Simple Speaks His Mind
Simple Takes a Wife
Simple Stakes a Claim
Tambourines to Glory
The Best of Simple
Simple's Uncle Sam
The Sweet Flypaper of Life
    (with Roy DeCarava)

Something in Common and Other Stories

By

LANGSTON HUGHES

American Century Series

HILL AND WANG * NEW YORK

A division of Farrar, Straus and Giroux

FIRST AMERICAN CENTURY SERIES EDITION FEBRUARY 1963

The following stories are from *The Ways of White Folks*, reprinted with the permission of the publisher, Alfred A. Knopf, Inc.: "Little Dog," "A Good Job Gone," "Father and Son."

The following stories are from *Laughing to Keep from Crying*, published by Henry Holt and Company: "Who's Passing for Who?," "African Morning," "Pushcart Man," "Why, You Reckon?," "Saratoga Rain," "Spanish Blood," "Heaven to Hell," "Sailor Ashore," "Slice Him Down," "Tain't So," "Professor," "Powder-White Faces," "Rouge High," "On the Way Home," "Mysterious Madame Shanghai," "Never Room with a Couple," "Tragedy at the Baths," "Trouble with the Angels," "On the Road," "Big Meeting," "Something in Common."

The following stories are from *The Langston Hughes Reader*, published by George Braziller, Inc.: "Thank You, M'am," "Patron of the Arts."

Other stories originally appeared in magazines as follows: "Gumption" in *The New Yorker* under the title "Oyster's Son"; "The Gun" in the *Brooklyn Daily Eagle* under the title "Flora Belle"; "Sorrow for a Midget" in *The Literary Review* of Fairleigh Dickinson University; "Fine Accommodations" in *Negro Story* under the title "The Negro in the Drawingroom"; "Breakfast in Virginia" in *Common Ground* under the title "I Thank You for This."

Sixteenth printing, 1987

To Gwendolyn

My thanks to The New Yorker, Esquire, The American Spectator, Story Magazine, Common Ground, The American Mercury, The Crisis, The Literary Review, Negro Story, Stag, The African, Scribner's Fiction Parade, *and* The Brooklyn Daily Eagle *in whose pages some of these stories first appeared.*

Contents

Something in Common

Thank You, M'am

She was a large woman with a large purse that had everything in it but a hammer and nails. It had a long strap, and she carried it slung across her shoulder. It was about eleven o'clock at night, dark, and she was walking alone, when a boy ran up behind her and tried to snatch her purse. The strap broke with the sudden single tug the boy gave it from behind. But the boy's weight and the weight of the purse combined caused him to loose his balance. Instead of taking off full blast as he had hoped, the boy fell on his back on the sidewalk and his legs flew up. The large woman simply turned around and kicked him right square in his blue-jeaned sitter. Then she reached down, picked the boy up by his shirt front, and shook him until his teeth rattled.

After that the woman said, "Pick up my pocketbook, boy, and give it here."

She still held him tightly. But she bent down enough to permit him to stoop and pick up her purse. Then she said, "Now ain't you ashamed of yourself?"

Firmly gripped by his shirt front, the boy said, "Yes'm."

The woman said, "What did you want to do it for?"

The boy said, "I didn't aim to."

She said, "You a lie!"

By that time two or three people passed, stopped, turned to look, and some stood watching.

"If I turn you loose, will you run?" asked the woman.

"Yes'm," said the boy.

"Then I won't turn you loose," said the woman. She did not release him.

"Lady, I'm sorry," whispered the boy.

"Um-hum! Your face is dirty. I got a great mind to wash your face for you. Ain't you got nobody home to tell you to wash your face?"

"No'm," said the boy.

"Then it will get washed this evening," said the large woman, starting up the street, dragging the frightened boy behind her.

He looked as if he were fourteen or fifteen, frail and willow-wild, in tennis shoes and blue jeans.

The woman said, "You ought to be my son. I would teach you right from wrong. Least I can do right now is to wash your face. Are you hungry?"

"No'm," said the being-dragged boy. "I just want you to turn me loose."

"Was I bothering *you* when I turned that corner?" asked the woman.

"No'm."

"But you put yourself in contact with *me*," said the woman. "If you think that that contact is not going to last awhile, you got another thought coming. When I get through with you, sir, you are going to remember Mrs. Luella Bates Washington Jones."

Sweat popped out on the boy's face and he began to struggle. Mrs. Jones stopped, jerked him around in front of her, put a half nelson about his neck, and continued to drag him up the street. When she got to her door, she dragged the boy inside, down a hall, and into a large kitchenette-furnished room at the rear of the house. She switched on the light and left the door open. The boy could hear other roomers laughing and talking in the large house. Some of their doors were open, too, so he knew he and the woman were not alone. The woman still had him by the neck in the middle of her room.

She said, "What is your name?"

"Roger," answered the boy.

"Then, Roger, you go to that sink and wash your face," said the woman, whereupon she turned him loose—at last. Roger looked at the door—looked at the woman—looked at the door—*and went to the sink.*

"Let the water run until it gets warm," she said. "Here's a clean towel."

"You gonna take me to jail?" asked the boy, bending over the sink.

"Not with that face, I would not take you nowhere," said the woman. "Here I am trying to get home to cook me a bite to eat, and you snatch my pocketbook! Maybe you ain't been to your supper either, late as it be. Have you?"

"There's nobody home at my house," said the boy.

"Then we'll eat," said the woman. "I believe you're hungry —or been hungry—to try to snatch my pocketbook!"

"I want a pair of blue suede shoes," said the boy.

"Well, you didn't have to snatch *my* pocketbook to get some suede shoes," said Mrs. Luella Bates Washington Jones. "You could of asked me."

"M'am?"

The water dripping from his face, the boy looked at her. There was a long pause. A very long pause. After he had dried his face and not knowing what else to do, dried it again, the boy turned around, wondering what next. The door was open. He could make a dash for it down the hall. He could run, run, run, *run!*

The woman was sitting on the day bed. After a while she said, "I were young once and I wanted things I could not get."

There was another long pause. The boy's mouth opened. Then he frowned, not knowing he frowned.

The woman said, "Um-hum! You thought I was going to say *but,* didn't you? You thought I was going to say, *but I didn't snatch people's pocketbooks.* Well, I wasn't going to say that." Pause. Silence. "I have done things, too, which I would not tell you, son—neither tell God, if He didn't already know. Everybody's got something in common. So you set down while I fix us something to eat. You might run that comb through your hair so you will look presentable."

In another corner of the room behind a screen was a gas plate and an icebox. Mrs. Jones got up and went behind the screen. The woman did not watch the boy to see if he was going to run now, nor did she watch her purse, which she left behind her on the day bed. But the boy took care to sit on the far side of the room, away from the purse, where he thought she could easily see him out of the corner of her eye if she wanted to. He did not trust the woman *not* to trust him. And he did not want to be mistrusted now.

"Do you need somebody to go to the store," asked the boy, "maybe to get some milk or something?"

"Don't believe I do," said the woman, "unless you just want sweet milk yourself. I was going to make cocoa out of this canned milk I got here."

"That will be fine," said the boy.

She heated some lima beans and ham she had in the icebox, made the cocoa, and set the table. The woman did not ask the boy anything about where he lived, or his folks, or anything else that would embarrass him. Instead, as they ate, she told him about her job in a hotel beauty shop that stayed open late, what the work was like, and how all kinds of women came in and out, blondes, redheads, and Spanish. Then she cut him a half of her ten-cent cake.

"Eat some more, son," she said.

When they were finished eating, she got up and said, "Now here, take this ten dollars and buy yourself some blue suede shoes. And next time, do not make the mistake of latching onto *my* pocketbook *nor nobody else's*—because shoes got by devilish ways will burn your feet. I got to get my rest now. But from here on in, son, I hope you will behave yourself."

She led him down the hall to the front door and opened it. "Good night! Behave yourself, boy!" she said, looking out into the street as he went down the steps.

The boy wanted to say something other than, "Thank you, m'am," to Mrs. Luella Bates Washington Jones, but although his lips moved, he couldn't even say that as he turned at the foot of the barren stoop and looked up at the large woman in the door. Then she shut the door.

Little Dog

Miss Briggs had a little apartment all alone in a four-story block just where Oakwood Drive curved past the park and the lake. Across the street, beneath her window, kids skated in winter, and in the spring the grass grew green. In summer, lovers walked and necked by the lake in the moonlight. In fall brown and red-gold leaves went skithering into the water when the wind blew.

Miss Briggs came home from work every night at eight, unless she went to the movies or the Women's Civics Club. On Sunday evenings she sometimes went to a lecture on Theosophy. But she was never one to gad about, Miss Briggs. Besides, she worked too hard. She was the head bookkeeper for the firm of Wilkins and Bryant, Wood, Coal and Coke. And since 1930, when they had cut down the staff, she had only one assistant. Just two of them now to take care of the books, bills, and everything. But Miss Briggs was very efficient. She had been head bookkeeper for twenty-one years. Wilkins and Bryant didn't know what they would do without her.

Miss Briggs was proud of her record as a bookkeeper. Once the City Hall had tried to get her, but Wilkins and Bryant said, "No, indeed. We can pay as much as the city, if not more. You stay right here with us." Miss Briggs stayed. She was never a person to move about much or change jobs.

As a young girl she had studied very hard in business school. She never had much time to go out. A widowed mother, more or less dependent on her then, later became completely dependent—paralyzed. Her mother had been dead for six years now.

Perhaps it was the old woman's long illness that had got Miss Briggs in the habit of staying home every night in her youth, instead of going out to the theatre or to parties. They had never been able to afford a maid even after Miss Briggs became so well paid—for doctors' bills were such a drain, and in those last

5

months a trained nurse was needed for her mother—God rest
her soul.

Now, alone, Miss Briggs usually ate her dinner in the Rose
Bud Tea Shoppe. A number of genteel businesswomen ate
there, and the colored waiters were so nice. She had been served
by Joe or Perry, flat-footed old Negro gentlemen, for three or
four years now. They knew her tastes, and would get the cook
to make little special dishes for her if she wasn't feeling very
well.

After dinner, with a walk of five or six blocks from the Rose
Bud, the park would come into view with its trees and lights.
The Lyle Apartments loomed up. A pretty place to live, facing
the park. Miss Briggs had moved there after her mother died.
Trying to keep house alone was just a little too much. And there
was no man in view to marry. Most of them would want her
only for her money now, at her age, anyway. To move with another woman, Miss Briggs thought, would be a sort of sacrilege
so soon after her mother's death. Besides, she really didn't know
any other woman who, like herself, was without connections.
Almost everybody had somebody, Miss Briggs reflected. Every
woman she knew had either a husband, or sisters, or a friend
of long standing with whom she resided. But Miss Briggs had
nobody at all. Nobody.

Not that she thought about it very much. Miss Briggs was
too used to facing the world alone, minding her own business,
and going her own way. But one summer, while returning from
Michigan, where she had taken her two weeks' rest, as she came
through Cleveland, on her way from the boat to the station
there, she happened to pass a dog shop with a window full of
fuzzy little white dogs. Miss Briggs called to the taxi man to
stop. She got out and went in. When she came back to the taxi,
she carried a little white dog named Flips. At least, the dealer
said he had been calling it Flips because its ears were so floppy.

"They just flip and flop," the man said, smiling at the tall
middle-aged woman.

"How much is he?" Miss Briggs asked, holding the puppy up.

"I'll let you have him for twenty-five dollars," the man said.

Miss Briggs put the puppy down. She thought that was a pretty steep price. But there was something about Flips that she liked, so she picked him up again and took him with her. After all, she allowed herself very few indulgences. And somehow, this summer, Miss Briggs sort of hated going back to an empty flat—even if it did overlook the park.

Or maybe it was because it overlooked the park that had made it so terrible a place to live lately. Miss Briggs had never felt lonely, not *very* lonely, in the old house after her mother died. Only when she moved to the flat did her loneliness really come down on her. There were some nights there, especially summer nights, when she thought she couldn't stand it, to sit in her window and see so many people going by, couple by couple, arms locked; or else in groups, laughing and talking. Miss Briggs wondered why she knew no one, male or female, to walk out with, laughing and talking. She knew only the employees where she worked, and with whom she associated but little (for she hated to have people know her business). She knew, of course, the members of the Women's Civics Club, but in a cultural sort of way. The warmth of friendship seldom mellowed her contacts there. Only one or two of the clubwomen had ever called on her. Miss Briggs always believed in keeping her distance, too. Her mother used to say she'd been born poor but proud, and would stay that way.

"Folks have to amount to something before Clara takes up with them," old Mrs. Briggs always said. "Men'll have a hard time getting Clara."

Men did. Now, with no especial attractions to make them keep trying, Miss Briggs, tall and rail-like, found herself left husbandless at an age when youth had gone.

So, in her forty-fifth year, coming back from a summer boardinghouse in Michigan, Miss Briggs bought herself a little white dog. When she got home, she called on the janitor and asked him to bring her up a small box for Flips. The janitor, a towheaded young Swede, brought her a grapefruit crate from the A & P. Miss Briggs put it in the kitchen for Flips.

She told the janitor to bring her, too, three times a week, a

dime's worth of dog meat or bones, and leave it on the back
porch where she could find it when she came home. On other
nights Flips ate dog biscuits.

Flips and Miss Briggs soon settled on a routine. Each evening
when she got home she would feed him. Then she would take
him for a walk. This gave Miss Briggs an excuse for getting out,
too. In warm weather she would walk around the little lake
fronting her apartment with Flips on a string. Sometimes she
would even smile at other people walking around the lake with
dogs at night. It was nice the way dogs made things friendly.
It was nice the way people with dogs smiled at her occasionally
because she had a dog, too. But whenever (as seldom happened)
someone in the park, dog or no dog, tried to draw her into conversation, Miss Briggs would move on as quickly as she could
without being rude. You could never tell just who people were,
Miss Briggs thought, or what they might have in their minds.
No, you shouldn't think of taking up with strange people in
parks. Besides, she was head bookkeeper for Wilkins and Bryant, and in these days of robberies and kidnapings maybe they
just wanted to find out when she went for the payroll, and how
much cash the firm kept on hand. Miss Briggs didn't trust people.

Always, by ten o'clock, she was back with Flips in her flat.
A cup of hot milk then maybe, with a little in a saucer for Flips,
and to bed. In the morning she would let Flips run down the
back steps for a few minutes, then she gave him more milk, left
a pan of water, and went to work. A regular routine, for Miss
Briggs took care of Flips with great seriousness. At night when
she got back from the Rose Bud Tea Shoppe, she fed him biscuits; or if it were dog meat night, she looked out on the back
porch for the package the janitor was paid to leave. (That is,
Miss Briggs allowed the Swede fifty cents a week to buy bones.
He could keep the change.)

But one night, the meat was not there. Miss Briggs thought
perhaps he had forgotten. Still, he had been bringing it regularly for nearly two years. Maybe the warm spring this year

made the young janitor listless, Miss Briggs mused. She fed Flips biscuits.

But two days later, another dog meat night, the package was not there either. "This is too much!" thought Miss Briggs. "Come on, Flipsy, let's go downstairs and see. I'm sure I gave him fifty cents this week to buy your bones."

Miss Briggs and the little white beast went downstairs to ask why there was no meat for her dog to eat. When they got to the janitor's quarters in the basement, they heard a mighty lot of happy laughter and kids squalling, and people moving. They didn't sound like Swedes, either. Miss Briggs was a bit timid about knocking, but she finally mustered up courage with Flips there beside her. A sudden silence fell inside.

"You Leroy," a voice said. "Go to de door."

A child's feet came running. The door opened like a flash and a small colored boy stood there grinning.

"Where—where is the janitor?" Miss Briggs said, taken aback.

"You mean my papa?" asked the child, looking at the gaunt white lady. "He's here." And off he went to call his father.

Surrounded by children, a tall broad-shouldered Negro of perhaps forty, gentle of face and a little stooped, came to the door.

"Good evenin'," he said pleasantly.

"Why, are you the janitor?" stammered Miss Briggs. Flips had already begun to jump up on him with friendly mien.

"Yes'm, I'm the new janitor," said the Negro in a softly beautiful voice, kids all around him. "Is there something I can help you to do?"

"Well," said Miss Briggs, "I'd like some bones for my little dog. He's missed his meat two times now. Can you get him some?"

"Yes'm, sure can," said the new janitor, "if all the stores ain't closed." He was so much taller than Miss Briggs that she had to look up at him.

"I'd appreciate it," said Miss Briggs, "please."

As she went back upstairs she heard the new janitor calling in his rich voice, "Lora, you reckon that meat store's still open?" And a woman's voice and a lot of children answered him.

It turned out that the store was closed. So Miss Briggs gave the Negro janitor ten cents and told him to have the meat there the next night when she came home.

"Flips, you shan't starve," she said to the little white dog, "new janitor or no new janitor."

"Wruff!" said Flips.

But the next day when she came home there was no meat on the back porch either. Miss Briggs was puzzled, and a little hurt. Had the Negro forgotten?

Scarcely had she left the kitchen, however, when someone knocked on the back door and there stood the colored man with the meat. He was almost as old as Miss Briggs, she was certain of it, looking at him. Not a young man at all, but he was awfully big and brown and kind looking. So sort of sure about life as he handed her the package.

"I thought some other dog might get it if I left it on the porch," said the colored man. "So I kept it downstairs till you come."

Miss Briggs was touched. "Well, thank you very much," she said.

When the man had gone, she remembered that she had not told him how often to get meat for the dog.

The next night he came again with bones, and every night from then on. Miss Briggs did not stop him, or limit him to three nights a week. Just after eight, whenever she got home, up the back porch steps the Negro would come with the dog meat. Sometimes there would be two or three kids with him. Pretty little brown-black rather dirty kids, Miss Briggs thought, who were shy in front of her, but nice.

Once or twice during the spring the janitor's wife, instead, brought the dog meat up on Saturday nights. Flips barked rudely at her. Miss Briggs didn't take to the creature, either. She was fat and yellow, and certainly too old to just keep on having children as she evidently did. The janitor himself was so solid and big and strong! Miss Briggs felt better when he brought her the bones for her dog. She didn't like his wife.

That June, on warm nights, as soon as she got home, Miss Briggs would open the back door and let the draft blow through. She could hear the janitor better coming up the rear stairs when he brought the bones. And, of course, she never said more than good evening to him and thank you. Or here's a dollar for the week. Keep the change.

Flips ate an awful lot of meat that spring. "Your little dog's a regular meat-hound," the janitor said one night as he handed her the bones; and Miss Briggs blushed, for no good reason.

"He does eat a lot," she said. "Good night."

As she spread the bones out on paper for the dog, she felt that her hands were trembling. She left Flips eating and went into the parlor, but found that she could not keep her mind on the book she was reading. She kept looking at the big kind face of the janitor in her mind, perturbed that it was a Negro face, and that it stayed with her so.

The next night she found herself waiting for the dog meat to arrive with more anxiety than Flips himself. When the colored man handed it to her, she quickly closed the door, before her face got red again.

"Funny old white lady," thought the janitor as he went back downstairs to his basement full of kids. "Just crazy about that dog," he added to his wife. "I ought to tell her it ain't good to feed a dog so much meat."

"What do you care, long as she wants to?" asked his wife.

The next day in the office Miss Briggs found herself making errors over the books. That night she hurried home to be sure and be there on time when he brought the dog meat up, in case he came early.

"What's the matter with me," she said sharply to herself, "rushing this way just to feed Flips? Whatever is the matter with me?" But all the way through the warm dusky streets, she seemed to hear the janitor's deep voice saying, "Good evenin'," to her.

Then, when the Negro really knocked on the door with the

meat, she was trembling so that she could not go to the kitchen to get it. "Leave it right there by the sink," she managed to call out. "Thank you, Joe."

She heard the man going back downstairs sort of humming to himself, a kid or so following him. Miss Briggs felt as if she were going to faint, but Flips kept jumping up on her, barking for his meat.

"Oh, Flips," she said, "I'm so hungry." She meant to say, "*You're* so hungry." So she repeated it. "You're so hungry! Heh, Flipsy, dog?"

And from the way the little dog barked, he must have been hungry. He loved meat.

The next evening, Miss Briggs was standing in the kitchen when the colored man came with the bones.

"Lay them down," she said, "thank you," trying not to look at him. But as he went downstairs, she watched through the window his beautifully heavy body finding the rhythm of the steps, his big brown neck moving just a little.

"Get down!" she said sharply to Flips barking for his dinner.

To herself she said earnestly, "I've got to move. I can't be worried being so far from a meat shop, or from where I eat my dinner. I think I'll move downtown where the shops are open at night. I can't stand this. Most of my friends live downtown anyway."

But even as she said it, she wondered what friends she meant. She had a little white dog named Flips, that was all. And she was acquainted with other people who worked at Wilkins and Bryant, but she had nothing to do with them. She was the head bookkeeper. She knew a few women in the Civics Club fairly well. And the Negro waiters at the Rose Bud Shoppe.

And this janitor!

Miss Briggs decided that she could not bear to have this janitor come upstairs with a package of bones for Flips again. She was sure he was happy down there with his portly yellow wife and his house full of children. Let him stay in the basement, then, where he belonged. She never wanted to see him again, never.

The next night Miss Briggs made herself go to a movie before coming home. And when she got home, she fed Flips dog biscuits. That week she began looking for a new apartment, a small one for two, her and the dog. Fortunately, there were plenty to be had, what with people turned out for not being able to pay their rent—which would never happen to her, thank God! She had saved her money. When she found an apartment, she deposited the first month's rent at once. On her coming Saturday afternoon off, she planned to move.

Friday night, when the janitor came up with the bones, she decided to be just a little pleasant to him. Probably she would never see him again. Perhaps she would give him a dollar for a tip, then. Something to remember her by.

When he came upstairs, she was aware a long time of his feet approaching. Coming up, up, up, bringing bones for her dog. Flips began to bark. Miss Briggs went to the door. She took the package in one hand. With the other she offered the bill.

"Thank you so much for buying bones for my little dog," she said. "Here, here is a dollar for your trouble. You keep it all."

"Much obliged, m'am," said the astonished janitor. He had never seen Miss Briggs so generous before. "Thank you, m'am! He sure do eat a heap o' bones, your little dog."

"He almost keeps me broke buying bones," Miss Briggs said, holding the door.

"True," said the janitor. "But I reckon you don't have much other expenses on hand, do you? No family and all like me?"

"You're right," answered Miss Briggs. "But a little dog is so much company, too."

"Guess they are, m'am," said the janitor, turning to go. "Well, good night, Miss Briggs. I'm much obliged."

"Good night, Joe."

As his broad shoulders and tall brown body disappeared down the stairs, Miss Briggs slowly turned her back, shut the door, and put the bones on the floor for Flipsy. Then suddenly she began to cry.

The next day she moved away as she had planned to do. The janitor never saw her any more. For a few days the walkers in

the park beside the lake wondered where a rather gaunt middle-
aged woman who used to come out at night with a little white
dog had gone. But in a very short while the neighborhood had
completely forgotten her.

Rock, Church

Elder William Jones was one of them rock-church preachers
who know how to make the spirit rise and the soul get right.
Sometimes in the pulpit he used to start talking real slow, and
you'd think his sermon warn't gonna be nothing; but by the
time he got through, the walls of the temple would be almost
rent, the doors busted open, and the benches turned over from
pure shouting on the part of the brothers and sisters.

He were a great preacher, was Reverend William Jones. But
he warn't satisfied—he wanted to be greater than he was. He
wanted to be another Billy Graham or Elmer Gantry or a resur-
rected Daddy Grace. And that's what brought about his down-
fall—ambition!

Now, Reverend Jones had been for nearly a year the pastor
of one of them little colored churches in the back alleys of
St. Louis that are open every night in the week for preaching,
singing, and praying, where sisters come to shake tambourines,
shout, swing gospel songs, and get happy while the Reverend
presents the Word.

Elder Jones always opened his part of the services with "In
His Hand," his theme song, and he always closed his services
with the same. Now, the rhythm of "In His Hand" was such
that once it got to swinging, you couldn't help but move your
arms or feet or both, and since the Reverend always took up
collection at the beginning and ending of his sermons, the dancing movement of the crowd at such times was always toward

the collection table—which was exactly where the Elder wanted
it to be.

> *"In His hand!*
> *In His hand!*
> *I'm safe and sound*
> *I'll be bound—*
> *Settin' in Jesus' hand!"*

"Come one! Come all! Come, my Lambs," Elder Jones would
shout, "and put it down for Jesus!"

Poor old washer-ladies, big fat cooks, long lean truck drivers
and heavy-set roustabouts would come up and lay their money
down, two times every evening for Elder Jones.

That minister was getting rich right there in that St. Louis
alley.

> *"In His hand!*
> *In His hand!*
> *I'll have you know*
> *I'm white as snow—*
> *Settin' in Jesus' hand!"*

With the piano just a-going, tambourines a-flying, and people
shouting right on up to the altar.

"Rock, church, rock!" Elder Jones would cry at such intensely lucrative moments.

But he were too ambitious. He wouldn't let well enough
alone. He wanted to be a big shot and panic Harlem, gas
Detroit, sew up Chicago, then move on to Hollywood. He
warn't satisfied with just St. Louis.

So he got to thinking, "Now, what can I do to get everybody
excited, to get everybody talking about my church, to get the
streets outside crowded and my name known all over, even unto
the far reaches of the nation? Now, what can I do?"

Billy Sunday had a sawdust trail, so he had heard. Reverend
Becton had two valets in the pulpit with him as he cast off garment after garment in the heat of preaching, and used up dozens of white handkerchiefs every evening wiping his brow while

calling on the Lord to come. Meanwhile, the Angel of Angelus
Temple had just kept on getting married and divorced and making the front pages of everybody's newspapers.

"I got to be news, too, in my day and time," mused Elder
Jones. "This town's too small for me! I want the world to hear
my name!"

Now, as I've said before, Elder Jones was a good preacher—
and a good-looking preacher, too. He could cry real loud and
moan real deep, and he could move the sisters as no other black
preacher on this side of town had ever moved them before. Besides, in his youth, as a sinner, he had done a little light hustling
around Memphis and Vicksburg—so he knew just how to appeal to the feminine nature.

Since his recent sojourn in St. Louis, Elder Jones had been
looking for a special female Lamb to shelter in his private fold.
Out of all the sisters in his church, he had finally chosen Sister
Maggie Bradford. Not that Sister Maggie was pretty. No, far
from it. But Sister Maggie was well fed, brownskin, good-
natured, fat, and *prosperous*. She owned four two-family houses
that she rented out, upstairs and down, so she made a good living. Besides, she had sweet and loving ways as well as the interest of her pastor at heart.

Elder Jones confided his personal ambitions to said Sister
Bradford one morning when he woke up to find her by his side.

"I want to branch out, Maggie," he said. "I want to be a
really big man! Now, what can I do to get the 'tention of the
world on me? I mean, in a religious way?"

They thought and they thought. Since it was a Fourth of
July morning, and Sister Maggie didn't have to go collect rents,
they just lay there and thought.

Finally, Sister Maggie said, "Bill Jones, you know something
I ain't never forgot that I seed as a child? There was a preacher
down in Mississippi named old man Eubanks who one time got
himself dead and buried and then rose from the dead. Now, I
ain't never forgot that. Neither has nobody else in that part of
the Delta. That's something mem'rable. Why don't you do
something like that?"

"How did he do it, Sister Maggie?"

"He ain't never told nobody how he do it, Brother Bill. He say it were the Grace of God, that's all."

"It might a-been," said Elder Jones. "It might a-been."

He lay there and thought awhile longer. By and by he said, "But honey, I'm gonna do something better'n that. I'm gonna be nailed on a cross."

"Do, Jesus!" said Sister Maggie Bradford. "Jones, you's a mess!"

Now, the Elder, in order to pull off his intended miracle, had, of necessity, to take somebody else into his confidence, so he picked out Brother Hicks, his chief deacon, one of the main pillars of the church long before Jones came as pastor.

It was too bad, though, that Jones never knew that Brother Hicks (more familiarly known as Bulldog) used to be in love with Sister Bradford. Sister Bradford neglected to tell the new reverend about any of her former sweethearts. So how was Elder Jones to know that some of them still coveted her, and were envious of him in their hearts?

"Hicks," whispered Elder Jones in telling his chief deacon of his plan to die on the cross and then come back to life, "that miracle will make me the greatest minister in the world. No doubt about it! When I get to be world renowned, Bulldog, and go traveling about the firmament, I'll take you with me as my chief deacon. You shall be my right hand, and Sister Maggie Bradford shall be my left. Amen!"

"I hear you," said Brother Hicks. "I hope it comes true."

But if Elder Jones had looked closely, he would have seen an evil light in his deacon's eyes.

"It will come true," said Elder Jones, "if you keep your mouth shut and follow out my instructions—exactly as I lay 'em down to you. I trust you, so listen! You know and I know that I ain't gonna *really* die. Neither is I *really* gonna be nailed. That's why I wants you to help me. I wants you to have me a great big cross made, higher than the altar—so high I has to have a step-ladder to get up to it to be nailed thereon, and you to nail me. The higher the better, so's they won't see the straps—cause I'm gonna be tied on by straps, you hear. The light'll be rose-colored so they can't see the straps. Now, here you come and do the nailin'—nobody else but you. Put them nails *between* my fingers and toes, not through 'em—*between*—and don't nail too deep. Leave the heads kinder stickin' out. You get the jibe?"

"I get the jibe," said Brother Bulldog Hicks.

"Then you and me'll stay right on there in the church all night and all day till the next night when the people come back to see me rise. Ever so often, you can let me down to rest a little bit. But as long as I'm on the cross, I play off like I'm dead, particularly when reporters come around. On Monday night, hallelujah! I will rise, and take up collection!"

"Amen!" said Brother Hicks.

Well, you couldn't get a-near the church on the night that Reverend Jones had had it announced by press, by radio, and by word of mouth that he would be crucified *dead,* stay dead, and rise. Negroes came from all over St. Louis, East St. Louis, and mighty nigh everywhere else to be present at the witnessing of the miracle. Lots of 'em didn't believe in Reverend Jones, but lots of 'em *did.* Sometimes false prophets can bamboozle you so you can't tell yonder from whither—and that's the way Jones had the crowd.

The church was packed and jammed. Not a seat to be found, and tears were flowing (from sorrowing sisters' eyes) long before the Elder even approached the cross which, made out of new lumber right straight from the sawmill, loomed up behind the pulpit. In the rose-colored lights, with big paper lilies that Sister Bradford had made decorating its head and foot, the cross looked mighty pretty.

Elder Jones preached a mighty sermon that night, and hot as it was, there was plenty of leaping and jumping and shouting in that crowded church. It looked like the walls would fall. Then when he got through preaching, Elder Jones made a solemn announcement. As he termed it, for a night and a day, his last pronouncement.

"Church! Tonight, as I have told the world, I'm gonna die. I'm gonna be nailed to this cross and let the breath pass from me. But tomorrow, Monday night, August the twenty-first, at twelve P.M., I am coming back to life. Amen! After twenty-four hours on the cross, hallelujah! And all the city of St. Louis can be saved—if they will just come out to see me. Now, before I mounts the steps to the cross, let us sing for the last time "In His Hand"—cause I tell you, that's where I am! As we sing, let everybody come forward to the collection table and help this church before I go. Give largely!"

The piano tinkled, the tambourines rang, hands clapped. Elder Jones and his children sang:

> *"In His hand!*
> *In His hand!*
> *You'll never stray*
> *Down the Devil's way—*
> *Settin' in Jesus' hand!*
>
> *Oh, in His hand!*
> *In His hand!*
> *Though I may die*
> *I'll mount on high—*
> *Settin' in Jesus' hand!"*

"Let us pray." And while every back was bowed in prayer, the Elder went up the stepladder to the cross. Brother Hicks followed with the hammer and nails. Sister Bradford wailed at the top of her voice. Woe filled the Amen Corner. Emotion rocked the church.

Folks outside was saying all up and down the street, "Lawd, I wish we could have got in. Listen yonder at that noise! I wonder what *is* going on!"

Elder Jones was about to make himself famous—that's what was going on. And all would have went well had it not been for Brother Hicks—a two-faced rascal. Somehow that night the Devil got into Bulldog Hicks and took full possession.

The truth of the matter is that Hicks got to thinking about Sister Maggie Bradford, and how Reverend Jones had worked up to be her No. 1 Man. That made him mad. The old green snake of jealousy began to coil around his heart, right there in the meeting, right there on the steps of the cross. Lord, have mercy! At the very high point of the ceremonies!

Hicks had the hammer in one hand and his other hand was full of nails as he mounted the ladder behind his pastor. He was going up to nail Elder Jones on that sawmill cross.

"While I'm nailin', I might as well nail him right," Hicks thought. "A low-down klinker—comin' here out of Mississippi to take my woman away from me! He'll never know the pleasure of my help in none o' his schemes to out-Divine Father! No, sir!"

Elder Jones had himself all fixed up with a system of straps round his waist, round his shoulder blades, and round his wrists and ankles, hidden under his long black coat. These straps fastened in hooks on the back of the cross, out of sight of the audience, so he could just hang up there all sad and sorrowful-looking, and make out like he was being nailed. Brother Bulldog Hicks was to plant the nails *between* his fingers and toes. Hallelujah! Rock, church, rock!

Excitement was intense.

All went well until the nailing began. Elder Jones removed his shoes and socks and, in his bare black feet, bade farewell to his weeping congregation. As he leaned back against the cross and allowed Brother Hicks to compose him there, the crowd began to moan. But it was when Hicks placed the first nail between Elder Jones's toes that they became hysterical. Sister Bradford outyelled them all.

Hicks placed that first nail between the big toe and the next toe of the left foot and began to hammer. The foot was well strapped down, so the Elder couldn't move it. The closer the head of the nail got to his toes, the harder Hicks struck it. Finally the hammer collided with Elder Jones's foot, *bam* against his big toe.

"Aw-oh!" he moaned under his breath. "Go easy, man!"

"Have mercy," shouted the brothers and sisters of the church. "Have mercy on our Elder!"

Once more the hammer struck his toe. But the all-too-human sound of his surprised and agonized "Ouch!" was lost in the tumult of the shouting church.

"Bulldog, I say, go easy," hissed the Elder. "This *ain't* real."

Brother Hicks desisted, a grim smile on his face. Then he turned his attention to the right foot. There he placed another nail between the toes, and began to hammer. Again, as the nail went into the wood, he showed no signs of stopping when the hammer reached the foot. He just kept on landing cruel metallic blows on the Elder's bare toenails until the preacher howled with pain, no longer able to keep back a sudden hair-raising cry. The sweat popped out on his forehead and dripped down on his shirt.

At first the Elder thought, naturally, that it was just a slip of the hammer on the deacon's part. Then he thought the man must have gone crazy—like the rest of the audience. Then it hurt him so bad, he didn't know what he thought—so he just hollered, "Aw-ooo-oo-o!"

It was a good thing the church was full of noise, or they would have heard a strange dialogue.

"My God, Hicks, what are you doing?" the Elder cried, staring wildly at his deacon on the ladder.

"I'm nailin' you to the cross, Jones! And man, I'm *really* nailin'."

"Aw-oow-ow! Don't you know you're hurting me? I told you *not* to nail so hard!"

But the deacon was unruffled.

"Who'd you say's gonna be your right hand when you get down from here and start your travelings?" Hicks asked.

"You, brother," the sweating Elder cried.

"And who'd you say was gonna be your left hand?"

"Sister Maggie Bradford," moaned Elder Jones from the cross.

"Naw she ain't," said Brother Hicks, whereupon he struck the Reverend's toe a really righteous blow.

"Lord, help me!" cried the tortured minister. The weeping

congregation echoed his cry. It was certainly real. The Elder *was* being crucified!

Brother Bulldog Hicks took two more steps up the ladder, preparing to nail the hands. With his evil face right in front of Elder Jones, he hissed: "I'll teach you nappy-headed jack-leg ministers to come to St. Louis and think you-all can walk away with any woman you's a mind to. I'm gonna teach you to leave my women alone. Here—here's a nail!"

Brother Hicks placed a great big spike right in the palm of Elder Jones's left hand. He was just about to drive it in when the frightened Reverend let out a scream that could be heard two blocks away. At the same time he began to struggle to get down. Jones tried to bust the straps, but they was too strong for him.

If he could just get one foot loose to kick Brother Bulldog Hicks!

Hicks lifted the hammer to let go when the Reverend's second yell, this time, was loud enough to be heard in East St. Louis. It burst like a bomb above the shouts of the crowd—and it had its effect. Suddenly the congregation was quiet. Everybody knew that was no way for a dying man to yell.

Sister Bradford realized that something had gone wrong, so she began to chant the song her beloved pastor had told her to chant at the propitious moment after the nailing was done. Now, even though the nailing was not done, Sister Bradford thought she had better sing:

> *"Elder Jones will rise again,*
> *Elder Jones will rise again,*
> *Rise again, rise again!*
> *Elder Jones will rise again,*
> *Yes, my Lawd!"*

But nobody took up the refrain to help her carry it on. Everybody was too interested in what was happening in front of them, so Sister Bradford's voice just died out.

Meanwhile Brother Hicks lifted the hammer again, but Elder Jones spat right in his face. He not only spat, but suddenly called his deacon a name unworthy of man or beast. Then he let out another frightful yell and, in mortal anguish, called, "Sister Maggie Bradford, lemme down from here! I say, come and get . . . me . . . down . . . *from here!*"

Those in the church that had not already stopped moaning and shouting did so at once. You could have heard a pin drop. Folks were petrified.

Brother Hicks stood on the ladder, glaring with satisfaction at Reverend Jones, his hammer still raised. Under his breath the panting Elder dared him to nail another nail, and threatened to kill him stone-dead with a forty-four if he did.

"Just lemme get loost from here, and I'll fight you like a natural man," he gasped, twisting and turning like a tree in a storm.

"Come down, then," yelled Hicks, right out loud from the ladder. "Come on down! As sure as water runs, Jones, I'll show you up for what you is—a woman-chasing no-good low-down faker! I'll beat you to a batter with my bare hands!"

"Lawd, have mercy!" cried the church.

Jones almost broke a blood vessel trying to get loose from his cross. "Sister Maggie, come and lemme down," he pleaded, sweat streaming from his face.

But Sister Bradford was covered with confusion. In fact, she was petrified. What could have gone wrong for the Elder to call on her like this in public in the very midst of the thing that was to bring him famous-glory and make them all rich, preaching throughout the land with her at his side? Sister Bradford's head was in a whirl, her heart was in her mouth.

"Elder Jones, you means you really wants to get down?" she asked weakly from her seat in the Amen Corner.

"Yes," cried the Elder, "can't you hear? I done called on you twenty times to let me down!"

At this point Brother Hicks gave the foot nails one more good hammering. The words that came from the cross were not to be found in the Bible.

In a twinkling, Sister Bradford was at Jones's side. Realizing at last that the Devil must've done got into Hicks (like it used to sometimes in the days when she knowed him), she went to

the aid of her battered Elder, grabbed the foot of the ladder, and
sent Hicks sprawling across the pulpit.

"You'll never crucify my Elder," she cried, "not for real."
Energetically she began to cut the straps away that bound the
Reverend. Soon poor Jones slid to the floor, his feet too sore
from the hammer's blows to even stand on them without help.

"Just lemme get at Hicks," was all Reverend Jones could
gasp. "He knowed I didn't want them nails that close." In the
dead silence that took possession of the church, everybody heard
him moan, "Lawd, lemme get at Hicks," as he hobbled away
on the protecting arm of Sister Maggie.

"Stand back, Bulldog," Sister Maggie said to the deacon, "and
let your pastor pass. Soon as he's able, he'll flatten you out like
a shadow—but now, I'm in charge. Stand back, I say, and let
him pass!"

Hicks stood back. The crowd murmured. The minister made
his exit. Thus ended the ambitious career of Elder William
Jones. He never did pastor in St. Louis any more. Neither did
he fight Hicks. He just snuck away for parts unknown.

Little Old Spy

A number of years ago, toward the end of one of Cuba's reac-
tionary regimes, on the evening of my second day in Havana,
I realized I was being followed. I had walked too far for the
same little old man, trailing a respectable distance behind me,
to be there accidentally. I noticed him first standing quite close
to me when I stopped to buy a paper at the big newsstand across
from the Alhambra. He seemed to be trying to see what I was
buying.

Then I forgot about him. I walked down the Prado in the
warm dusk, looking at the American tourists on parade, watching the fine cars that passed, and seeing the lights catch fire from

sunset. When I got to the bandstand by the fort at the water-front, I stopped, leaned against the wall, and put my foot out for a ragged little urchin to shine. I was lighting a cigarette when the little old man of the newsstand strolled by in front of me. He stopped a few paces beyond, and called a boy to shine his shoes, too. Even then I thought nothing of his being there. But I did notice his strange getup, the tight suit, the cream-colored spats, and the floppy Panama with its bright band that a youth, but not an old man, could have worn well. He was a queer withered little old Cuban, certainly sixty at least, but dressed like a fop of twenty.

A mile away on the Malecon—for I continued to walk along the sea wall—I looked at my watch and saw the hour approaching seven, when I was to meet some friends at the Florida Café. I turned to retrace my steps. In turning, whom should I face on the sidewalk but the little old man! Then I became suspicious. He said nothing, and strolled on as though he had not seen me. But when I looked back after walking perhaps a quarter-mile toward the center, there he was, a respectable distance behind.

Later that evening at the restaurant, midway through the salad, I noticed him alone at a far table, sipping coffee and looking sort of out of place in the fashionable dining room.

"Say, who is that fellow?" I asked my friend, the newspaper editor, as we sat with his cousin, the poet, and a little dancer named Mata. Carlos, the editor, looked across the restaurant toward the table I indicated.

"Don't everybody look," I said as Mata and Jorge began bending their necks, too. "It might embarrass him."

But when Carlos turned his head toward us again and answered in a whispering voice, "A spy," none of us could keep our eyes from glancing quickly across the café.

"Yes," Carlos affirmed, "a government spy."

"But why should he be following me?" I asked.

"He has been following you?"

"All afternoon."

"Maybe he thinks you're Communist," Carlos said. "That's what they are afraid of here."

"But they've got a lot more to be afraid of than that," Jorge
added.

"I guess they have," I answered, for everybody knew Cuba
was on the verge of a revolution. All the schools were closed, and
the public buildings guarded. The "they" we so discreetly re-
ferred to meant the government and the tyrant at its head. But
nobody mentioned the tyrant's name in public; and nobody
talked very loud, if they talked at all.

For months there had been political murders in the streets of
the capital, riots in the provinces, and American gunboats in
the harbors. Mobs were becoming bolder, crying in public
places, "Down with the Yankees! Down with the government
that supports them!" But the tourists seemed blissfully unaware
of all this. They still flocked to the casino, wore their fine
clothes through quaint streets of misery, danced nightly rhumbas at the big hotels, and took tours into the countryside, ex-
claiming before the miserable huts of the sugar-cane cutters,
"How picturesque! How cute!"

"Yes," went on Carlos (this time in English), pouring a beer.
"He ees spy. I know heem. On newspaper you know everybody.
But he ees no dangerous."

"Not dangerous?" I said.

"Not, joust a poor little *viejo,* once pimp, now spy."

"Oh," I said.

"But tomorrow the government will know with whom you
dined," said Mata, "and that maybe will be dangerous."

"Why?" I asked.

"To dine with anyone in Havana is dangerous"—Jorge
laughed—"unless it is with the big boss himself. Everybody
else, except the police, are against the government. And that
paper of my cousin's"—indicating Carlos—"*caramba!* It has
been suppressed ten times."

"But I thought it was your best paper."

"It is—but they think they are our *best* government."

Just then the waiter came, bringing more beer. We switched
our conversation into Spanish again and the domestic troubles

of the Pickford-Fairbanks ménage—then of great interest to the readers of Carlos's paper.

"But what shall I do about the spy?" I asked when the waiter had gone. "I never imagined such open spying."

"They are that way down here," Carlos said. "Not very subtle."

"Make friends with him," suggested Jorge, eating a *flan*. "That would be amusing."

"Buy heem a few drinks," said Carlos, "I know his kind. All they looking for, after all, ees easiest way to get few drinks. The government ees full of drunkards."

Meanwhile the little spy kept mournfully sipping his coffee across the room. Evidently his allowance for spying called for nothing better than coffee when his job took him into an expensive restaurant. I pitied him sitting there looking at all the good food going by and getting nothing.

"Say," I said to Carlos and Jorge, "won't it be dangerous for you and Mata, sitting here with me—if I'm suspected of being a dangerous man?"

"To sit with anybody is dangerous in Havana," Jorge replied. "But they can't lock up everyone. Or kill all of us. After all, it is not writers like my cousin and me that they are really afraid of. Or visiting dancers like Mata. No, it is the workers. You see, they can stop refineries from running. They can keep ships from being loaded, and sugar cane from being cut. They can hit in the pocketbook—and that's all our damned government's here for—to protect foreign dividends."

"Sure, I know that," I said. "But why's that man watching me?"

"Because strangers who don't at once make for the casino to start gambling are watched. *Poor* strangers may be sympathetic with our revolution. They may be bearers of messages from our group in exile. That's why they watch you."

"But if you want heem to forget all about it, buy heem few drinks." Carlos shrugged. "We kill all their best spies. We don't bother with little old bums like heem. Bullets too valuable."

The little man across the way took out a pack of cheap cigarettes and began to smoke. Carlos, Mata, Jorge, and I sat talking until almost midnight. Well-dressed Americans and portly
Cubans passed and repassed between the tables. A famous Spanish actress came in with her man on her arm. There was music
somewhere at the back of the café, and talk, laughter, and clatter of dishes everywhere. We stopped thinking about the spy
and began to speak of Mayakovsky—for Jorge, who was putting
his verse into Spanish, declared him the greatest poet of the
twentieth century, but Carlos disagreed in favor of Lorca, so a
discussion sprang up.

When I left my friends, the little brown man was right at my
heels. He trailed behind me until I finally got into a taxi. As
the car drew off, I knew he was taking down the license number. Later the police would find out from the chauffeur where I
had been driven.

I was not a little flattered to be so assiduously spied upon. At
home in Harlem I was nobody, just a Negro writer. Down
here in Havana I was suddenly of governmental importance.
And I knew pretty well why. The government of Cuba had
grown suddenly terribly afraid of its Negro population, its black
shine boys and cane-field hands, its colored soldiers and sailors
who made up most of the armed forces, its taxi drivers and street
vendors. At last, after all the other elements of the island's population had openly revolted against the tyrant in power, the
Negroes had begun to rise with the students and others to drive
the dictator from Cuba.

For a strange New York Negro to come to Havana might
mean—*quién sabe?*—that he had come to help stir them up—
for the Negroes of Harlem were reputed in Cuba to be none too
docile and none too dumb. Had not Marcus Garvey come out
of Harlem to arouse the whole black world to a consciousness of
its potential strength?

"They," the Cuban dictatorship, were afraid of Negroes from
Harlem. The American steamship lines at that time would not
sell colored persons tickets to Cuba. The immigration at the

port of Havana tried to keep them out if they got that far. But here was I—and I was being shadowed.

The next day I went downstairs to breakfast in the café-bar of my hotel. The iron shutters were up and the whole front of the building open to the street, dust, and sunshine.

Across the way in a Spanish wineshop, I saw the little old man of the day before, waiting patiently.

"Today," I thought to myself, "we will make friends. There ought to be an amusing story in you, old top, if I can get it out."

But after breakfast, for the fun of it, I gave him a merry chase first. By streetcar, by taxi, on foot, down narrow old streets and up broad new ones, all over the central part of Havana, he trotted after me. I had a number of errands to do, and I did them in as zigzag a manner as possible. Once I lost him. But just as I was beginning to regret it (for the game was not unamusing), I looked around, and there, not ten feet away from me in El Centro, was the little old man, puffing and blowing to be sure, but nevertheless there. I laughed. But the sweating little spy did not seem to find the situation entertaining. One of his spats had become unbuttoned from running, and his watch chain was hanging.

That afternoon I had tea with Señora Barrios, the Chilean novelist, my spy waiting patiently the while outside the hedge of her Vedado villa. No taxi being in sight when I emerged, I walked along toward the center of the city, giving the old man some exercise.

On a quiet corner near the statue of Gomez, I sighted a little bar, and went across for a drink before dinner. My withered dandy stood forlornly without.

"It'll be fun to tire him," I thought. "I'll sit here drinking nice cool beers until he can stand it no longer and will have to come in, too. Then I'll invite him to have a drink and see what happens."

It worked. The little old man could not forever stand on that corner and watch me drinking comfortably within. I knew his throat was dry. At last he entered, wiping his brow, and called for an anisette at the small bar.

"Have a Bacardi with me," I invited. "I don't like to drink
alone."

The little old man started, stared, seemed hesitant as to
whether he should answer at all or not, and finally slid into the
chair across from my own. The waiter brought us two drinks
and put them on the marble-topped table.

"Hot," I said pleasantly.

"*Si, señorito,* like steam," the little old man answered.

"You've been walking quite a lot, too." I laughed.

"Too much for my age," the old man said. "You Americanos
are *muy activo.* That's no good in this climate."

"Have another drink," I said.

The old man accepted with alacrity. Just as Carlos said, he
loved his Bacardi. He smiled and nodded as I called the waiter.

"Say," I said, "you have a hell of a job."

"I know it," he said, "they had me for cutting a woman. I
caught her giving her money to some other man after all I did
for her, so I nearly killed her.

"Aren't you pretty old for that girl racket, *señor?*"

"Not too old to knife one if she crosses me. They had me in
jail, locked up. But I said to them, 'I'm no good here, not to you
nor me either. I know languages, I know people, I'm smart'—
so the Porra turned me out to help them scent revolutionists.
Now they've switched me to the foreign squad. I get two dollars
a day for just running around behind you. 'They' don't like
strange foreigners."

We were speaking in Spanish, but when I switched to English, he understood me equally well.

He spoke the English of the wharf rats and the bad Spanish
of one who wants to speak Castilian. He was provincial and
grandiloquent. But when he began to speak of women, as he
did shortly, he was poetical, too.

For years he had been a procurer on the waterfront, I learned
as we drank. Even to his own wife, when he had one, he would
bring lovers from among the sailors. The crumpled bills in his
hand, the round silver dollars, meant more to him than any
woman could ever mean, I gathered from his talk.

That afternoon he was quite out of breath from trailing me. He needed to rest, drink, sit, and talk to somebody. I was interested, so I began to ask him questions as I kept his glass filled.

"Those women," I said, "that you exploited, didn't they care?"

"Couldn't care," he said. "Most of 'em are poor, some of 'em are black, all of 'em loved me. They couldn't afford to care. Without me they might have died, anyhow. I looked out for them. Man, when I was young, the money they brought me! Whew-oo-o!"

As he told his story, I discovered that the little brown man was the very essence of those people who want a good time in life—and don't care how they get it. He had no morals. He had no qualms about using for gain the women who loved him or sought his protection. But as he grew older, naturally they sought the favors of younger men; new kings arose in the brothels. Then he took to intimidations, to knives and beatings to hold his power. When he could no longer pay off the police, they put him in jail, so he became a spy.

"Drink," I said.

"*Si, señor.*"

As he put his glass down, he twirled his little wax mustache and looked at me across the marble table in the darkening café. Outside the street lights had come on and the tropical evening deepened into night.

"Come, let us go to San Isidro Street, *señorito*," said the little man. "Along about now the girls are coming out."

"What's there," I asked, "in San Isidro Street?"

"Just women," said the little man, "of the waterfront."

"Pretty?" I asked.

"Yes," said the little man, "very pretty."

"So!" I said. "Have a drink."

This time I asked the waiter to bring a whole bottle of rum and leave it on our table. As the little man partook, he became more and more grandiloquent on the subject of women.

"The women of Cuba," he said, "are like the pomegranates of Santa Clara. Their souls are jeweled, *joven*, their blood is red, their lips are sweet. And sweetest of all are the mulattoes of Camagüey, *Americanito*. They are the sweetest of all."

"Why the mulattoes?" I said.

"Because," said the old man, "they are a mixture of two worlds, two extremes, two bloods. You see, *señorito*, the passion of the blacks and the passion of the whites combine in the smoldering heat that is *la mulata*. The rose of Venus blooms in her body. She's pain and she's pleasure. You see, *señorito*, I know. In the pure Negro soul and body are separate. In the white they work badly together. But in the mulatto they strangle each other—and their strangulation produces that sweet juice that is a yellow woman's love."

With this amazing observation the little brown man, once a merchant in bodies, lifted his glass of rum and drank. He swayed a little in his chair as he put the glass down. He looked at me with funny far-off eyes. "I wish I were young again," he said. "Come, let's go down to San Isidro Street."

"All right, wait a minute."

I got up and left the table. The little brown man's head was in his arms when I looked back. His eyes were closed. I slipped the barman a bill and went out, leaving more than half a bottle of Bacardi on the table.

That night I delivered all the messages that the exiles in the Latin-American quarter of Harlem had sent by me to their revolutionary coworkers in Havana.

On the boat to New York two days later, off the coast of Georgia, the wireless brought the news that the Cuban government was falling, and that a "pack of Negresses from the waterfront had torn the clothes off the backs of a party of cabinet wives as they came to visit their husbands in jail."

"I wonder," I thought to myself, "what the women of San Isidro Street would have done to that withered little old man had I gone there with him that night and whispered to them that he was a spy?" They probably would have torn him to pieces and given his gold watch chain to some younger man. On the end of the chain I felt sure he had no watch.

A Good Job Gone

It was a good job. Best job I ever had. Got it my last year in high
school and it took me damn near through college. I'm sure sorry
it didn't last. I made good money, too. Made so much I changed
from City College to Columbia my sophomore year. Mr. Lloyd
saw to it I got a good education. He had nothing against the
Negro race, he said, and I don't believe he did. He certainly
treated me swell, from the time I met him till that high brown
I'm gonna tell you about drove him crazy.

Now, Mr. Lloyd was a man like this: he had plenty of money,
he liked his licker, and he liked his women. That was all. A
damn nice guy—till he got hold of this jane from Harlem. Or
till she got hold of him. My people—they won't do. They'd
mess up the Lord if He got too intimate with 'em. Poor
Negroes! I guess I was to blame. I should of told Mr. Lloyd she
didn't mean him no good. But I was minding my own business, and I minded it too well.

That was one of the things Mr. Lloyd told me when I went
to work there. He said, "Boy, you're working for me—nobody
else. Keep your mouth shut about what goes on here, and I'll
look out for you. You're in school, ain't you? Well, you won't
have to worry about money to buy books and take your friends
out—if you stay with me."

He paid me well, and I ate and slept in. He had a four-room
apartment, as cozy a place as you'd want to see, looking right
over Riverside Drive. Swell view. In the summer when Mr.
Lloyd was in Paris, I didn't have a damn thing to do but eat and
sleep, and air the furniture. I got so tired that I went to summer
school.

"What you gonna be, boy?" he said.

I said, "A dentist, I reckon."

He said, "Go to it. They make a hell of a lot of money—if
they got enough sex appeal."

He was always talking about sex appeal and lovin'. He knew
more dirty stories, Mr. Lloyd did! And he liked his women
young and pretty. That's about all I'd do, spend my time cleaning up after some woman he'd have around, or makin' sandwiches and drinks in the evenings. When I did something extra, he'd throw me a fiver any time. I made oodles o' money.
Hell of a fine guy, Mr. Lloyd, with his 40–11 pretty gals—right
out of the Copa or the pages of *Playboy*—sweet and willing.

His wife was paralyzed, so I guess he had to have a little
outside fun. They lived together in White Plains. But he had a
suite in the Hotel Roosevelt, and a office down on Broad. He
says, when I got the job, "Boy, no matter what you find out
about me, where I live or where I work, don't *you* connect up
with no place but here. No matter what happens on Riverside
Drive, don't you take it no further."

"Yes, sir, Mr. Lloyd," I said, I knew where my bread was but-
tered. So I never went near the office or saw any of his other
help but the chauffeur—and him a Jap.

Only thing I didn't like about the job, he used to bring some
awfully cheap women there sometimes—big timers, but cheap
inside. They didn't know how to treat a servant. One of 'em
used to nigger and darkie me around, till I got her told right
quietly one time, and Mr. Lloyd backed me up.

The boss said, "This is no ordinary boy, Lucille. True, he's
my servant, but I've got him in Columbia studying to be a dentist, and he's just as white inside as he is black. Treat him right,
or I'll see why." And it wasn't long before this Lucille dame was
gone, and he had a little Irish girl with blue eyes he treated mean
as hell.

Another thing I didn't like, though. Sometimes I used to
have to drink a lot with him. When there was no women
around, and Mr. Lloyd would get one of his blue spells and start
talking about his wife, and how she hadn't walked for eighteen
years, just laying flat on her back, after about an hour of this
he'd want me to start drinking with him. And when he felt
good from licker, he'd start talking about women in general,
and he'd ask me what they were like in Harlem. Then he'd tell

me what they were like in Montreal, and Havana, and Honolulu. He'd even had Gypsy women in Spain, Mr. Lloyd.

Then he would drink and drink, and make me drink with him. And we'd both be so drunk, I couldn't go to classes the next morning, and he wouldn't go to the office all day. About four o'clock he'd send me for some clam broth and a *New Yorker,* so he could sober up on cartoons. I'd give him an alcohol rub, then he'd go off to the Roosevelt and have dinner with the society folks he knew. I might not see him again for days. But he'd slip me a greenback usually.

"Boy, you'll never lose anything through sticking with me! Here," and it would be a fiver.

Sometimes I wouldn't see Mr. Lloyd for weeks. Then he'd show up late at night with a chippie, and I'd start making drinks and sandwiches and smoothing down the bed. Then there'd be a round o' women, six or eight different ones in a row, for days. And me working my hips off keeping 'em fed and lickered up. This would go on till he got tired, and had the blues again. Then he'd beat the hell out of one of 'em and send her off. Then we'd get drunk. When he sobered up, he'd telephone for his chauffeur and drive to White Plains to see his old lady, or down to the hotel, where he lived with a secretary. And that would be that.

He had so damn much money, Mr. Lloyd. I don't see where folks get so much cash. But I don't care so long as they're giving some of it to me. And if it hadn't been for this colored woman, boy, I'd still be sitting pretty.

I don't know where he got her. Out of one of the Harlem night clubs, I guess. They came bustin' in about four o'clock one morning. I heard a woman laughing in the living room, and I knew it was a colored laugh—one of ours. So deep and pretty, it couldn't have been nothing else. I got up, of course, like I always did when I heard Mr. Lloyd come in. I broke some ice, and took 'em out some drinks.

Yep, she was colored, all right. One of those golden browns, like an Alabama moon. Swell-looking kid. She had the old man standing on his ears. I never saw him looking so happy before.

She kept him laughing till daylight, hugging and kissing. She had a hot line, that kid did, without seemin' serious. He fell for it. She hadn't worked in Harlem after-hours spots for nothing. Jesus! She was like gin and vermouth mixed. You know!

We got on swell, too, that girl and I. "Hi, pal," she said when she saw me bringing out the drinks. "If it ain't old Harlem, on the Drive."

She wasn't a bit hinkty like so many folks when they're light-complexioned and up in the money. If she hadn't been the boss's girl, I'd have tried to make her myself. But she had a black boy friend—a numbers writer on 135th Street—so she didn't need me. She was in love with him. Used to call him up soon as the boss got in the elevator bound for the office.

"Can I use this phone?" she asked me that very morning.

"Sure, madam," I answered.

"Call me Pauline," she said, "I ain't white." And we got on swell. I cooked her some bacon and eggs while she called up her sweetie. She told him she'd hooked a new butter-and-egg man with bucks.

Well, the days went on. Each time the boss would show up with Pauline. It looked like blondes didn't have a break—a sugar-brown had crowded the white babies out. But it was good for Mr. Lloyd. He didn't have the blues. And he stopped asking me to drink with him, thank God!

He was crazy about this Pauline. Didn't want no other woman. She kept him laughing all the time. She used to sing him bad songs that didn't seem bad when she was singing them, only seemed funny and good-natured. She was nice, that girl. A gorgeous thing to have around the house.

But she knew what it was all about. Don't think she didn't. "You've got to kid white folks along," she said to me. "When you're depending on 'em for a living, make 'em *think* you like it."

"You said it," I agreed.

And she really put the bee on Mr. Lloyd. He bought her everything she wanted, and was as faithful to her as a husband. Used to ask me when she wasn't there, what I thought she needed. I don't know what got into him, he loved her like a dog.

She used to spend two or three nights a week with him—and the others with her boy friend in Harlem. It was a hell of a long time before Mr. Lloyd found out about this colored fellow. When he did, it was pure accident. He saw Pauline going into the movies with him at the Capitol one night—a tall black good-looking guy with a diamond on his finger. And it made the old man sore.

That same night Mr. Lloyd got a ring-side table at the Cabin Club in Harlem. When Pauline came dancing out in the two o'clock revue, he called her, and told her to come there. He looked mad. Funny, boy, but that rich white man was jealous of the colored guy he had seen her with. Mr. Lloyd, jealous of a jig! Wouldn't that freeze you?

They had a hell of a quarrel that morning when they came to the apartment. First time I ever heard them quarrel. Pauline told him finally he could go to hell. She told him, yes, she loved that black boy, that he was the only boy she loved in the wide world, the only man she wanted.

They were all drunk, because between words they would drink licker. I'd left two bottles of Haig & Haig on the tray when I went to bed. I thought Pauline was stupid, talking like that, but I guess she was so drunk she didn't care.

"Yes, I love that colored boy," she hollered. "Yes, I love him. You don't think you're buying my heart, do you?"

And that hurt the boss. He'd always thought he was a great lover, and that women liked him for something else besides his money. (Because most of them wanted his money, nobody ever told him he wasn't so hot. His girls all swore they loved him, even when he beat them. They all let *him* put *them* out. They hung on till the last dollar.)

But that little yellow devil of a Pauline evidently didn't care what she said. She began cussing the boss. Then Mr. Lloyd slapped her. I could hear it way back in my bedroom where I was sleeping, with one eye open.

In a minute I heard a crash that brought me to my feet. I ran out, through the kitchen, through the living room, and opened

Mr. Lloyd's door. Pauline had thrown one of the whisky bottles at him. They were battling like hell in the middle of the floor.

"Get out of here, boy!" Mr. Lloyd panted. So I got. But I stood outside the door in case I was needed. A white man beating a Negro woman wasn't so good. If she wanted help, I was there. But Pauline was a pretty tough little scrapper herself. It sounded like the boss was getting the worst of it. Finally, the tussling stopped. It was so quiet in there I thought maybe one of them was knocked out, so I cracked the door to see. The boss was kneeling at Pauline's feet, his arms around her knees.

"My God, Pauline, I love you!" I heard him say. "I want you, child. Don't mind what I've done. Stay here with me. Stay, stay, stay."

"Lemme out of here!" said Pauline, kicking at Mr. Lloyd.

But the boss held her tighter. Then she grabbed the other whisky bottle and hit him on the head. Of course, he fell out. I got a basin of cold water and put him in bed with a cloth on his dome. Pauline took off all the rings and things he'd given her and threw them at him, lying there on the bed like a ghost.

"A white bastard!" she said. "Just because they pay you, they always think they own you. No white man's gonna own me. I laugh with 'em and they think I like 'em. Hell, I'm from Arkansas where the crackers lynch niggers in the streets. How could I like 'em?"

She put on her coat and hat and went away.

When the boss came to, he told me to call his chauffeur. I thought he was going to a doctor, because his head was bleeding. But the chauffeur told me later he spent the whole day driving around Harlem trying to find Pauline. He wanted to bring her back. But he never found her.

He had a lot of trouble with that head, too. Seems like a piece of glass or something stuck in it. I didn't see him again for eight weeks. When I did see him, he wasn't the same man. No, sir, boy, something had happened to Mr. Lloyd. He didn't seem quite right in the head. I guess Pauline dazed him for life, made a fool of him.

He drank more than ever and had me so high I didn't know B from Bull's Foot. He had his white women around again, but he'd got the idea from somewhere that he was the world's greatest lover, and that he didn't have to give them anything but himself—which wasn't so forty for them little Broadway gold diggers who wanted diamonds and greenbacks.

Women started to clearing out early when they discovered Mr. Lloyd had gone romantic—and cheap. There were scandals and fights and terrible goings on when the girls didn't get their presents and checks. But Mr. Lloyd just said, "To hell with them," and drank more than ever, and let the pretty girls go. He picked up women off the streets and then wouldn't pay them, cheap as they are. Late in the night he would start drinking and crying about Pauline. The sun would be rising over the Hudson before he'd stop his crazy carryings on—making me drink with him and listen to the nights he'd spent with Pauline.

"I loved her, boy! She thought I was trying to buy her. Some black buck had to come along and cut me out. But I'm just as good a lover as that black boy any day."

And he would begin to boast about the women he could have —without money, too. (Wrong, of course.) But he sent me to Harlem to find Pauline.

I couldn't find her. She'd gone away with her boy friend. Some said they went to Memphis. Some said Chicago. Some said Los Angeles. Anyway, she was gone—that kid who looked like an Alabama moon.

I told Mr. Lloyd she was gone, so we got drunk again. For more'n a week, he made no move to go to the office. I began to be worried, cutting so many classes, staying up all night to drink with the old man, and hanging around most of the day. But if I left him alone, he acted like a fool. I was scared. He'd take out women's pictures and beat 'em and stamp on 'em and then make love to 'em and tear 'em up. Wouldn't eat. Didn't want to see anybody.

Then, one night, I knew he was crazy—so it was all up. He grabs the door like it was a woman, and starts to kiss it. I couldn't make him stop pawing at the door, so I telephoned his chauffeur.

The chauffeur calls up one of Mr. Lloyd's broker friends. And they take him to the hospital.

That was last April. They've had him in the sanatorium ever since. The apartment's closed. His stuff's in storage, and I have no more job than a snake's got hips. Anyway, I went through college on what I had saved, but I don't know how the hell I'll get to dental school. I just wrote Ma down in Atlanta and told her times was hard. There ain't many Mr. Lloyds, you can bet your life on that.

The chauffeur told me yesterday he's crazy as a loon now. Sometimes he thinks he's a stud-horse chasing a mare. Sometimes he's a lion. Poor man, in a padded cell! He was a swell guy when he had his right mind. But a yellow woman sure did drive him crazy. For me, well, it's just a good job gone!

Say, boy, gimme a smoke, will you? I hate to talk about it.

Who's Passing for Who?

One of the great difficulties about being a member of a minority race is that so many kindhearted, well-meaning bores gather around to help you. Usually, to tell the truth, they have nothing to help with, except their company—which is often appallingly dull.

Some members of the Negro race seem very well able to put up with it, though, in these uplifting years. Such was Caleb Johnson, colored social worker, who was always dragging around with him some nondescript white person or two, inviting them to dinner, showing them Harlem, ending up at the Savoy— much to the displeasure of whatever friends of his might be out that evening for fun, not sociology.

Friends are friends and, unfortunately, overearnest uplifters are uplifters—no matter what color they may be. If it were the

white race that was ground down instead of Negroes, Caleb
Johnson would be one of the first to offer Nordics the sympathy
of his utterly inane society, under the impression that somehow
he would be doing them a great deal of good.

You see, Caleb, and his white friends, too, were all bores. Or
so we, who lived in Harlem's literary bohemia during the "Negro
Renaissance," thought. We literary ones in those days consid-
ered ourselves too broad-minded to be bothered with questions
of color. We liked people of any race who smoked incessantly,
drank liberally, wore complexion and morality as loose garments,
and made fun of anyone who didn't do likewise. We snubbed
and high-hatted any Negro or white luckless enough not to understand Gertrude Stein, Ulysses, Man Ray, the theremin, Jean
Toomer, or George Antheil. By the end of the 1920's Caleb was
just catching up to Dos Passos. He thought H. G. Wells good.

We met Caleb one night in Small's. He had three assorted
white folks in tow. We would have passed him by with but a
nod had he not hailed us enthusiastically, risen, and introduced
us with great acclaim to his friends, who turned out to be school-
teachers from Iowa, a woman and two men. They appeared
amazed and delighted to meet all at once two Negro writers and
a black painter in the flesh. They invited us to have a drink
with them. Money being scarce with us, we deigned to sit down
at their table.

The white lady said, "I've never met a Negro writer before."

The two men added, "Neither have we."

"Why, we know any number of *white* writers," we three dark
bohemians declared with borèd nonchalance.

"But Negro writers are much more rare," said the lady.

"There are plenty in Harlem," we said.

"But not in Iowa," said one of the men, shaking his mop of
red hair.

"There are no good *white* writers in Iowa either, are there?"
we asked superciliously.

"Oh yes, Ruth Suckow came from there."

Whereupon we proceeded to light in upon Ruth Suckow as
old hat and to annihilate her in favor of Kay Boyle. The way we

flung names around seemed to impress both Caleb and his white guests. This, of course, delighted us, though we were too young and too proud to admit it.

The drinks came and everything was going well, all of us drinking, and we three showing off in a high-brow manner, when suddenly at the table just behind us a man got up and knocked down a woman. He was a brownskin man. The woman was blonde. As she rose, he knocked her down again. Then the red-haired man from Iowa got up and knocked the colored man down.

He said, "Keep your hands off that white woman."

The man got up and said, "She's not a white woman. She's my wife."

One of the waiters added, "She's not white, sir, she's colored."

Whereupon the man from Iowa looked puzzled, dropped his fists, and said, "I'm sorry."

The colored man said, "What are you doing up here in Harlem anyway, interfering with my family affairs?"

The white man said, "I thought she was a white woman."

The woman who had been on the floor rose and said, "Well, I'm not a white woman, I'm colored, and you leave my husband alone."

Then they both lit in on the gentleman from Iowa. It took all of us and several waiters, too, to separate them. When it was over, the manager requested us to kindly pay our bill and get out. He said we were disturbing the peace. So we all left. We went to a fish restaurant down the street. Caleb was terribly apologetic to his white friends. We artists were both mad and amused.

"Why did you say you were sorry," said the colored painter to the visitor from Iowa, "after you'd hit that man—and then found out it wasn't a white woman you were defending, but merely a light colored woman who looked white?"

"Well," answered the red-haired Iowan, "I didn't mean to be butting in if they were all the same race."

"Don't you think a woman needs defending from a brute, no matter what race she may be?" asked the painter.

"Yes, but I think it's up to you to defend your own women."

"Oh, so you'd divide up a brawl according to races, no matter who was right?"

"Well, I wouldn't say that."

"You mean you wouldn't defend a colored woman whose husband was knocking her down?" asked the poet.

Before the visitor had time to answer, the painter said, "No! You just got mad because you thought a black man was hitting a *white* woman."

"But she *looked* like a white woman," countered the man.

"Maybe she was just passing for colored," I said.

"Like some Negroes pass for white," Caleb interposed.

"Anyhow, I don't like it," said the colored painter, "the way you stopped defending her when you found out she wasn't white."

"No, we don't like it," we all agreed except Caleb.

Caleb said in extenuation, "But Mr. Stubblefield is new to Harlem."

The red-haired white man said, "Yes, it's my first time here."

"Maybe Mr. Stubblefield ought to stay out of Harlem," we observed.

"I agree," Mr. Stubblefield said. "Good night."

He got up then and there and left the café. He stalked as he walked. His red head disappeared into the night.

"Oh, that's too bad," said the white couple who remained. "Stubby's temper just got the best of him. But explain to us, are many colored folks really as fair as that woman?"

"Sure, lots of them have more white blood than colored, and pass for white."

"Do they?" said the lady and gentleman from Iowa.

"You never read Nella Larsen?" we asked.

"She writes novels," Caleb explained. "She's part white herself."

"Read her," we advised. "Also read the *Autobiography of an Ex-Coloured Man*." Not that we had read it ourselves—because we paid but little attention to the older colored writers—but we knew it was about passing for white.

We all ordered fish and settled down comfortably to shocking

our white friends with tales about how many Negroes there
were passing for white all over America. We were determined to
épater le bourgeois real good via this white couple we had cornered, when the woman leaned over the table in the midst of
our dissertations and said, "Listen, gentlemen, you needn't spread
the word, but me and my husband aren't white either. We've
just been *passing* for white for the last fifteen years."

"What?"

"We're colored, too, just like you," said the husband. "But it's
better passing for white because we make more money."

Well, that took the wind out of us. It took the wind out of
Caleb, too. He thought all the time he was showing some fine
white folks Harlem—and they were as colored as he was!

Caleb almost never cursed. But this time he said, "I'll be
damned!"

Then everybody laughed. And laughed! We almost had hys-
terics. All at once we dropped our professionally self-conscious
"Negro" manners, became natural, ate fish, and talked and
kidded freely like colored folks do when there are no white folks
around. We really had fun then, joking about that red-haired
guy who mistook a fair colored woman for white. After the fish
we went to two or three more night spots and drank until five
o'clock in the morning.

Finally we put the light-colored people in a taxi heading
downtown. They turned to shout a last good-by. The cab was
just about to move off when the woman called to the driver to
stop.

She leaned out the window and said with a grin, "Listen, boys!
I hate to confuse you again. But, to tell the truth, my husband
and I aren't really colored at all. We're white. We just thought
we'd kid you by passing for colored a little while—just as you
said Negroes sometimes pass for white."

She laughed as they sped off toward Central Park, waving,
"Good-by!"

We didn't say a thing. We just stood there on the corner in
Harlem dumbfounded—not knowing now *which* way we'd

been fooled. Were they really white—passing for colored? Or colored—passing for white?

Whatever race they were, they had had too much fun at our expense—even if they did pay for the drinks.

African Morning

Maurai took off his calico breechcloth of faded blue flowers. He took two buckets of water and a big bar of soap into the backyard and threw water all over himself until he was clean. Then he wiped his small golden body on an English towel and went back into the house. His mother had told him always to wear English clothes whenever he went out with his father, or was sent on an errand into the offices of the Export Company or onto one of the big steamships that came up the Niger to their little town. So Maurai put on his best white shirt and a pair of little white sailor trousers that his mother had bought him before she died.

She hadn't been dead very long. She was black, pure African, but Maurai was a half-breed, and his father was white. His father worked in the bank. In fact, his father was the president of the bank, the only bank for hundreds of miles on that part of the coast, up the hot Niger delta in a town where there were very few white people. And no other half-breeds.

That was what made it so hard for Maurai. He was the only half-native, half-English child in the village. His black mother's people didn't want him now that she was dead; and his father had no relatives in Africa. They were all in England, far away, and they were white. Sometimes when Maurai went outside of the stockade, the true African children pelted him with stones for being a half-breed and living inside the enclosure with the English, where the mutterings of independence had not yet penetrated, nor the voice of Azikiwe from far-off Lagos. When Maurai's mother was alive, she would fight back for Maurai and protect him, but now he had to fight for himself.

In the pale fresh morning, the child crossed the large, square, foreign enclosure of the English section toward that corner where the bank stood, one entrance within the stockade and another on the busy native street. The boy thought curiously how the whites had built a fence around themselves to keep the natives out—as if black people were animals. Only servants and women could come in, as a rule. And already his father had brought another young black woman to live in their house. She was only a child, very young and shy, and not wise like his mother had been.

There were already quite a few people in the bank this morning transacting business, for today was Steamer Day, and Maurai had come to take a letter to the captain for his father. In his father's office there were three or four assistants surrounding the president's desk, and as Maurai opened the door, he heard the clink of gold. They were counting money there on the desk, a great pile of golden coins, and when they heard the door close, they turned quickly to see who had entered.

"Wait outside, Maurai," said his father sharply, his hands on the gold, so the little boy went out into the busy main room of the bank again. Evidently they did not want him to see the gold.

Maurai knew that in his village the English did not allow Africans to possess gold—but to the whites it was something very precious. They were always talking about it, always counting it and wrapping it and sending it away by boat, or receiving it from England.

If a black boy stole a coin of gold, they would give him a great many years in prison to think about it. This Maurai knew. And suddenly he thought, looking at his own small hands, "Maybe that's why the black people hate me, because I am the color of gold."

Just then his father came out of his office and handed him the letter. "Here, Maurai, take this note to Captain Higgins of the *Drury* and tell him I shall expect him for tea at four."

"Yes, sir," said Maurai as he went out into the native street and down toward the river where the masts of the big boat towered.

On the dock everyone was busy. There were women selling things to eat and boys waiting for sailors to come ashore. Winches rattled, and the cranes lifted up their loads of palm oil and cocoa beans. Ebony-black men, naked to the waist, the sweat pouring off them, loaded the rope hampers before they swung up and over and down into the dark hole of the big ship. Their sweat fell from shining black bodies onto the bags of cocoa beans and went away to England and came back in gold for the white men to count in banks as though it were the most precious thing in the world.

Maurai went up the steep swinging stairway at the side of the ship, past the sailors leaning over the deck rail, and on up to the bridge and the captain's office. The captain took the letter from the little golden boy without a word.

As Maurai descended from the bridge, he could see directly down into the great dark holes where went the palm oil and the cocoa beans, and where more sweating ebony-black men were stowing away the cargo for its trip to England.

One of the white sailors grabbed Maurai on the well deck and asked, "You take me see one fine girl?" because he naturally thought Maurai was one of the many little boys who are regularly sent to the dock on Steamer Days by the prostitutes, knowing only one or two vile phrases in English and the path to the prostitute's door. The sailors fling them a penny, perhaps, if they happen to like the black girls to whom the child leads them.

"I am not a guide boy," said Maurai as he pulled away from the sailor and went on down the swinging stairs to the dock. There the boys who were runners for the girls in the palm huts laughed and made fun of this little youngster who was neither white nor black. They called him an ugly yellow name. And Maurai turned and struck one of the boys in the face.

But they did not fight fair, these dock boys. A dozen of them began to strike and kick at Maurai, and even the black women squatting on the wharf selling fruits and sweetmeats got up and

joined the boys in their attack, while the sailors leaning on the
rail of the English steamer had great fun watching the excitement.

The little black boys ran Maurai away from the wharf in a
trail of hooting laughter. In the wide grassy street he wiped the
blood from his nose and looked down at his white shirt, torn
and grimy from the blows of the wharf rats. He thought how,
even in his English clothes, a sailor had taken him for a prostitute's boy and had asked him to find "one fine girl" for him.

The little mulatto youngster went slowly up the main street
past the bank where his father worked, past the house of the
man who sells parrots and monkeys to the sailors, on past the big
bayamo tree where the vendors of palm wine have their stands,
on to the very edge of town—which is the edge of the jungle,
too—and down a narrow path through a sudden tangle of vines
and flowers, until he came to a place where the still backwaters
of the lagoon formed a pool on whose grassy banks the feet of
the obeah dancers dance in nights of moon.

Here Maurai took off his clothes and went into the water,
cool to his bruised little body. He swam well, and he was not
afraid of snakes or crocodiles. He was not afraid of anything but
white people and black people—and gold. Why, he wondered
in the water, was his body the color of gold? Why wasn't he
black or white—like his mother or like his father, one or the
other—but not just (he remembered that ugly word of the wharf
rats) a *bastard* of gold?

Filling his lungs with air and holding his breath, down, down,
Maurai went, letting his naked body touch the cool muddy bottom of the deep lagoon.

"Suppose I were to stay here forever," he thought, "in the
dark, at the bottom of this pool?"

But, against his will, his body shot upward like a cork, and
his skin caught the sun in the middle of the big pool, and he
kept on swimming around and around, loath to go back to the
house in the enclosure where his father would soon be having
the white captain to tea in the living room, but where he, Mau-

rai, and the little dark girl with whom his father slept, would, of course, eat in the kitchen.

But since he had begun to be awfully hungry and awfully tired, he came out of the water to lie down on the grassy bank and dry in the sun. And probably because he was only twelve years old, Maurai began to cry. He thought about his mother who was dead and his father who would eventually retire and go back to England, leaving him in Africa—where nobody wanted him.

Out of the jungle two bright birds came flying, and stopped to sing in a tree above his head. They did not know that a little boy was crying on the ground below them. They paid no attention to the strange sounds that came from that small golden body on the bank of the lagoon. They simply sang a moment, flashed their bright wings, and flew away.

Pushcart Man

The usual Saturday night squalls and brawls were taking place as the Pushcart Man trucked up Eighth Avenue in Harlem. A couple walking straggle-legged got into a fight. A woman came to take her husband home from the corner saloon, but he didn't want to go. A man said he had paid for the last round of drinks. The bartender said he hadn't. The squad car came by. A midget stabbed a full-grown man. Saturday night jumped.

"Forgive them, Father, for they know not what they do," said a Sanctified Sister passing through a group of sinners.

"Yes, they do know what they do," said a young punk, "but they don't give a damn!"

"Son, you oughtn't to use such language!"

"If you can't get potatoes, buy tomatoes," yelled the Pushcart Man. "Last call! Pushing this cart on home!"

"Have you got the *Times*?" asked a studious young man at a newsstand where everybody was buying the *Daily News*.

"I got the *News* or *Mirror*," said the vendor.

"No," said the young man, "I want the *Times*."

"You can't call my mother names and live with me," said a dark young fellow to a light young girl.

"I did not call your mother a name," said the girl. "I called *you* one."

"You called *me* a son of a——"

"Such language!" said the Sanctified Sister.

"He just ain't no good," explained the girl. "Spent half his money already and ain't brought home a thing to eat for Sunday."

"Help the blind, please," begged a kid cup-shaker, pushing a blind man ahead of him.

"That man ain't no more blind than me," declared a fellow in a plaid sport shirt.

"I once knew a blind man who made more money begging than I did working," said a guy leaning on a mailbox.

"You didn't work very hard," said the Sport Shirt. "I never knowed you to keep a job more than two weeks straight. Hey, Mary, where you going?"

"Down to the store to get a pint of ice cream." A passing girl paused. "My mama's prostrate with the heat."

An old gentleman whose eyes followed a fat dame in slacks muttered, "Her backside looks like a keg of ale."

"It's a shame," affirmed a middle-aged shopper on her way into the chicken store, "slacks and no figure."

"If you don't like pomatoes, buy totatoes!" cried the Push-cart Man.

"This bakery sure do make nice cakes," said a little woman to nobody in particular, "but they's so high."

"Don't hit me!" yelled a man facing danger, in the form of two fists.

"Stop backing up!"

"Then stop coming forward—else I'll hurt you." He was cornered. A crowd gathered.

"You children go on home," chided a portly matron to a flock of youngsters. "Fights ain't for children."

"You ain't none of my mama."

"I'm glad I ain't."

"And we don't have to go home."

"You-all ought to be in bed long ago! Here it is midnight!"

"There ain't nobody at my house."

"You'd be home if I was any relation to you," said the portly lady.

"I'm glad you ain't."

"Hit me! Just go on and hit me—and I'll cut you every way there is," said the man.

"I ain't gonna fight you with my bare fists 'cause you ain't worth it."

"Break it up! Break it up! Break it up!" barked the cop. They broke it up.

"Let's go play in a Hundred Forty-third Street," said a little bowlegged boy. "There's blocks of ice down there we can sit on and cool off."

"If you don't get potatoes, buy tomatoes," cried the Pushcart Man.

A child accidentally dropped a pint of milk on the curb as he passed. The child began to cry.

"When you get older," the Pushcart Man consoled the child, "you'll be glad it wasn't Carstairs you broke. Here's a quarter. Buy some more milk. I got tomatoes, potatoes," cried the push-cart vendor. "Come and get 'em—'cause I'm trucking home."

Why, You Reckon?

Well, sir, I ain't never been mixed up in nothin' wrong before nor since, and I don't intend to be again, but I was hongry that night. Indeed, I was! Depression times before the war plants

opened up and money got to circulating again and that Second
World War had busted out.

I was goin' down a Hundred Thirty-third Street in the snow
when another colored fellow what looks hongry sidetracks me
and says, "Say, buddy, you wanta make a little jack?"

"Sure," I says. "How?"

"Stickin' up a guy," he says. "The first white guy what comes
out o' one o' these speak-easies and looks like bucks, we gonna
grab him!"

"Oh no," says I.

"Oh yes, we will," says this other guy. "Man, ain't you hongry? Didn't I see you down there at the charities today, not gettin' nothin'—like me? You didn't get a thing, did you? Hell, no!
Well, you gotta take what you want, that's all, reach out and
take it," he says. "Even if you are starvin', don't starve like a fool.
You must be in love with white folks or somethin'. Else scared.
Do you think they care anything about you?"

"No," I says.

"They sure don't," he says. "These here rich folks comes up
to Harlem spendin' forty or fifty bucks in the night clubs and
speak-easies and don't care nothin' 'bout you and me out here
in the street, do they? Huh? Well, one of 'em's gonna give up
some money tonight before he gets home."

"What about the cops?"

"To hell with the cops!" said the other guy. "Now, listen,
now. I live right here, sleep on the ash pile back of the furnace
down in this basement. Don't nobody never come down there
after dark. They let me stay here for keepin' the furnace goin'
at night. It's kind of a fast house upstairs, you understand. Now,
you grab this here guy we pick out, push him down to the basement door, right here, I'll pull him in, we'll drag him on back
yonder to the furnace room and rob him, money, watch, clothes,
and all. Then push him out in the rear court. If he hollers—
and he sure will holler when that cold air hits him—folks'll just
think he's some drunken white man what's fell out with some
chocolate baby upstairs and has had to run and leave his clothes

behind him. But by that time we'll be long gone. What do you say, boy?"

Well, sir, I'm tellin' you, I was so tired and hongry and cold that night I didn't hardly know what to say, so I said all right, and we decided to do it. Looked like to me 'bout that time a Hundred Thirty-third Street was just workin' with people, taxis cruisin', women hustlin', white folks from downtown lookin' for hot spots.

It were just midnight.

This guy's front basement door was right near the door of the Dixie Bar where that woman sings the kind of blues ofays is crazy about.

Well, sir! Just what we wanted to happen happened right off. A big party of white folks in furs and things come down the street. They musta parked their car on Lenox, 'cause they wasn't in no taxi. They was walkin' in the snow. And just when they got right by us, one o' them white women says, "Ed-*ward*," she said, "oh, darlin', don't you know I left my purse and cigarettes and compact in the car. Please go and ask the chauffeur to give 'em to you." And they went on in the Dixie. The boy started toward Lenox again.

Well, sir, Edward never did get back no more that evenin' to the Dixie Bar. No, pal, uh-hum! 'Cause we nabbed him. When he come back down the street in his evenin' clothes and all, with a swell black overcoat on that I wished I had, just a-tippin' so as not to slip up and fall on the snow, I grabbed him. Before he could say Jack Robinson, I pulled him down the steps to the basement door, the other fellow jerked him in, and by the time he knew where he was, we had that white boy back yonder behind the furnace in the coalbin.

"Don't you holler," I said on the way down.

There wasn't much light back there, just the raw gas comin' out of a jet, kind of blue-like, blinkin' in the coal dust. Took a few minutes before we could see what he looked like.

"Ed-*ward*," the other fellow said, "don't you holler in this coalbin."

But Edward didn't holler. He just sat down on the coal. I reckon he was scared weak-like.

"Don't you throw no coal, neither," the other fellow said. But Edward didn't look like he was gonna throw coal.

"What do you want?" he asked by and by in a nice white-folks kind of voice. "Am I kidnaped?"

Well, sir, we never thought of kidnapin'. I reckon we both looked puzzled. I could see the other guy thinkin' maybe we *ought* to hold him for ransom. Then he musta decided that that weren't wise, 'cause he says to this white boy, "No, you ain't kidnaped," he says. "We ain't got no time for that. We's hongry right *now*, so, buddy, gimme your money."

The white boy handed out of his coat pocket amongst other things a lady's pretty white beaded bag that he'd been sent after. My partner held it up.

"Doggone," he said, "my gal could go for this. She likes purty things. Stand up and lemme see what else you got."

The white guy got up and the other fellow went through his pockets. He took out a wallet and a gold watch and a cigarette lighter, and he got a swell key ring and some other little things colored folks never use.

"Thank you," said the other guy when he got through friskin' the white boy, "I guess I'll eat tomorrow! And smoke right now," he said, opening up the white boy's cigarette case. "Have one," and he passed them swell fags around to me and the white boy, too. "What kind is these?" he wanted to know.

"Benson's Hedges," said the white boy, kinder scared-like, 'cause the other fellow was makin' an awful face over the cigarette.

"Well, I don't like 'em," the other fellow said, frownin' up. "Why don't you smoke decent cigarettes? Where do you get off, anyhow?" he said to the white boy standin' there in the coalbin. "Where do you get off comin' up here to Harlem with these kind of cigarettes? Don't you know no colored folks smoke these kind of cigarettes? And what're you doin' bringin' a lot of purty rich women up here wearin' white fur coats? Don't you know it's more'n we colored folks can do to get a black fur coat, let alone a white one? I'm askin' you a question," the other fellow said.

The poor white fellow looked like he was gonna cry. "Don't you know," the colored fellow went on, "that I been walkin' up and down Lenox Avenue for three or four months tryin' to find some way to earn money to get my shoes half-soled? Here, look at 'em." He held up the palms of his feet for the white boy to see. There were sure big holes in his shoes. "Looka here!" he said to that white boy. "Still you got the nerve to come up here to Harlem all dressed up in a tuxedo suit with a stiff shirt on and diamonds shinin' out of the front of it, and a silk muffler on and a big heavy overcoat! Gimme that overcoat," the other fel-low said.

He grabbed the white guy and took off his overcoat.

"We can't use that M.C. outfit you got on," he said, talking about the tux. "But we might be able to make earrings for our janes out of them studs. Take 'em off," he said to the white kid.

All this time I was just standin' there, wasn't doin' nothin'. The other fellow had taken all the stuff, so far, and had his arms full.

"Wearin' diamonds up here to Harlem, and me starvin'!" the other fellow said. "Goddamn!"

"I'm sorry," said the white fellow.

"Sorry?" said the other guy. "What's your name?"

"Edward Peedee McGill, III," said the white fellow.

"What third?" said the colored fellow. "Where's the other two?"

"My father and grandfather," said the white boy. "I'm the third."

"I had a father and a grandfather, too," said the other fellow, "but I ain't no third. I'm the first. Ain't never been one like me. I'm a new model." He laughed out loud.

When he laughed, the white boy looked real scared. He looked like he wanted to holler. He sat down in the coal agin. The front of his shirt was all black where he took the diamonds

out. The wind came in through a broken pane above the coalbin and the white fellow sat there shiverin'. He was just a kid—
eighteen or twenty maybe—runnin' around to night clubs.

"We ain't gonna kill you." The other fellow kept laughin'.
"We ain't got the time. But if you sit in that coal long enough,
white boy, you'll be black as me. Gimme your shoes. I might
maybe can sell 'em."

The white fellow took off his shoes. As he handed them to
the colored fellow, he had to laugh, hisself. It looked so crazy
handin' somebody else your shoes. We all laughed.

"But I'm laughin' last," said the other fellow. "You two can
stay here and laugh if you want to, both of you, but I'm gone.
So long!"

And, man, don't you know he went on out from that basement and took all that stuff! Left me standin' just as empty-
handed as when I come in there. Yes, sir! He left me with that
white boy standin' in the coal. He'd done took the money, the
diamonds, and everythin', even the shoes! And me with nothin'!
Was I stung? I'm askin' you!

"Ain't you gonna gimme none?" I hollered, runnin' after him
down the dark hall. "Where's my part?"

I couldn't even see him in the dark—but I *heard* him.

"Get back there," he yelled at me, "and watch that white boy
till I get out o' here. Get back there," he hollered, "Or I'll knock
your livin' gizzard out! I don't know you."

I got back. And there me and that white boy was standin' in
a strange coalbin, him lookin' like a picked chicken—and me
feelin' like a fool. Well, sir, we both had to laugh again.

"Say," said the white boy, "is he gone?"

"He ain't here," I said.

"Gee, this was exciting," said the white fellow, turning up his
tux collar. "This was thrilling!"

"What?" I says.

"This is the first exciting thing that's ever happened to me,"
said the white guy. "This is the first time in my life I've ever had
a good time in Harlem. Everything else has been fake, a show.
You know, something you pay for. This was real."

"Say, buddy," I says, "if I had your money, I'd be always having a good time."

"No, you wouldn't," said the white boy.

"Yes, I would, too," I said, but the white boy shook his head. Then he asked me if he could go home, and I said, "Sure! Why not?" So we went up the dark hall. I said, "Wait a minute."

I went up and looked, but there wasn't no cops or nobody much in the streets, so I said, "So long," to that white boy. "I'm glad you had a good time." And left him standin' on the sidewalk in his stocking feet, waitin' for a taxi.

I went on up the street hongrier than I am now. And I kept thinkin' about that boy with all his money. I said to myself, "What do you suppose is the matter with rich white folks? Why you reckon they ain't happy?"

Saratoga Rain

The wind blew. Rain swept over the roof. Upstairs the man and woman lay close together. He held her in his arms, drowsily, sleepily, head half buried in the covers, the scent of bodies between them. The rain came down.

She said, "Ben, I love you." To her, thirty years of muddy yesterdays were as nothing.

He said, "I like you, too, babe." And all the dice on all the tables from Reno to Saratoga were forgotten.

It was early morning. The rain came down. They didn't care. They were together in the darkened room, heads half buried in the covers. They had each other. They didn't remember now the many cliffs they'd had to climb nor the lurking tomorrows of marsh and danger.

They would never be angels and have wings—that they knew for sure. But at the moment they had each other.

That moment, that rainy morning, not even that whole day

would last very long. Indeed, it might never repeat itself. Things had a way of moving swiftly with each of them, leaving memories, raising scars, and passing on. But they did not choose to remember now the aching loneliness of time, warm in bed as they were, with the rain falling outside.

They did not choose to remember (for her) the stableboy who had been her lover last night, nor the jockey who had been so generous with his money the week before but had fallen yesterday in the steeplechase, lost his mount, and broken his neck.

They did not (for him) choose to remember the swift rattle of crooked dice in the fast fading game at the corner, the recollection of the startled look on that Florida simpleton's face when he saw his month's pay gone.

For neither of them now the memory of muddy water in the gutter of life, because on this early August morning the rain fell straight out of the sky—clean.

The room is pleasantly dark and warm, the house safe, and though neither of them will ever be angels with wings, at the moment they have each other.

"I like you," Ben said.

"I love you," she whispered.

Spanish Blood

In that amazing city of Manhattan where people are forever building things anew, during prohibition times there lived a young Negro called Valerio Gutierrez whose mother was a Harlem laundress, but whose father was a Puerto Rican sailor. Valerio grew up in the streets. He was never much good at school, but he was swell at selling papers, pitching pennies, or shooting pool. In his teens he became one of the smoothest dancers in the Latin-American quarter north of Central Park. Long before the rhumba became popular, he knew how to do it in the real Cuban way that made all the girls afraid to dance with him. Besides, he was very good-looking.

At seventeen, an elderly Chilean lady who owned a beauty parlor called La Flor began to buy his neckties. At eighteen, she kept him in pocket money and let him drive her car. At nineteen, younger and prettier women—a certain comely Spanish widow, also one Dr. Barrios's pale wife—began to see that he kept well dressed.

"You'll never amount to nothin'," Hattie, his brown-skinned mother said. "Why don't you get a job and work? It's that foreign blood in you, that's what it is. Just like your father."

"*Qué va?*" Valerio replied, grinning.

"Don't you speak Spanish to me," his mama said. "You know I don't understand it."

"O.K., Mama," Valerio said, "*Yo voy a trabajar.*"

"You better *trabajar,*" his mama answered. "And I mean work, too! I'm tired o' comin' home every night from that Chinee laundry and findin' you gone to the dogs. I'm gonna move out o' this here Spanish neighborhood anyhow, way up into Harlem where some real *colored* people is, I mean American Negroes. There ain't nobody settin' a decent example for you down here 'mongst all these Cubans and Puerto Ricans and things. I don't care if your father was one of 'em, I never did like 'em real well."

"Aw, Ma, why didn't you ever learn Spanish and stop talking like a spook?"

"Don't you spook me, you young hound, you! I won't stand it. Just because you're straight-haired and yellow and got that foreign blood in you, don't you spook me. I'm your mother and I won't stand for it. You hear me?"

"Yes, m'am. But you know what I mean. I mean stop talking like most colored folks—just because you're not white, you don't have to get back in a corner and stay there. Can't we live nowhere else but way up in Harlem, for instance? Down here in a Hundred Sixth Street, white and colored families live in the same house—Spanish-speaking families, some white and some black. What do you want to move farther up in Harlem for, where everybody's all black? Lots of my friends down here are Spanish and Italian, and we get along swell."

"That's just what I'm talkin' about," said his mother. "That's just why I'm gonna move. I can't keep track of you, runnin' around with a fast foreign crowd, all mixed up with every what-cha-ma-call-it, lettin' all shades o' women give you money. Besides, no matter where you move or what language you speak, you're still colored less'n your skin is white."

"Well, I won't be," said Valerio, "I'm American, Latin American."

"Huh!" said his mama. "It's just by luck that you even got good hair."

"What's that got to do with being American?"

"A mighty lot," said his mama, "in America."

They moved. They moved up to 143rd Street, in the very middle of "American" Harlem. There Hattie Gutierrez was happier—for in her youth her name had been Jones, not Gutierrez, just plain colored Jones. She had come from Virginia, not Latin America. She had met the Puerto Rican seaman in Norfolk, had lived with him there and in New York for some ten or twelve years and borne him a son, meanwhile working hard to keep him and their house in style. Then one winter he just disappeared, probably missed his boat in some far-off port town, settled down with another woman, and went on dancing rhumbas and drinking rum without worry.

Valerio, whom Gutierrez left behind, was a handsome child, not quite as light as his father, but with olive-yellow skin and Spanish-black hair, more foreign than Negro. As he grew up, he became steadily taller and better-looking. Most of his friends were Spanish-speaking, so he possessed their language as well as English. He was smart and amusing out of school. But he wouldn't work. That was what worried his mother, he just wouldn't work. The long hours and low wages most colored fellows received during depression times never appealed to him. He could live without struggling, so he did.

He liked to dance and play billiards. He hung out near the

Cuban theater at 110th Street, around the pool halls and gambling places, in the taxi dance emporiums. He was all for getting the good things out of life. His mother's moving up to black 143rd Street didn't improve conditions any. Indeed, it just started the ball rolling faster, for here Valerio became what is known in Harlem as a big-timer, a young sport, a hep cat. In other words, a man-about-town.

His sleek-haired yellow star rose in a chocolate sky. He was seen at all the formal invitational affairs given by the exclusive clubs of Harlem's younger set, although he belonged to no clubs. He was seen at midnight shows stretching into the dawn. He was even asked to Florita Sutton's famous Thursday midnight-at-homes where visiting dukes, English authors, colored tap dancers, and dinner-coated downtowners vied for elbow room in her small Sugar Hill apartment. Hattie, Valerio's mama, still kept her job ironing in the Chinese laundry—but nobody bothered about his mama.

Valerio was a nice enough boy, though, about sharing his income with her, about pawning a ring or something someone would give him to help her out on the rent or the insurance policies. And maybe, once or twice a week, Mama might see her son coming in as she went out in the morning or leaving as she came in at night, for Valerio often slept all day. And she would mutter, "The Lord knows, 'cause I don't, what will become of you, boy! You're just like your father!"

Then, strangely enough, one day Valerio got a job. A good job, too—at least, it paid him well. A friend of his ran an after-hours night club on upper St. Nicholas Avenue. Gangsters owned the place, but they let a Negro run it. They had a red-hot jazz band, a high-yellow revue, and bootleg liquor. When the Cuban music began to hit Harlem, they hired Valerio to introduce the rhumba. That was something he was really cut out to do, the rhumba. That wasn't work. Not at all, *hombre!* But it was a job, and his mama was glad.

Attired in a yellow silk shirt, white satin trousers, and a bright red sash, Valerio danced nightly to the throbbing drums and seed-filled rattles of the tropics—accompanied by the orchestra's usual instruments of joy. Valerio danced with a little brown Cuban girl in a red dress, Concha, whose hair was a mat of darkness and whose hips were nobody's business.

Their dance became the talk of the town—at least, of that part of the town composed of night-lifers—for Valerio danced the rhumba as his father had taught him to dance it in Norfolk when he was ten years old, innocently—unexpurgated, happy, funny, but beautiful, too—like a gay, sweet longing for something that might be had, some time, maybe, some place or other.

Anyhow, business boomed. Ringside tables filled with people who came expressly to see Valerio dance.

"He's marvelous," gasped ladies who ate at the Ritz any time they wanted to.

"That boy can dance," said portly gentlemen with offices full of lawyers to keep track of their income tax. "He can dance!" And they wished they could, too.

"Hot stuff," said young rum-runners, smoking reefers and drinking gin—for these were prohibition days.

"A natural-born eastman," cried a tan-skin lady with a diamond wrist watch. "He can have anything I got."

That was the trouble! Too many people felt that Valerio could have anything they had, so he lived on the fat of the land without making half an effort. He began to be invited to fashionable cocktail parties downtown. He often went out to dinner in the East Fifties with white folks. But his mama still kept her job in the Chinese laundry.

Perhaps it was a good thing she did in view of what finally happened, for to Valerio the world was nothing but a swagger world tingling with lights, music, drinks, money, and people who had everything—or thought they had. Each night, at the club, the orchestra beat out its astounding songs, shook its rattles, fingered its drums. Valerio put on his satin trousers with the fiery red sash to dance with the little Cuban girl who always had a look of pleased surprise on her face, as though amazed to find dancing so good. Somehow she and Valerio made their rhumba, for all their hip-shaking, clean as a summer sun.

Offers began to come in from other night clubs, and from small producers as well. "Wait for something big, kid," said the man who ran the cabaret. "Wait till the Winter Garden calls you."

Valerio waited. Meanwhile, a dark young rounder named Sonny, who wrote number bets for a living, had an idea for making money off of Valerio. They would open an apartment together where people could come after the night clubs closed —come and drink and dance—and love a little if they wanted to. The money would be made from the sale of drinks—charging very high prices to keep the riffraff out. With Valerio as host a lot of good spenders would surely call. They could get rich.

"O.K. by me," said Valerio.

"I'll run the place," said Sonny, "and all you gotta do is just be there and dance a little, maybe—you know—and make people feel at home."

"O.K.," said Valerio.

"And we'll split the profit two ways—me and you."

"O.K."

So they got a big Seventh Avenue apartment, furnished it with deep, soft sofas and lots of little tables and a huge icebox and opened up. They paid off the police every week. They had good whisky. They sent out cards to a hundred downtown people who didn't care about money. They informed the best patrons of the cabaret where Valerio danced—the white folks who thrilled at becoming real Harlem initiates going home with Valerio.

From the opening night on, Valerio's flat filled with white people from midnight till the sun came up. Mostly a sporty crowd, young blades accompanied by ladies of the chorus, racetrack gentlemen, white cabaret entertainers out for amusement after their own places closed, musical-comedy stars in search of new dance steps—and perhaps three or four brownskin ladies-of-the-evening and a couple of chocolate gigolos, to add color.

There was a piano player. Valerio danced. There was impromptu entertaining by the guests. Often famous radio stars would get up and croon. Expensive night-club names might rise to do a number—or several numbers if they were tight enough. And sometimes it would be hard to stop them when they really got going.

Occasionally guests would get very drunk and stay all night, sleeping well into the day. Sometimes one might sleep with Valerio.

Shortly all Harlem began to talk about the big red roadster Valerio drove up and down Seventh Avenue. It was all nickel-plated—and a little blonde revue star known on two continents had given it to him, so folks said. Valerio was on his way to becoming a gigolo de luxe.

"That boy sure don't draw no color lines," Harlem commented. "No, sir!

"And why should he?" Harlem then asked itself rhetorically. "Colored folks ain't got no money—and money's what he's after, ain't it?"

But Harlem was wrong. Valerio seldom gave a thought to money—he was having too good a time. That's why it was well his mama kept her job in the Chinese laundry, for one day Sonny received a warning, "Close up that flat of yours, and close it damn quick!"

Gangsters!

"What the hell?" Sonny answered the racketeers. "We're payin' off, ain't we—you and the police, both? So what's wrong?"

"Close up, or we'll break you up," the warning came back. "We don't like the way you're running things, black boy. And tell Valerio to send that white chick's car back to her—and quick!"

"Aw, nuts!" said Sonny. "We're paying the police! You guys lay off."

But Sonny wasn't wise. He knew very well how little the police count when gangsters give orders, yet he kept right on. The profits had gone to his head. He didn't even tell Valerio they had been warned, for Sonny, who was trying to make enough money to start a numbers bank of his own, was afraid the boy might quit. Sonny should have known better.

One Sunday night about 3:30 A.M, the piano was going like mad. Fourteen couples packed the front room, dancing close and warm. There were at least a dozen folks whose names you'd know if you saw them in any paper, famous from Hollywood to Westport.

They were feeling good.

Sonny was busy at the door, and a brown bar-boy was collecting highball glasses as Valerio came in from the club where he still worked. He went in the bedroom to change his dancing shoes, for it was snowing and his feet were cold.

"O, rock me, pretty mama, till the cows come home . . ."

sang a sleek-haired Harlemite at the piano.

"Rock me, rock me, baby, from night to morn . . ."

when, just then, a crash like the wreck of the Hesperus resounded through the hall and shook the whole house as five Italian gentlemen in evening clothes who looked exactly like gangsters walked in. They had broken down the door.

Without a word they began to smash up the place with long axes each of them carried. Women began to scream, men to shout, and the piano vibrated, not from jazz-playing fingers, but from axes breaking its hidden heart.

"Lemme out," the piano player yelled. "Lemme out!" But there was panic at the door.

"I can't leave without my wrap," a woman cried. "Where is my wrap? Sonny, my ermine coat!"

"Don't move," one of the gangsters said to Sonny.

A big white fist flattened his brown nose.

"I ought to kill you," said a second gangster. "You was warned. Take this!"

Sonny spit out two teeth.

Crash went the axes on furniture and bar. Splintered glass

flew, wood cracked. Guests fled, hatless and coatless. About that time the police arrived.

Strangely enough, the police, instead of helping protect the place from the gangsters, began themselves to break, not only the furniture, but also the *heads* of every Negro in sight. They started with Sonny. They laid the barman and the waiter low. They grabbed Valerio as he emerged from the bedroom. They beat his face to a pulp. They whacked the piano player twice across the buttocks. They had a grand time with their night sticks. Then they arrested all the colored fellows (and no whites) as the gangsters took their axes and left. That was the end of Valerio's apartment.

In jail Valerio learned that the woman who gave him the red roadster was being kept by a gangster who controlled prohibition's whole champagne racket and owned dozens of rum-running boats.

"No wonder!" said Sonny, through his bandages. "He got them guys to break up our place! He probably told the police to beat hell out of us, too!"

"Wonder how he knew she gave me that car?" asked Valerio innocently.

"White folks know everything," said Sonny.

"Aw, stop talking like a spook," said Valerio.

When he got out of jail, Valerio's face had a long night-stick scar across it that would never disappear. He still felt weak and sick and hungry. The gangsters had forbidden any of the night clubs to employ him again, so he went back home to Mama.

"Umm-huh!" she told him. "Good thing I kept my job in that Chinee laundry. It's a good thing. . . . Sit down and eat, son. . . . What you gonna do now?"

"Start practicing dancing again. I got an offer to go to Brazil —a big club in Rio."

"Who's gonna pay your fare way down yonder to Brazil?"

"Concha," Valerio answered—the name of his Cuban rhumba partner whose hair was a mat of darkness. "Concha."

"A woman!" cried his mother. "I might a-knowed it! We're weak that way. My God, I don't know, boy! I don't know!"

"You don't know what?" asked Valerio, grinning.

"How women can help it," said his mama. "The Lord knows you're *just* like your father—and I took care o' him for ten years. I reckon it's that Spanish blood."

"*Qué va!*" said Valerio.

Gumption

You young folks don't remember the depression, but I do. No jobs for nobody. That winter there wasn't a soul working in our house but my wife, and she was evil as she could be! She was doing a few washings now and then for the white folks—before hand laundry went out of style—so we kinder made out. But she didn't like to see me sitting around, even if I couldn't find a job. There wasn't no work to be got in our town, nor any other place, for that matter. We had a couple of roomers, a man and his girl friend, but they were out of a job also. And, like me and my wife, they hadn't been in town long enough to get any consideration, since the relief folks were hard on strangers. All of us was just managing to get by on beans and mush all winter.

One cold February morning we was sitting around the stove in the kitchen trying to keep warm, the roomers and me, my wife was ironing, when who should pass by outside in the alley but old man Oyster and his son.

"There goes Oyster and that boy of his," I said, "ragged as a jaybird, both of 'em."

"They ain't even on relief work, is they?" Jack, the roomer, asked.

"They did have a few hours' work a month," I answered. "They messed up, though."

"Messed up, you call it, heh?" my wife put in, in her nervous way. "Well, they got gumption, anyhow. They told them white folks up yonder in the office just what they thought of 'em. That's what they did."

"And look at 'em now," I said, "going through the alley looking for something to eat."

"Well, they got gumption," my wife yelled, "and that's something!"

"You can't eat gumption," Jack remarked, which made my wife mad.

"You can't eat sitting-around-on-your-rumpus, neither," she broke out, slamming her iron down on the white man's shirt and looking real hard at our roomer—a look that said, You oughtn't to talk, cause you ain't paid your rent for a month.

I sure was glad I hadn't said nothing, boy.

"What's it all about?" Jack's girl asked. "What's old man Oyster done to get in bad with them relief folks, Miss Clara?"

She had heard about it before from me, but she just wanted to get my wife to running her mouth—and keep her mind off the fact that they hadn't paid their rent that month.

"You ain't heard?" my wife said, choosing a new hot iron. "It's a story worth telling, to my mind, cause they got *gumption* —them Oysters." She looked hard at Jack and me. "Now, old man Oyster—this story goes way back, child—he ain't never amounted to much, just poor and honest. But he always did want to make something out of that boy o' his'n, Charlie—little and runty as he was. He worked hard to do it, too. He portered, bellhopped, did road work, did anything he could get to do. Kept that boy in school after his wife died, washed his ears, kept him clean, tried to make a gentleman out of him—and that boy did pretty well. Grew up and took a commercial bookkeeping-typewriter course in the school, and come out Grade A. *Grade A,* I'm telling you. Graduated and got a job with the white folks. Yes, sir! First time I ever heard tell of a colored boy typewriting or keeping books or anything like that in this white man's town. But Mr. Bartelson what owned the coalyard and fuel office where young Oyster worked, he was from Maine and didn't have no prejudice to speak of, so he give this colored boy a chance in his place. And was them white truck drivers jealous—seeing a Negro working in the office and they out driving trucks! But old man Oyster's boy was *prepared*. I'm telling you, *prepared!* He had a good education and could do the work, black as he was. And he was lucky to find somebody to give him a break, because you know and I know you don't see no colored men working in white folks' offices nowhere hardly.

"Well, sir, old man Oyster was proud as he could be of his boy. We was all proud. The church was proud. The white business school what graduated him was proud. Everything went fine for two or three years. Oyster and Charlie even started to buy a little house, cause the old man was working on the road digging for forty cents a hour. Then the depression came. They stopped building roads, and folks stopped buying fuel to keep warm by. Poor old man Bartelson what owned the coalyard finally had to close up, bankrupted and broke—which left young Oyster without a job, like the rest of us. Old man Oyster was jobless, too, cause the less roads they built and sewers they laid, the less work they gave to colored folks, and give it to the white instead. You know how it is—first to be fired and last to be hired."

Clara was just a-ironing and a-talking. "Then along come this Government relief and WPA and everybody thought times was surely gonna get better. Well, they ain't got no better, leastwise not for colored. Everybody in this town's on relief now but me and you-all—what ain't been here long enough to be on it. I've still got a few washings to do and a little house cleaning now and then, thank God! But look at Sylvester," pointing at me. "They done cut every porter off at the bus station but one. And Syl is jobless as a greyhound.

"Anyhow, to go ahead with Oyster, it were a crying shame to see this poor old man and that fine young colored boy out o' work —and they both ambitious, and steady, and good race men. Well, when relief opened up and they started giving out so many hours of work a month, they put old man Oyster back on the road. Now, his boy, Charlie, ain't never done no kind of work like road work, being a office man. But he thought he'd

have to do it, too, and Charlie wasn't objecting, mind you—
when the Government opened up a office for what they calls
white-collar workers. All the white folks what's been doing
office work in good times, insurance people and store clerks and
such, they went there to get the kind o' work they was used to
doing. Oyster's son went, too. But don't you know they dis-
criminated against him! Yes, sir—the Government discriminat-
ing him because he were black! They said, 'You're not no office
worker,' in spite of all the proofs Charlie had that he were in
Mr. Bartelson's office for three years—the letter Bartelson gave
him and all. But they sent old man Oyster's boy right on out
yonder to work on the road with his father.

"Well, that made the old man mad. He said, 'What am I working all these years for you, educating you to come out here and
dig on the road with me, and you with a education?'

"The old man stopped his work then and there that morning,
laid off, and went right on up to that government office to see the
white man about it. And that's where the trouble commenced!"

Clara was just a-talking and a-ironing. "The Government
white man said, 'You ought to be glad for your boy to get any
kind o' work, these days and times. You can't be picking and
choosing now.'

"But old man Oyster stood there and argued with the man
for his son's rights. That's why I say he's got *gumption*. He said,
'I ain't asking to be picking and choosing, and I ain't asked
nothing for *myself*. I'm speaking about that boy o' mine.
Charlie's got a education. True, he's colored, but he's worked
for three years in a office for one of the finest white men that
ever lived and breathed, Mr. Bartelson. Charlie's got experience.
My boy's a typewriter and a bookkeeper. What for you send him
out to work on a road with me? Ain't this the place what's giving
all the white folks jobs doing what they *used* to doing and know
how to do? My boy ain't know nothing about no pick and shovel.
Why don't you treat Charlie Oyster like you do the rest of the
people and give him some o' his kind o' work?'

" 'We have no office jobs here for Negroes,' said the man,

right flat out like that. 'That's why I sent your son over to where they give out road work. I classify all Negroes as laborers on our relief rolls.'

"Well, that made old man Oyster mad as hell. He said, 'Drat it, I'm a citizen! Is that what WPA is for—to bring more discrimination than what is? I want to know why my boy can't be a typewriter like the rest of 'em what's got training, even if it is on relief. If he could work in a white man's office, ain't he good enough to get work from you—and you the gobernment?'

"Well, this made the white man mad, and he yelled, 'You must be one o' them Communists, ain't you?' And he pressed some kind o' buzzer and sent out for a cop.

"Now, old man Oyster ain't never had no trouble of any kind in this town before, but when them cops started to put their hands on him and throw him out o' that office, he raised sand. He was right, too! But them cops didn't see it that way, and one of 'em brought his stock down on that old man's head and knocked him out.

"When Oyster come to, he was in jail.

"Then old man Oyster's son showed he was a man! Charlie heard about the trouble when he come home from off the road that evening, and he went to the jail to see his papa, boiling mad. When he heard how it was, that white man calling the cops in to beat up his father, he said, 'Pa, I'll be in jail here with you tomorrow.' And sure enough, he was. He went up to that there white-collar relief office the next morning and beat that white man so bad, he ain't got over it yet.

" 'The idea,' young Oyster said, 'of you having my father knocked down and dragged out because he came here to talk to you like a citizen about our rights! Who are you anyway, any more'n me? Try to throw me out o' yere and I'll beat you to a pulp first!'

"Well, that man reached for the buzzer again to call some more cops. When he reached, young Oyster had him! It would a-done me good to see the way that black boy give that white man a fit—cause he turned him every way but loose. When the cops come, they put Charlie in jail all right—but that white man was beat by then! The idea of relief coming here adding prejudice to what we already got, and times as hard as they is."

Clara planked down her iron on the stove. "Anyhow, they didn't keep them Oysters in jail very long, neither father or son. Old Judge Murray give 'em a month apiece, suspended sentence, and let 'em out. But when they got out o' jail, don't you know them relief people wouldn't give Oyster and his boy no more work a-tall! No, sir! They told 'em they wasn't feeding no black reds. Now old man Oyster nor Charlie neither ain't never heard o' Communists—but that's what they called 'em, just cause they went up there and fought for what they ought to have. They didn't win—they're out there in the alleys now hauling trash. But they got gumption!"

"You can't live on gumption," I said, trying to be practical.

"No, but you can choke on shame!" my wife yelled, looking hard at Jack and me. "I ain't never seen you-all fighting for nothing yet. Lord knows you both bad enough off to go out and raise hell somewhere and get something!" She put the iron down with a bang. "If I had a young boy, I'd want him to be like Oyster's son, and not take after none of you—sitting around behind the stove talking 'bout you 'can't live on gumption.' *You* can't live on it cause you ain't got none, that's why! Get up from behind that stove, get out o' here, both of you, and bring me something back I can use—bread, money, or a job, I don't care which. Get up and go on! Scat!"

She waved her iron in the air and looked like she meant to bring it down on my head instead of on a shirt. So Jack and me had to leave that nice warm house and go out in the cold and scuffle. There was no peace at home that morning, I mean. I had to try and work up a little gumption.

Heaven to Hell

There we was dancin' up the steps of glory, my husband, Mackenzie, and me, our earthly troubles over, when who should we meet comin' down but Nancy Smothers!

"That hussy!" I said, "how did she get up here?"

She had her white wings all folded around her, lookin' just like an Easter lily, 'cept that her face was chocolate.

"Nancy Smothers, if you come a-near my husband, I'm gonna crown you!" I said, "I done stood enough from you down on earth, let alone meetin' you in heaven."

All this while Mackenzie ain't said a word. Shame! He knowed he's done wrong with that woman. Mackenzie lifted up his wings like as if he was gonna fly, but I dared him!

"Don't you lift a feather, you dog, you! Just hold your horses! I'm gonna ask God how come this Harlem hussy got to heaven anyhow."

Mackenzie and I went on up the golden stairs. I could see him strainin' his eyeballs, tryin' to look back without turning his head.

Nancy Smothers switched on down the steps, I reckon.

But I never did find out how she got in heaven—because just then I come out from under the ether.

I looked up and saw a pretty white nurse standin' there by my bed just like a angel. I hollered, "Where is Mackenzie? Was he hurt much, too? You know, he was drivin' when we hit that pole!"

The nurse said, "Don't worry, madam. Your husband's all right. He just got a broken arm when the car turned over. But he'll be in to see you by and by. They're keepin' him in the Men's Ward overnight."

"I'm glad he's safe," I said, "I sure am glad!"

Then the nurse said, "This lady's been here with you a long

73

time, sitting by your bed. An old friend of yours, she says. She brought you some flowers."

So I turned my eyes—and there sat Nancy Smothers, right beside of my bed! Just as long-faced and hypocritical as she could be!

"Nancy," I said, "where am I—in heaven *or in hell?*"

"You's still on earth, Amelia," Nancy said sweetly, "and, honey, I just come from the Men's Ward where I seen Mackenzie. He says to tell you he's doin' well."

Even with three broken ribs I would have tried to kill Nancy —that hussy, bringing me messages from my own Mackenzie —but there was that nice white nurse standing beside me like an angel, and I always did hate to act up in front of white folks.

All I said was, "Nancy, I wish you'd been with us in that wreck! Then I could a-got some pleasure out of it. I'd just love to see you all crippled up."

"Shss-ss-s!" said the nurse. "You're weak! You mustn't talk so loud!"

"You shouldn't excite yourself, dear," said Nancy, rising, "so I'll be going on home. I know you're out of your head."

"I wish you'd go to . . ."

"Shss-sss-s-s!" said the nurse.

Then I realized I was startin' to act up in front of that nice sweet white nurse, so I tried to smile. "Good-by, Nancy."

She said, "Good-by, Amelia," her eyes gleamin' like a chesscat's. That snake! Snake!

When the nurse took my temperature again, she said, "That's strange, madam! Your fever's gone away up!"

"Strange, nothin'," I thought to myself.

But then how could that pretty young nurse know I was layin' there worryin' myself to death about whether Nancy Smothers went on home or not—*or if the hussy went back in the Men's Ward to set beside Mackenzie?*

Love can be worse than hell.

Sailor Ashore

"What's your story, Morning Glory?"

"Like your tail, Nightingale."

Azora answered the sailor with as impudent a couplet as she could muster on short notice. This rhymed jive was intended as a compliment, for the sailor was big, brown, and handsome, except that he had sad eyes. Azora was coffee-and-cream colored, leaning slightly to the heavy side.

The sailor took her in with his eyes and decided she would do. Their stools were side by side. The bar was cozy. He was just a little drunk.

"Hold your attitude," he said.

"Solid," affirmed Azora.

"Have a drink?"

"What you think?"

"Well, all reet! That's down my street! Name it!"

"White Horse. Send it trotting!"

"Get a commission?"

"Sure," said Azora. She thought she might as well tell the truth. This bird was probably hep anyhow. But that shouldn't keep him from spending money. Shore leave was short and gay spots scarce after midnight. Colored folks didn't have many after-hour places to go on Central Avenue for, with elections coming, the politicians were cleaning up the city.

"Yes," said Azora, "I get a commission. What's it to you?"

"Set her up," said the sailor to the bartender. "And gimme a gin. What's your name, Miss Fine Brown Frame?"

"Azora."

"Mine's Bill."

"Bill, how are you?"

"Like a ship left to drift. I been looking for you all night. Shall we drink some more here—or go to your house?"

"My house? You act like you know me."

"I feel like I know you. Where's the liquor store?"

"Two doors down, bootleg, extra charge."

"Let's dig it."

Outside the moon was brighter than the street lights, the stars big in the sky. The girl put her arm through Bill's.

"I don't live far," Azora said.

"I'll keep up with you."

"I'm fast as greased lightning and slippery as a pig," jived Azora. "Play my name and you liable to catch a gig."

"Ain't you from Chicago?" asked the sailor.

"Thirty-ninth and State," said Azora.

"I knowed it. All they do in Chicago's play policy. But out here on the Coast the Chinaman's got everything sewed up."

"Tight as Dick's hatband."

"If you beat that Chinese lottery with all them spots to mark —you really beat something," commented the sailor.

The lights in the liquor joint were hard as tin. "What kind of whisky you like, Azora, when you ain't boosting bar sales?"

"Any kind, honey."

They bought a pint and started home to her room. Away from the bright lights of the bar, in the cool night air, the sailor suddenly fell silent. Under the street lights Azora noticed that his face, when he wasn't talking or smiling, was very sad. Well, sometimes she felt sad, too, but she tried not to look it.

She lived in one of those little two-room boxes that sit back in yards in Los Angeles behind two or three more little houses. It was cozy inside. She turned the radio on and got out her tray of glasses. They drank. But the sailor remained quiet. He looked into the brown whisky as if he was looking for something. Maybe he is drunk, Azora thought, or just sleepy. He kept looking down, frowning.

"Why don't you look at me?" Azora asked.

"I don't see no crystal ball in your eyes," the sailor answered.

"Crystal ball?"

"Yah, I'm trying to see my future."

"What old future?"

"My black future."

"What about mine, honey?"

"Yours is sewed up," said the sailor.

"Sewed up?"

"Sure, you ain't gonna be nothing. Neither am I."

"Honey, what makes you talk so serious? We come here to have some fun," said the woman.

"We're colored, ain't we?"

"Sure! Colored as we can be."

"Then we can't get nowhere in this white man's country," said the sailor.

"Yes, we can, too. There ain't no use talking like that, baby. I got a little boy, and I'm sure gonna make something out of him."

"I ain't talking about your little boy, Azora. I'm talking about you and me. We ain't gonna be nothing."

"You're something now, honey—a big, strong, fine stud." She leaned toward him. "What does them stripes mean on your arm?"

"Nothing. A colored sailor can have all the stripes he wants on his arm. The white man still cusses him out."

"Who cussed you out, honey? You had trouble on your ship today? Is that why, all of a sudden, you so grouchy?"

"Yah, I had trouble. Looks like they think I'm a dog to 'buse around."

"Well, let's not talk about it no more. Leave your troubles aboard."

"Suppose I do leave 'em aboard? I run into 'em all over again ashore," he muttered. "Look how far from the docks I have to come to have a little fun. Can't even get a decent drink out at the port. The bars won't serve Negroes."

"Boy, you talk like you just now finding out you're colored. Now, me, I've been colored a long time."

"So've I, but——"

"But what?"

"I don't know. To listen at the radio, you would think we never had no Jim Crow and lynchings and prejudice in America at all. Even the Southerners are talking about liberty and freedom. White folks is funny, Azora, especially when they get all noble and speechifying."

"True. But I can deal with 'em, can't you?"

"Naw, they got me in a squirrel cage."

"You take it too serious. I work for white folks every day, cook and scrub. It's hard work, too."

"Then what you doing out ballyhooing all night long?"

"Saturday, ain't it? Besides, suppose I hadn't been out, I wouldn't've run into you."

"You got something there! How old's your kid you mentioned?"

"Eleven. Sixth grade in school. He's a fine boy."

"Un-hum. Wish I had a kid."

"Never been married?"

"No." The sailor shook his head.

"I'm a grass widow. I got nobody, either, now. You reckon you and me could get along?"

"I been looking for a girl like you. Fix that last drink."

She mixed the whisky and soda.

"I've only got three months more to go in the Navy."

"I've been on my job in Beverly Hills for ten years."

"No wonder you got such a sweet little shack. How come you've got no old man?"

"Colored men's all too much like you—got your mind on not being nothing. Always complaining, always discouraged. Always talking about this is a white man's world."

"This *is* a white man's world, ain't it?"

"No, it ain't! I'm in it, too! I'm colored—and I'm gonna make something out of my son."

"You always talking about your son. I'm talking about us now."

"There ain't no just us. There's us—and everybody else. If things is bad, change 'em! You a man, ain't you?"

"I hope so."

"Then talk like a man."

The sad look deepened in the sailor's eyes.

"You a mighty hard chick to get along with," he said.

"What did you ask me tonight when we first met in that bar?"

"I said, 'What's your story, Morning Glory?' " remembered the sailor.

"You've heard my tale, Nightingale," said the girl.

"The whisky is all gone," said the sailor. "I better go—seeing as how I ain't man enough for you."

He looked around for his cap, found it, and opened the door. Azora didn't try to stop him.

"Thanks for the inspiring conversation," he said as he closed the door.

He got a few steps down the path between the houses when he heard her knob turn. A rectangle of light fell into the yard, with Azora's shadow silhouetted in the middle.

She called, "Say, listen, sailor! Wait a minute! Com'ere!"

Her voice was harder than before. He turned and saw her standing in the doorway. Slowly he came back to the steps.

"Listen, sailor," said Azora, "ain't neither one of us gonna be nothing! I lied when I told you I had a son. I ain't got nobody. I don't work in Beverly Hills. I work on the streets and in bars. I ain't nothing but a hustler."

"I knowed what you was the minute I saw you," said the sailor.

"Yeah? Well, listen, kid! If I ever *did* have a son—and if I ever do have a job—if I wasn't what I am—I'd make something out of my son, if I had one! I swear to God I would, sailor!"

The man looked at the woman in the doorway a long time.

"I say, I swear to God I would," she repeated as he walked away.

Slice Him Down

In Reno in the thirties, among the colored folks of the town, there were two main social classes—those who came to the city on a freight train and those who did not. The latter, or cushion-riders, were sometimes inclined to turn flat noses high at those who rode the rods by way of entry to the city. Supercilious glances on the part of old settlers and chair-car arrivals tobogganed down broad Negro noses at the black bums who, like the white bums, both male and female, streamed through Nevada during the depression years on their way to or from the Coast, to remain a while, if the law would let them, in THE BIGGEST LITTLE CITY IN THE WORLD—RENO—according to the official sign in electric lights near the station.

But, of course, the rod-riders got off nowhere near the station. If they were wise, bums from the East got off at Sparks, several miles from the famous mecca of unhappy wives, then they footed it into Reno. (Only passengers with tickets, coaches or Pullmans, can afford the luxury of alighting directly at any station, anywhere.)

Terry and Sling came in one day on a fast freight from Salt Lake. Before that they had come from Cheyenne. And before that, from Chicago—and then the line went south and got lost somewhere in a tangle of years and cottonfields and God-knows-what fantasies of blackness.

They were Southern shines. Sure, shines—darkies—niggers—Terry and Sling. At least, that's what the railroad bulls called them often enough on the road. And you don't deny anything to a railroad bull, do you? They hit too hard and shoot too fast. And, after all, why argue over a name? It's only when your belly's full and your pride's up that you want people to call you Mr. Terry, Mr. Sling . . . Mr. Man.

80

"What's your name, boy?" asked a colored voice in the near-darkness.

"What you care? You might be a detective."

Terry grinned from ear to ear at the compliment. He put one hand in a raggedy pocketless pocket and scratched himself.

"You's a no-name boy like me, heh, fella? Well, maybe you is equally as bad as me, too? Mean and hongry and bad! Listen, let's me and you travel together, since we's on the road. What shall I call you?"

"Call me Sling."

Freights were being made up in the Chicago railroad yards at dusk. Rattlers on rollers going somewhere—must be better than here, Lawd, better than here.

"I'm tough, too," said Sling, eying a passing string of box-cars. "I eats pig iron for breakfast."

"Huh! I use cement for syrup on hot cakes made o' steel," said Terry.

"That's why I'm leavin' town," said scarred-up Sling, " 'cause I spit in a bozo's eye yesterday and killed him stone dead! I spit bullets."

Just then they grabbed a westbound freight on the wing. They lied all the way to Omaha as they squatted in the corner of an open-lathed empty car where plenty of cattle had left plenty of smells on their various trips to the Chicago market.

"Why, man, I done killed me so many mens in my day that I'm scared I'll kill myself some time by accident," said Sling. "When I shaves myself, I tries not to look mean—to keep from pullin' my own razor across my own throat. I'm a bad jigaboo, son."

"Huh! You ain't nowheres near as bad·as me," Terry lied, long tall lies, all the way from Omaha to Cheyenne. "Lemme tell you 'bout the last duster that crossed my path. He were an Al Capone—machine gun and all—and I just mowed him down with my little thirty-two on a forty-four frame. Man, I made lace curtains out of his a-nat-toe-mie!"

"Why?"

" 'Cause he were white, and I were mad 'cause he were messin' with my State Street gal."

"Man, you let women mess you up that way?"

"I did that time."

"They ain't worth fightin' about."

"I know it—but I does fight about 'em."

"I does, too, man, but I ain't gonna no mo'. I'm through fightin' 'bout women."

"Me, too."

"Then we's buddies. Womens done messed me up too much."

"And me."

By that time the coal car they were in was running too slow for anybody's good, nearing a town. What town? On the map, Cheyenne.

But no map ever made would have a dot on it for the alley where the garbage can was at the A-1 Café's back door that gave up only a half-dozen rinds of raw squash, a handful of bacon skins, and a few bread crusts to feed two long tall black boys named Terry and Sling.

"Let's get on down the road, boy." As the stars came out.

"Dust my broom, pal."

"Swing your feet, Terry. Let's make this early evenin' rattler."

> *Aw, do it freight train!*
> *Wheelers roll!*
> *Dog-gone my hard,*
> *Unlucky soul!*

Reno! THE BIGGEST LITTLE CITY IN THE WORLD blazing its name in lights at night in a big arch of a sign all the way across the street. But they couldn't read the sign too well. Hunger and rain and a bad education all stood between them and the reading of that sign.

Autumn in Reno! Dog-bite my onions! Stacks of shining silver dollars on the tables—even in depression times—wheels spinning in gambling places, folks winning, losing, winning. THE BANK CLUB: big plate-glass windows on the main street.

Stand right on the sidewalk and look in at the Bank Club. Dice, keno, roulette, piles of silver. Pretty sight.

"There must not be no law in Reno."

"Must ain't," said Sling.

"Must be all the cartwheels in the world in Reno."

"Must is," said Sling.

"Here we stays in Reno."

"Here we stays, Terry," said Sling.

As luck would have it, they got jobs, settled in Reno, got a room, got gambling change, got girls. And there the trouble began—with the girls.

Terry was shining shoes at a stand in front of the station. Sling was elbow-greasing the floor of a Chinese lottery and dice joint, acting as general janitor, bouncer, and errand boy all in one. Between them they made ten or twelve dollars a week, not bad in those times. Suits on credit—three dollars down. Two-tone shoes. Near-silk shirts. Key chains—without keys. Who cares about keys? You *wear* the chains. String 'em across your breast! Hang 'em from your pockets. Man, they shine like silver! Shine like gold—them chains! You can't wear keys.

"Boy, you ought to see my gal! Three quarters cat—and didn't come here on no freight train, neither," said Terry, putting a stocking cap on his head to make his hair lay down.

"You come on a rattler, so hush," said Sling. "My gal did, too, so don't bring that up!"

"All right, pal! Take it easy! You know I'm a bad man."

"Almost as bad as I is, ain't you?" said Sling, spraying his armpits with rose-colored talcum from a tall ten-cent store box.

"You mean as bad as you would like to be," kidded Terry, at the same time wishing, in his heart of hearts, that he had a big knife scar somewhere on his body like the one Sling had halfway across his neck and down his shoulder blade—a true sign of battle. "You'd like to be tough," kidded Terry.

But Sling let that pass. He was kinda tired and in no mood for joking, nor quarreling, either. A Chinaman sure can work you hard in one day! Poor *hockaway* gets worked hard everywhere by everybody. Almost too tired to wash up and go see my gal. Dog-gone! That's why he used so much talcum powder, he was so tired.

Meanwhile, Terry put on his derby at a cocky angle, got that off his mind, and looked around under the bed for his shoes. As he tied his brown-and-white oxfords, he kept thinking in his mind how his sweet mama didn't come to Reno on no freight train. No, sir! Not that dame o' mine! Angelina Walls is her name, Mrs. Angelina Walls. Cooks for a white lady from Frisco who come to Reno to get unchained and brought along her maid. And the maid done fell for me! Ha! Ha! Angelina! Fell for a smooth black papa with a deep Chicago line. Old young Terry's done got himself a woman, sure enough.

"Boy, lend me your honey-brown tie, will you?"

"Aw-right," said Sling.

Tonight Sling's thoughts were on his lady love, too, tired as he was. Dark and Indian-looking, his particular girl. She didn't work much, neither. Just rested. She made her living—somehow. Wore a rabbitskin coat and a gold wrist watch. . . . Sure, she come to town on a freight train—but she rode in taxis on rainy nights! Had a nice room. Had a good heart. Liked an old long tall boy by the name of Sling, with a razor scar across his shoulder. Hot dog!

Her name was Charlie-Mae. Charlie-Mae what? I dunno! Nobody was ever heard to call her by her last name, if she had one. She might have had one, maybe. Who knows? Probably did. Charlie-Mae—Indian-looking girl in a rabbitskin coat with a gold wrist watch, Lawd!

"Let's haul it to the club," said Terry, "soon's I go get Angelina."

"I'll pick you up," said Sling, "by and by. You truck on down."

So Terry tapped on down the street in his derby hat and honey-colored tie to get Mrs. Walls.

Shortly thereafter, in a sky-blue suit with wide shoulders, Sling went looking for Charlie-Mae, key chain just a-swinging, shining, and swinging.

Both boys really looked hot in the gorgeous sense—but the

sad facts were that it was late November by now and neither one of them had yet worked up to an overcoat to cover their outer finery. So it should be recorded that before donning their stylish suits and ties and hats, they had put on underneath clean shirts various sweaters, sweat shirts, and other warm but unsightly garments from their meager store in order the better to face the cold Nevada wind.

Saturday night in Reno. Back-alley Reno. Colored Reno by the railroad tracks where you can hear the trains go by. Where do they go, them trains? Where do they come from? What is there where them trains go better than here, Lawd, better than here? Colored folks always live down by the railroad tracks, but is there any train anywhere runnin' where a man ain't black? Far or near, Lawd, is it better than here—Reno on a Saturday night?

"Anyhow, who gives a damn about being black when he's hard and tough as I is?" said Terry, leaving the house near the park where he had called at the white lady's back door for his girl friend.

"Well, for a woman it ain't easy being black," said Mrs. Angelina Walls. "I could a-been much better educated, had I been white. Now, down South where I growed up, there wasn't any schools hardly for colored. But as it were, I learned to read and write, and I holds my head high. I ain't common! I come here on a train, myself!"

"You all right with me," Terry said proudly as they walked down the street toward the alley where the colored club was located. "A high-toned woman like you's all right with me."

"Then don't mix me with no dirt," said Mrs. Angelina Walls. "That's one reason I don't like to go to this old club. Any-and-everybody goes there. Womens right off the street. Bums right off the freight."

"They sure do," said Terry, feeling kinda shamed to take her there, educated as she was. "But they ain't no place else for jigs to go in Reno."

"You right, honey," said Mrs. Angelina Walls. "We has to get a glass o' beer somewhere and dance a little bit once in a while."

"We sho' do."

"You can have a right smart good time at that there club," said Sling as he and his girl came down the steps of the third-rate Japanese rooming house where she lived.

"We sho' can," said Charlie-Mae, buttoning her rabbit fur. "Um-m! This air smells good tonight."

"Would smell better if it weren't so cold," said Sling. "I never did like for winter to start coming."

"I do," said Charlie-Mae. "It's better for my business. I don't always have a nice affectionate fella like you to look after me."

"But you got me now," said Sling, "so you don't have to worry."

"When we gonna start living together?"

"Soon's I get my next pay from that Chinaman in the dice house. But I kinda hate to move away from Terry, 'cause me and him's been real good buddies. He's mighty nigh as bad a man as I is, and don't neither one of us take no foolishness. I'm tellin' you, Charlie-Mae," Sling lied, "you ought to seen how we used to do them railroad bulls when we was on the road together. We used to slice 'em right down! I mean, cut 'em to ribbons and leave their carcass in the railroad yard if they messed with us."

"You did?"

"Sho' did."

"You and Terry?"

"Me and Terry! We used to slice them bulls right down."

"But Terry ain't got no scars."

"He sho' ain't," said Sling. "I just now thought o' that. I'm so bad, I done been scarred up two or three times, if not more."

' "That's a lovely cut on your right shoulder," said Charlie-Mae. "But, say! Listen, not changing the subject, Terry's sure got a funny taste in women, ain't he? Going around with that old stuck-up yellow hussy they calls Mrs. Angelina Walls. I heard her say she didn't speak to nobody what come here on a freight train, herself."

"She's got a high nose," said Sling. "But Terry, he's all right."

Packed and jammed, the club, on Saturday night. Little colored club in Reno. Six-foot bar and dance floor no bigger than a dime. Old piano with the front wide open, strings showing, and all the hammers of the notes bare, played by a little fat coal-black man in shirt sleeves with a glass of gin by his side. A young light-yellow boy beating drums out of this world!

Piano player singing as the dancers dance:

> "I'm goin' down de road and
> I won't look back a-tall.
> I say, Good-by, mama, it
> Ain't no use to call.
>
> "I'm goin' down to Frisco and
> I'm goin' by myself.
> I'm sorry for you, honey, but
> You sho' Lawd will be left."

Sling and Charlie-Mae dancing in a slow embrace. Mrs. Angelina Walls and Terry sitting at the bar drinking.

Angelina really shouldn't have had so many beers, with her education and reserve and all, but when you cook the whole week long for white folks over a hot stove, you need something on a Saturday night.

"A little recreation," she said, "a little recreation!"

"You right," said Terry, downing a straight whisky.

"Gimme another shetland," said Angelina. The barman drew a small glass of beer. "And don't you bother, baby," said Angelina as Terry reached in his pocket to pay for it. "I make more money'n you do. I'll pay. Hurry up and drink your'n so you can have a glass or two on me."

"O.K.," said Terry, tipsy enough to begin mixing his drinks. "Gimme a shetland, too."

As the music ended, several of the dancers flocked toward the bar, among them Sling and Charlie-Mae, arm in arm.

"Here comes the common herd," said Angelina, but Terry didn't grasp what she said. Charlie-Mae heard, however—and understood, too—as she sat down on a stool and turned her back.

"Gimme two shetlands," Sling called to the barman. "Hy there, buddy," he said to Terry, slapping his pal on the back, "you's huggin' the rail mighty close tonight. Why don't you dance?"

But before Terry could answer, Mrs. Walls explained. "The floor at this club's too full of riffraff for me," she said. "I come here to Reno on a *train*, myself." She was aiming directly at Charlie-Mae sitting beside her.

"That's more'n your boy friend did," said Sling, grinning at Terry.

"Well, if he didn't," said Mrs. Walls in a high half-drunken voice, "he's a real man right on. He earns a decent living shining shoes—not working down in no Chinese rat hole like you, cleaning up after gamblers, and running around with womens what don't know they name."

Sling was shamed into silence—but Charlie-Mae whirled around toward Mrs. Walls and slapped her face. Angelina's beer went all over her dress. Terry pushed Charlie-Mae from her stool. She landed on the floor.

"Don't you touch my woman," Sling yelled at his pal.

"Well, tell her not to touch *my* woman, then," said Terry. "Don't you know who I is? I'm badder'n usual tonight."

"Huh!" said Sling.

"Terry, protect me," Mrs. Walls cried, holding her well-slapped cheek. "A decent girl can't live in this town."

"No, they can't," said Charlie-Mae, rising, "not if they acts like you—and I'm around."

"Don't mess with her," warned Sling, glaring at Terry.

"Man, is you talking to me?" asked Terry of his friend.

"I'm bad," said Sling.

"Is you tryin' to tell *me* who's bad in this town? If there's anybody bad, it's Terry. I'm a terrible terrier this evenin', too!"

"Bark on!" said Sling.

"Listen, honey," pleaded Charlie-Mae loudly in Sling's ear, "do him like you said you did them railroad bulls—slice him down for knocking me off my stool."

Said Terry, "Slice who down?"

"Slice you down," said Sling, "if you fools around with me. You my buddy, and we don't want no trouble, but just leave me and Charlie-Mae alone, that's all, and take your old hinkty heifer out o' here where she belong, 'cause she can't stand no company sides herself. She's a fool!"

"Oh!" screamed Mrs. Walls. "You hear him, Terry? Hit him! Hit him for my sake!"

"If he do, he'll never hit another human," said Sling slowly.

"Boy," said Terry, "I'll pickle you in a minute in your own blood."

"And you'll be sliced baloney," said Sling.

"Not me!" cried Terry drawing a switch-blade and backing toward the wall. His knife was the kind that has a little button in it and double action. When you push the button once, the blade flies out halfway. When you push it twice, it flies out about six inches.

Switch-blades are dangerous weapons, but Sling was prepared. He drew a razor, a good old steel razor, slightly outmoded for shaving, but still useful for defense.

Didn't nobody holler, "Don't let 'em fight!"

On a Saturday night in a little club, down by the railroad track out West, in a town between the mountains, what could be more fun than a good fight with knives and razors? It didn't matter if they were buddies, them boys—didn't nobody holler, "Stop that fight!"

Women stood on stools and tables. The barman got on a beer keg behind the bar. The piano player brought his piano stool nearer the scene of combat.

Folks had to hold Charlie-Mae to keep her from attacking Angelina, for two fights at the same time would have spoilt the fun.

"You women wait," everybody said.

"Boy, I'm tellin' you, I mean business," warned Sling, his eyes red, his teeth shining, and his feelings hurt. "Don't come a-near me!"

"I done heard so much from you about how bad you is," said Terry. "I just want to see. You been my pal, but I believe you's lyin' about your badness."

His long face was a shiny oval under his derby. He was trembling.

"I'll cut you down," said Sling, "like you warn't no friend."

"Cut then—and don't talk," said Terry, " 'cause I'm quicker'n greased lightnin' and I'm liable to get you first."

Suddenly his knife flashed and Sling's left coat sleeve split like a torn ribbon—*swiss-ss-sh!* But at the same time Sling's razor made a moonlike upward movement and cut straight through the brim of Terry's derby, narrowly missing an eyebrow.

The crowd roared. It was getting good. Didn't nobody say, "Don't let them boys fight."

Sling, with a quick movement of his arm, sent the derby swirling through space and brought his weapon back into play for a slash at Terry's vitals, his flying razor cutting a wide gash straight across his friend's middle, slicing the front of Terry's pants open at the belt and exposing several layers of undergarments. But Terry's switch-blade went deep into Sling's fashionably padded shoulder before either stepped back.

Both began to bleed, but nobody fell. Their new and still unpaid-for suits got cut and stained. Blood dropped down on their two-tone shoes as the fighters stood apart, panting for a few moments.

A loud murmur went up from the crowd, and Mrs. Walls screamed, "My God!" as Sling's razor found the mark it had been looking for—a place where a cut would always show on a man so that people could say that he, Sling, had put it there. He slit the side of Terry's face right down, from temple to chin.

"Sling," Terry cried, "don't do that to me! Man, I'm bad! I'm telling you, I'm bad and I'll hurt you!"

"Lemme see," said Sling, panting against the bar, "I'se heard tell you's bad. Lemme see."

"I'll show you," said Terry, charging so swiftly that before Sling could sidestep, he ran his knife all the way up to the hilt in his companion's side—and left it there.

Sling looked down, saw where the knife had lodged, gasped, trembled, rolled his eyes up, and crumpled backward to the floor.

Terry saw his pal go down, taking the knife with him, embedded in his sky-blue coat, his mouth agape, his razor arm limp, his eyes like eggs. And something about the sight of that falling body made his own limbs begin to shake, his knees grow weaker, his bleeding jaw hurt more and more, and his throat fill up with his beating heart. Suddenly, he, too, passed out, sinking prone upon the floor.

"Here! Here! Here!" barked the bartender as he saw them both topple, "you two boys done fought enough now. Cut it out, I say! Cut it out!"

He jumped over the bar and pushed his way through the crowd. As Charlie-Mae shrieked hysterically and strong men turned their heads, the bartender stooped and pulled the knife from Sling's side.

"Funny," he said, frowning sharply, "there ain't no blood on this knife! Some of you-all take care o' Terry yonder while I see after this boy."

The bartender raised Sling up but his unseeing head fell limply backward. Others crowded near to help and to stare. They took off his sky-blue coat. One arm was bloody. They took off his vest, too, and unbuttoned his lemon-cream shirt. Underneath, he had on a gray sweat shirt. They pulled that off. Under the sweat shirt he wore a ragged purple sweater. They removed that.

"I don't see how any knife ever got to his skin," said one of the helpers, "with all these clothes he's got on."

"I don't believe it did," said the bartender. "His side ain't bleedin'."

And sure enough, when they finally got down to Sling's

cocoa-colored skin, he didn't have a scratch on his body—except
that old scar across his shoulder. His arm was cut slightly,
but his body proper was not harmed in the least.

"Pshaw! That there knife had to go through too many wrap-
pings. He ain't dead," said the bartender disappointedly.

"Boy, you wake up!"

He dropped Sling's head back on the floor with a bang, to
turn his attention to Terry. By now Terry was sitting up, a
towel tied around his sliced slit cheek.

"Did I kill him?" Terry moaned. "Is I done kilt my partner?"

"Naw, you ain't killed nobody," the bartender barked. "Both
you hucks get up off that floor and let things be as they were
before this mess started. Shame on you, lettin' a little blood scare
you—till you so weak you have to lay down. Sling, unroll them
eyes!"

By this time Sling's eyes were unrolled, and he felt his half-
naked body in amazement at finding it still whole. Only his
forearm bled a little where the fleshy part was cut. He sat up to
look anxiously across at Terry.

Terry looked back at Sling and then pointed to his wounded
jaw.

"Say, boy, is I got me a good scar?"

"Terry," Sling said, his voice shaking, "I thought I'd done
killed you."

"I said, boy, is I got me a good scar?"

"Man," Sling said generously, "you got a better scar than I
got now—'cause your'n is gonna be on your face where everybody can see it, and mine's just on my shoulder."

Terry grinned with delight. "All right, then," he said as he
rose from the floor. "We's got something in common. This
fight's been *some* good after all! Get up from there, Sling, and
put on your clothes. Let's have a drink."

As Sling gathered up his near-silk shirt and ragged sweater,
his well-sliced coat and wrinkled tie, Terry looked around for
his "company."

"Where's my lady friend?" he asked.

"Who? Angelina Walls?" some woman answered. "Why,

man, she runned out of here no sooner'n she seed you get cut!
She couldn't be mixed up in no murder trial. She's too respectable."

"A hinkty hussy!" said Sling.

"She is for true," said Terry. "Come on, boy, let's drink."

Sling, his lemon-colored shirttail out, looked around for his
woman. "Charlie-Mae," he said, glaring at his erstwhile sweetie
as she emerged all freshly powdered from the Ladies Room,
"this boy's my pal, and here you done liked to made me kill him,
right this evenin'. You get goin'!"

Charlie-Mae, heeding the look in Sling's eyes, got going.
Without a word she donned her rabbit fur and left.

The two big fellows, tattered and torn, key chains dangling
and sartorial effects awry, rested their elbows on the bar. They
grinned proudly at one another.

"Two shetlands," Sling said to the bartender.

"For two bad men," said Terry, " 'cause we really bad!"

"We slice 'em down," said Sling.

"We really slice 'em down," said Terry.

His Last Affair

Every five or six years, Henry Q. Marston came to New York.
He loved New York for the very good reason that he didn't
know anybody there. In his home town in Indiana Mr. Marston
knew everybody, from the Mayor who asked him to serve on
civic committees to the junk man who expected a ham at Christmas—for Marston was a wealthy man, a prominent citizen, and
a good Christian.

In Terre Haute his virtues were fully recognized. As a result,
his time was not his own. All the charities, from the Red Cross
to the foreign missions, all the lodges, clubs, and various organizations connected with the church, were constantly calling on

him. Besides, the demands of his business were many and time-
taking. He was a man of affairs.

Mr. Marston was in real estate, feed, grain, apples, and a
number of other commercial activities connected with the soil
of Indiana. He was a trustee of two or three banks. His offices
took up a whole floor in a downtown building, with branches
in Indianapolis and Gary. But Mr. Marston preferred to live in
the small city of Terre Haute, where he had lived all his life,
in spite of ambitious wives and daughters who always seemed to
want to live elsewhere, even in Chicago.

At fifty, fat, bluff, and bold, he had been married three times,
but had buried two wives. One wife, however, was still very
much alive, former president of the Federated Women's Clubs
of the state and a great worker in temperance and the church.
She was a large lady who wore glasses and presided over their
stately home with a firm and proper grace, caring for her own
children and stepchildren alike in a most capable manner.

Mr. Marston couldn't complain about his home life, for it
was exemplary, a model for all homes, and a pattern of Christian virtue. But every two or three years Mr. Marston just had
to get away! This spring his wife had gone to California to attend an important congress of clubwomen meeting in Pasadena.
She was gone three weeks. No sooner had she departed than
Mr. Marston went to New York. It had been a long time since
the smell of Broadway struck his small-town nostrils.

Mr. Marston needed Broadway like a colt needs a pasture. He
found it madder and gayer than ever, and there were still plenty
of hot spots for suckers. When Mr. Marston was spending
money in a town where he didn't know anybody, he didn't give
a damn about being a sucker. At home such sportiveness would
have been un-Christian, but in New York nobody cared, nobody
was even unduly impressed, and there were no prosaic hang-
overs in the way of requests for periodical donations, committees
demanding services, or missionaries asking him to pay and pray
for the heathen. Broadway didn't go in for salvation of any sort.
Self-sufficient, that street.

In New York Mr. Marston wined, dined, danced, and gambled until two of his three weeks were nearly up. He went to the Latin Quarter and the Peppermint Lounge. He had a few dates with ladies, but never at his own hotel, and never telling any of them his real name. Oh, he had a fine time being incognito in a town where he didn't know anybody.

Imagine his surprise when, early one morning, right on the corner of Forty-seventh and Broadway, where the lights are brighter than the noonday sun, somebody called his name. Somebody called his *right* name, "Hello, Henry Marston," in a sweetly feminine voice.

Mr. Marston wondered, "Now, who can that be?" He started to walk on, but curiosity got the best of him, so he turned to see. There on the corner stood a smartly dressed young woman, or rather a *young-looking* woman, tall and cool, saying, "Hello, Henry."

"Why—er—good evening," Mr. Marston replied, thinking perhaps it was one of his renters from Indiana, or an unknown lady of his church who would, of course, know him—a trustee. But this woman, although having a faint Midwestern aura about her, was distinctly New Yorkish. Mr. Marston was puzzled.

"How are you, Henry?" she said familiarly, offering a gloved hand. "It's been years since I've seen you."

That was a relief—years. But there was such a thrill to her hand that Mr. Marston said as he held it, "I'm mighty glad to see you *now*," wondering all the time who in the world she could be.

"Years and years," she said. "Don't you remember, Henry?"

An old schoolmate perhaps? Or some friend's daughter? Her age was indefinite. But Mr. Marston finally had to ask her when and where.

"Don't you really remember?" she said, smelling very sweet as her blue eyes looked into his.

He was ashamed, but he didn't. Maybe he could recollect if given time, he said. Evidently she felt he should have time, because she suggested stepping into Lindy's for coffee and a little chat. Because she was so charming, Mr. Marston agreed to go that far, at least, on the road to recollection.

"I seem to know you," he said, feeling in her nearness something pleasurably familiar.

"Quite well," the lady answered. "Don't you recall?"

"Here, in New York?" Mr. Marston asked, thinking perhaps of the days when he used to come to Manhattan under his own name, before he was so prominent or so wealthy.

"Oh, no," she said, "back home in Indiana."

"Indiana?"

"Yes, Indiana."

"Who are you?" asked Mr. Marston, unable to stand it any longer.

"Callie," the woman said simply.

"Callie!" gasped Mr. Marston. "Callie?" he cried staring at her.

"Calista now," she said, "Calista Lowery."

"Callie Lowery!"

"After all these years"—smiling. "Do you, perhaps, still love me?"

The trouble with that question was that Mr. Marston even now could not be sure whether he did or didn't. He could only sit and stare at her and notice the growing familiarity of her face and features, delicately powdered and even more beautiful; womanly, not girlish, but strange and vital as ever; and her hair twice as golden as it used to be. Callie!

The waiter came. They ordered dinner—for neither had eaten.

"We were waiting for each other," said Calista, smiling.

Henry was not hungry, confusion and surprise having taken his appetite away, although he ate, forcing the food down. He was too perturbed by—Calista. He remembered too well the last time he had seen her. Suddenly he recalled her mother's face, and his mother's face; the tears and cuss words of that awful day; and the fact that his father had had a pretty hard time getting him out of that scrape—his first "affair."

Back home in Indiana years ago in high school, he met Callie. She was from the wrong side of town, and wanted to be an actress. An incredible calling in those days, indecent and not befitting a lady—but glamorous to a young girl, and to a boy in high school who hadn't met many actresses. Every time a road show or a stock company came to town, Henry would be in the gallery of the Opera House; and Callie would be there, too, sometimes alone, sometimes with her mother. She was "sweet sixteen" then, poor but ambitious, and had never been kissed.

One night, when he had met her at the show alone, young Marston took her home—to the wrong side of town. He kissed her. He was never so thrilled before—or since. The memory of that thrill came back to him now as he looked at her across the table in Lindy's.

All that winter long ago, years ago now, before radio or the inroads of television, they met at the movies or in the gallery of the Opera House in their general admission seats, looking at *Under Two Flags* or *East Lynne*, *Uncle Tom's Cabin* or *Buster Brown*. Once they saw *Camille*, and Callie said, her eyes like stars, "Henry, one of my dreams is to go to Paris."

Henry agreed that he would like to go, also. Then, after the show, he walked her home through the snow to her side of town; and walked alone all the way back to his parents' house in a section where "decent" people lived.

One night in the spring Henry and Callie stopped in the park on their way home. They stopped several times thereafter. The next thing he knew, Callie was announcing dramatically, in the tragic manner of the leading lady in a stock company, "Henry, darling, I am with child!"

That bowled young Marston over—just about to graduate from high school as president of his class. That bowled over his father, too, when he heard of it. And it put his poor mother in bed for two weeks.

"That Lowery girl, my God! Why, she rouges and powders and wants to be an actress! I expect she smokes cigarettes. And nobody knows a thing about her family."

Well, they got Henry out of it by the hardest. There were

tears, scenes—and money paid to her gypsy-looking mama.
Then Callie and her mother went away to Chicago. He never
heard of them again. That was long, long ago, really long ago.

The scent of the old Opera House and Callie's hair came
back to him as he sat there at the table in Lindy's and looked
at her again. He wondered if her hair—now blonde—still
smelled as sweet, if her lips tasted the same. She had retained
her looks remarkably well, indeed she had improved, was slim
and smart in the best New York manner (although she must be
well over forty). In spite of himself, Henry compared her to
the three big wholesome small-town women he had married
and spent his life with. "Did you ever get to be an actress?" he
asked.

"Have you never heard of Calista Lowery?" she demanded
mockingly.

"I've heard of Callie," he said wryly. They both laughed.

"I am an actress, but not a very famous one," she said. "At
least, not a leading lady. I've played a lot of bit parts in stock,
and once or twice on Broadway, but nothing big. You were the
biggest thing in my life, Henry."

"I wish I had been," Mr. Marston said.

"I wish you had remained so," she answered. "Do you remember the Opera House?"

"I should say I do," Mr. Marston said, "and the park." Then
he leaned across the table. "Did we, Callie . . . did we—er
. . . ever have a child?"

"Don't you remember?" Callie said. "Your father wouldn't
let us."

Broadway, lane of lights, strange romances, and the beginning and end of funny fragile things. Hard surfaces, delicate
hearts. Birdland. Jazz bands that sob their mad caprices. Fancies
and dreams.

"Callie," Mr. Marston said, "let's walk in a park again."

During the week that remained to him in Manhattan, Mr.
Marston discovered that Calista's—Callie's complexion was
made by a popular beauty shop; that her hair smelled like a

French hairdresser's pomade; her lips were strawberry rouge; but her softness and her sweetness were still the same—the same as years ago, back home in Indiana.

Mr. Marston had never spent such a joyous seven days in New York, never spent such a seven days in his life, as the days of that week that was the last in Manhattan. Youth and romance came back all over again with Calista. They even went to see a play and sat in the gallery of the theatre just as in the past. Although the play wasn't anything like the old melodramas they had once loved, they were so absorbed in each other that they didn't notice its theme.

Then Mr. Marston had to go back home. His time was up.

In the meanwhile, he decided this would be just an interlude for them, or rather a postlude—for of course Mr. Marston couldn't keep this up now that he was married, had five children, was a pillar in the church and a leading citizen of the West. No, this would have to end when he got on the train.

Callie—Calista—agreed. But when she parted from the fat gray-haired Henry, she acted like her heart was broken. She let two tears stream down her well-enameled face. Mr. Marston could hardly stand to tear himself away. It was almost as bad as that first parting, years and years ago. But once on the train, as the miles retreated beneath the wheels while the Pullmans went forward toward Indiana, Henry gradually began to forget Callie—Calista Lowery—and to think of his wife. They would probably have chicken for dinner next Sunday. All the children would probably be there. And everybody would be delighted to see him home once more, safe and sound.

It was too bad poor Callie had not become an actress of fame. But at least she had become the shining Calista Lowery of New York, well dressed and beautiful, even at her age, and that was something toward an ambition generated in the gallery of the old Indiana Opera House. Beautiful—and dumb as ever, too, poor child. Suppose he had married her in his youth, in spite of his parents? Tut! Tut! She could never have managed his affairs as well as the three large ladies who had been his wives.

Probably he would not have prospered at all, Mr. Marston thought. There was something *too* alluring about Calista. There always had been. She took a man's mind off his work.

He arrived in Terre Haute in the morning, just in time to welcome Mrs. Marston, who came in on the afternoon train from Chicago. Henry's life settled down once more to the calm and comfortable routine that is the lot of a middle-aged man of business in a small city.

Then one afternoon about a fortnight later at his office, just when Mr. Marston was beginning to think about a game of golf, the telephone rang.

His secretary said, "Long distance calling you, Mr. Marston. A personal call from New York. Would you care to take it?"

He picked up the receiver and put it to his ear.

"Henry Quentin Marston speaking."

"Hello." A sweetly feminine voice came over the wire. "This is Callie, Henry darling. I am again with child."

"Good God!" Mr. Marston cried. "My God! What—what do you want?" the middle-aged man at the desk in Indiana asked, visions of his wife, his children, his home, his church, dancing before him.

"Darling," said Calista, "money."

"Money?" The sweat popped out on his forehead. "How—how—how much money?"

"The last time it was *so* little," Callie said. "Do you remember? Just enough to take mother and me to Chicago. This time I think I should really like to go to Paris. I have never been abroad—and Paris is one of my dreams. Our child could be born there, Henry."

"Would two thousand do?" asked Mr. Marston naïvely, having no one to guide him.

"Multiplied by ten," said Calista, "it *might* do."

"Oh-rr-r-r!" groaned Mr. Marston. "Callie! *Calista!* Callie!"

"I have no mother to protect me any more," the voice at the other end of the wire said sadly. "I have only some old lawyers now, Henry."

"Don't," said Henry trembling, "just a minute, wait."

"I'll try to wait a minute," said Calista.

"I—er—you—you shall have it, Callie," he panted, "I'll mail a draft to you this week."

"Better to my lawyers," the charming voice said, "just to make it legal." She gave him their address.

"All right," said Mr. Marston hoarsely, writing the number down. "O.K. All right."

"Perhaps you'll come to Europe," purred the lovely voice at his ear.

"Perhaps," panted Mr. Marston, "but I'm a very busy man."

"Then good-by, Henry," said the woman on the phone, considerately. "I'm so sorry, darling, to bother you with this."

When Mr. Marston could move from his chair, weak as he was, he wiped the sweat from his neck, rang for a glass of water, and prepared to arrange for the transfer of twenty thousand dollars to one Calista Lowery of New York.

A week later at the first-class canopy-covered entrance to a transatlantic jet, her hair newly waved, her face freshly fixed, an orchid at her neckline, and a smile of triumph on her lips, Callie emplaned for Paris—the city of her dreams.

" 'I am with child'—that is the best line I ever delivered," she said to herself. "I made it up myself—*both times!* I'm almost as good a playwright as I am an actress. But Henry's *such* a dumb leading man! And he never did even suspicion that I'm colored."

Tain't So

Miss Lucy Cannon was a right nice old white woman, so Uncle Joe always stated, except that she really did *not* like colored folks, not even after she come out West to California. She could never get over certain little Southern ways she had, and long as she knowed my Uncle Joe, who hauled her ashes for her, she never would call him *Mister*—nor any other colored man *Mister* neither, for that matter, not even the minister of the Baptist Church who was a graduate of San Jose State College. Miss Lucy Cannon just wouldn't call colored folks *Mister* nor *Missus,* no matter who they was, neither in Alabama nor in California.

She was always ailing around, too, sick with first one thing and then another. Delicate, and ever so often she would have a fainting spell, like all good Southern white ladies. Looks like the older she got, the more she would be sick and couldn't hardly get around—that is, until she went to a healer and got cured.

And that is one of the funniest stories Uncle Joe ever told me, how old Miss Cannon got cured of her heart and hip in just one cure at the healer's.

Seems like for three years or more she could scarcely walk—even with a cane—had a terrible bad pain in her right leg from her knee up. And on her left side, her heart was always just about to give out. She was in bad shape, that old Southern lady, to be as spry as she was, always giving teas and dinners and working her colored help to death.

Well, Uncle Joe says, one New Year's Day in Pasadena a friend of hers, a Northern lady who was kinda old and retired also and had come out to California to spend her last days, too, and get rid of some parts of her big bank full of money—this old lady told Miss Cannon, "Darling, you just seem to suffer so all the time, and you say you've tried all the doctors and all kinds of baths and medicines. Why don't you try my way of overcoming? Why don't you try faith?"

"Faith, honey?" says old Miss Lucy Cannon, sipping her jasmine tea.

"Yes, my dear," says the Northern white lady. "Faith! I have one of the best faith-healers in the world."

"Who is he?" asked Miss Lucy Cannon.

"She's a woman, dear," said old Miss Northern White Lady. "And she heals by power. She lives in Hollywood."

"Give me her address," said Miss Lucy, "and I'll go to see her. How much do her treatments cost?"

Miss Lucy warn't so rich as some folks thought she was.

"Only ten dollars, dearest," said the other lady. "Ten dollars a treatment. Go, and you'll come away cured."

"I have never believed in such things," said Miss Lucy, "nor disbelieved, either. But I will go and see." And before she could learn any more about the healer, some other friends came in and interrupted the conversation.

A few days later, however, Miss Lucy took herself all the way from Pasadena to Hollywood, put up for the week end with a friend of hers, and thought she would go to see the healer, which she did, come Monday morning early.

Using her customary cane and hobbling on her left leg, feeling a bit bad around the heart, and suffering terribly in her mind, she managed to walk slowly but with dignity a half-dozen blocks through the sunshine to the rather humble street in which was located the office and home of the healer.

In spite of the bright morning air and the good breakfast she had had, Miss Lucy (according to herself) felt pretty bad, racked with pains and crippled to the use of a cane.

When she got to the house she was seeking, a large frame dwelling, newly painted, she saw a sign thereon:

Miss Pauline Jones

"So that's her name," thought Miss Lucy. "Pauline Jones, Miss Jones."

Ring and Enter said a little card above the bell. So Miss Lucy entered. But the first thing that set her back a bit was that nobody received her, so she just sat down to await Miss Jones, the healer who had, she heard, an enormous following in Hollywood. In fact, that's why she had come early, so she wouldn't have to wait long. Now, it was only nine o'clock. The office was open—but empty. So Miss Lucy simply waited. Ten minutes passed. Fifteen. Twenty. Finally she became all nervous and fluttery. Heart and limb! Pain, pain, pain! Not even a magazine to read.

"Oh, me!" she said impatiently, "What is this? Why, I never!"
There was a sign on the wall that read:

BELIEVE

"I will wait just ten minutes more," said Miss Lucy, glancing
at her watch of platinum and pearls.

But before the ten minutes were up, another woman entered
the front door and sat down. To Miss Lucy's horror, she was a
colored woman! In fact, a big black colored woman!

Said Miss Lucy to herself, "I'll never in the world get used
to the North. Now here's a great—my friend says great—faith-
healer, treating darkies! Why, down in Alabama a Negro pa-
tient wouldn't dare come in here and sit down with white people like this!"

But, womanlike (and having still five minutes to wait), Miss
Lucy couldn't keep her mouth shut that long. She just had to
talk, albeit to a Negro, so she began on her favorite subject—
herself.

"I certainly feel bad this morning," she said to the colored
woman, condescending to open the conversation.

"Tain't so," answered the Negro woman placidly—which
sort of took Miss Lucy back a bit. She lifted her chin.

"Indeed, it is so," said she indignantly. "My heart is just
about to give out. My breath is short."

"Tain't so a-tall," commented the colored woman.

"Why!" gasped Miss Lucy, "such impudence! I tell you *it is
so!* I could hardly get down here this morning."

"Tain't so," said the Negro calmly.

"Besides my heart," went on Miss Lucy, "my right hip pains
me so I can hardly sit here."

"I say, tain't so."

"I tell you it *is* so," screamed Miss Lucy. "Where is the
healer? I won't sit here and suffer this—this impudence. I can't!
It'll kill me! It's outrageous."

"Tain't so," said the large black woman serenely, whereupon
Miss Lucy rose. Her pale face flushed a violent red.

"Where is the healer?" she cried, looking around the room.

"Right here," said the colored woman.

"What?" cried Miss Lucy. "You're the—why—you?"

"I'm Miss Jones."

"Why, I never heard the like," gasped Miss Lucy. "A *colored* woman as famous as you? Why, you must be lying!"

"Tain't so," said the woman calmly.

"Well, I shan't stay another minute," cried Miss Lucy.

"Ten dollars, then," said the colored woman. "You've had your treatment, anyhow."

"Ten dollars! That's entirely too much!"

"Tain't so."

Angrily Miss Lucy opened her pocketbook, threw a ten-dollar bill on the table, took a deep breath, and bounced out. She went three blocks up Sunset Boulevard, walking like the wind, conversing with herself.

" 'Tain't so,' " she muttered. " 'Tain't so!' I tell her I'm sick and she says, 'Tain't so!' "

On she went at a rapid gait, stepping like a young girl—so mad she had forgotten all about her infirmities, even her heart —when suddenly she cried, "Lord, have mercy, my cane! For the first time in three years, I'm *without* a cane!"

Then she realized that her breath was giving her no trouble at all. Neither was her leg. Her temper mellowed. The sunshine was sweet and warm. She felt good.

"Colored folks do have some funny kind of supernatural conjuring powers, I reckon," she said, smiling to herself. Immediately her face went grim again. "But the impudence of 'em! Soon's they get up North—calling herself *Miss* Pauline Jones. The idea! Putting on airs and charging me ten dollars for a handful of *tain't so's!*"

In her mind she clearly heard, "Tain't so!"

Father and Son

Colonel Thomas Norwood stood in his doorway at the Big House, looking down the dusty plantation road. Today his youngest son was coming home. A heavy Georgia spring filled the morning air with sunshine and earth-perfumes. It made the old man feel strangely young again. Bert was coming home.

Twenty years ago he had begotten him.

This boy, however, was not his real son, for Colonel Thomas Norwood had no real son, no white and legal heir to carry on the Norwood name; this boy was a son by his Negro mistress, Coralee Lewis, who kept his house and had borne him all his children.

Colonel Norwood never would have admitted, even to himself, that he was standing in his doorway waiting for this half-Negro son to come home. But in truth that is what he was doing. He was curious about this boy. How would he look after all these years away at school? Six or seven surely, for not once in that long time had he been allowed to come back to Big House Plantation. The Colonel had said then that never did he want to see the boy. But in truth he did—for this boy had been, after all, the most beautiful of the lot, the brightest and the baddest of the Colonel's five children, lording it over the other children, and sassing not only his colored mother, but his white father, as well. Handsome and mischievous, favoring too much the Colonel in looks and ways, this boy Bert, at fourteen, had got himself sent off to school to stay. Now a student in college (or what they call a college in Negro terms in Georgia), he was coming home for the summer vacation.

Today his brother, Willie, had been sent to the station to meet him in the new Ford. The ten o'clock train must have reached the Junction by now, thought the Colonel, standing in the door. Soon the Ford would be shooting back down the

road in a cloud of dust, curving past the tall white pillars of the
front porch, and around to the kitchen stoop where Cora would
greet her child.

Thinking thus, Colonel Norwood came inside the house,
closed the screen, and pulled at a bellcord hanging from the
wall of the great dark living room with its dignified but shabby
horsehair furniture of the nineties. By and by an old Negro
servant, whose name was Sam and who wore a kind of old-
fashioned butler's coat, came and brought the Colonel a drink.

"I'm going in my library where I don't want to be disturbed."

"Yes, suh," said the Negro servant.

"You hear me?"

"Yes, suh," said the servant, knowing that when Colonel
Norwood said "library," he meant he did not want to be disturbed.

The Colonel entered the small room where he kept his books
and papers of both a literary and a business nature. He closed
the door. He did this deliberately, intending to let all the
Negroes in the house know that he had no interest whatsoever
in the homecoming about to take place. He intended to remain
in the library several hours after Bert's arrival. Yet, as he bent
over his desk peering at accounts his storekeeper had brought
him, his head kept turning toward the window that gave on the
yard and the road, kept looking to see if a car were coming in a
cloud of dust.

An hour or so later, when shouts of welcome, loud warm
Negro-cries, laughter, and the blowing of an auto horn filled
the Georgia sunlight outside, the Colonel bent more closely
over his ledgers—but he did turn his eyes a little to catch the
dust sifting in the sunny air above the road where the car had
passed. And his mind went back to that little olive-colored kid
he had beaten one day in the stables years ago—the kid grown
up now, and just come home.

He had always been a little ashamed of that particular beating he had given the boy. But his temper had got the best of
him. That child, Bert, looking almost like a white child (a hell
of a lot favoring the Colonel), had come running out to the sta-

bles one afternoon when he was showing his horses to some guests from in town. The boy had come up to him crying, "Papa!" (He knew better, right in front of company.) "Papa, Ma says she's got dinner ready."

The Colonel had knocked him down under the feet of the horses right there in front of the guests. And afterwards he had locked him in the stable and beaten him severely. The boy had to learn not to call him Papa, and certainly not in front of white people from the town.

But it had been hard to teach Bert anything, the Colonel ruminated. Trouble was, the boy was too smart. There were other unpleasant memories of that same saucy ivory-skinned youngster playing about the front yard, even running through the Big House, in spite of orders that Coralee's children and all other pickaninnies keep to the back of the house, or down in the Quarters. But as a child, Bert had never learned his place.

"He's too damn much like me," the Colonel thought. "Quick as hell. Cora's been telling me he's leading his class at the Institute, and a football captain. . . . H-m-m-m, so they waste their time playing football at these darkie colleges. . . . Well, anyway, he must be a smart darkie. Got my blood in him."

The Colonel had Sam bring some food into the library. He pretended to be extremely busy, and did not give the old Negro, bursting with news, a chance to speak. The Colonel acted as though he were unaware of the presence of the newly arrived boy on the plantation; or if he were aware, completely uninterested and completely occupied.

But in the late afternoon the Colonel got up from his desk, went out into the parlor, picked up an old straw hat, and strolled through the front door, across the wide-porticoed porch with its white pillars, and down the road toward the South Field. The Colonel saw the brown backs of his Negroes in the green cotton. He smelt the earth-scent of a day that had been long and hot. He turned off by the edge of a field, went down to the creek, and back·toward the house along a path that took him through a grove of pecan trees skirting the old slave quarters, to the back door of the Big House.

Long before he approached the Big House, he could hear Negroes' voices, musical and laughing. Then he could see a small group of dark bare arms and faces about the kitchen stoop. Cora was sitting on a stool in the yard, probably washing fruit for jelly. Livonia, the fat old cook, was on the porch shelling peas for dinner. Seated on the stoop, and on the ground, and standing around, were colored persons the Colonel knew had no good reason to be there at that time of day. Some of them, when they saw the Colonel coming, began to move away, back toward the barns, or whatever work they were doing.

He was aware, too, standing in the midst of this group, of a tall young man in sporty white trousers, black-and-white oxfords, and a blue shirt. He looked very clean and well dressed, like a white man. The Colonel took this to be his son, and a certain vibration shook him from head to foot. Across the wide dusty yard, their eyes met. The Colonel's brows came together, his shoulders lifted and went back as though faced by an indignity just suffered. His chin went up. And he began to think, on the way toward them, how he would walk through this group like a white man. The Negroes, of course, would be respectful and afraid, as usual. He would say merely, "Good evening, Bert," to this boy, his son, then wait a moment, perhaps, and see what the boy said before passing on into the house.

Laughter died and dripped and trickled away, and talk quieted, and silence fell degree by degree, each step the white man approached. A strange sort of stiffness like steel nearing steel grew and straightened between the colored boy in the black-and-white shoes and the old Colonel who had just come from looking at his fields and his Negroes working.

"Good evening, Bert," the Colonel said.

"Good evening, Colonel Tom," the boy replied quickly, politely, almost eagerly. And then, like a puppet pulled by some perverse string, the boy offered his hand.

The Colonel looked at the strong young near-white hand held out toward him, and made no effort to take it. His eyes lifted to the eyes of the boy, his son, in front of him. The boy's eyes did not fall. But a slow flush reddened the olive of his skin as the old man turned without a word toward the stoop and into the house. The boy's hand went to his side again. A hum of dark voices broke the silence.

This happened between father and son. The mother, sitting there washing plums in a pail, did not understand what had happened. But the water from which she took the plums felt cool to her hands that were suddenly burning hot.

Coralee Lewis, sitting washing plums, had been Colonel Norwood's mistress for thirty years. She had lived in the Big House, supervised his life, given him children, and loved him. In his turn, he felt something very like love for her. Now, in his sixties, without Cora he would have been lost, but of course he did not realize that—consciously.

The history of their liaison, like that of so many between Negro women and white men in the South, began without love, at least on his part. For a long while its motif was lust—whose sweeter name, perhaps, is passion.

The Colonel had really known Cora all her life. As a half-grown boy, he had teased her as a baby, pulling her kinky braids and laughing at the way she rolled in the dust with the other pickaninnies born to the black servants and share-croppers on his father's plantation. He had seen her as a girl, barefooted and shy, brown face shining, bringing milk to the Big House night and morning, for her father took care of the cows. Her mother worked sometimes in the house but mostly in the fields. And Cora knew early how to pick cotton, too.

Then there came years when young Norwood had no contact with Cora: years when he had been away at military school; those first few years when he had come back from Macon with his new bride; those years of love and worry with the delicate and lovely woman he had wedded. During his early married life the Colonel could not truthfully remember ever having laid eyes on Cora, although she was about the place surely.

But Cora remembered often seeing the Colonel. Young and handsome, tall and straight, he drove over the plantation roads with the wisp of a pretty little lady he had married. She re-

membered him particularly well the day of his father's funeral,
when he came back from the burial—he and his wife, master
and mistress of the Big House now. How sad and worried young
Colonel Norwood looked that day, descending from the carriage.

And as the months went by, he began to look more and more
worried and weary. Servants' gossip from the Big House, drift-
ing down to the humbler Negroes in the cabins, said that a wall
had grown up between the young Colonel and his little wife,
who seemed to be wasting away day by day. A wall like a mist.
And the Negroes began to laugh that there were never no
children born to Mister and Missus. Then gossip began to say
that the young Colonel had taken up with the cook's daughter,
black but comely Livonia, who worked in the pantry. Then the
Quarters laughed all the more—for Livonia had four or five
Negro lovers, too. And she wasn't faithful to anybody—
just liked to love.

Cora heard all this, and in her mind a certain envy sprang
up. Livonia! Huh! Cora began to look more carefully into the
cracked mirror in her mother's cabin. She combed her hair and
oiled it better than before. She was seventeen then.

"Time you was takin' some pride about yo'self," said her
mother, noting the change.

"Yes'm," said Cora. And when she took milk to the Big
House now, she tried to look her best.

One night, there was a party there. A great many people
came from the Junction, and even seventy miles off from in
town, by horse and by carriage, by train, and even some by that
new-fangled autobuggy that most of the plantation hands had
never seen before. The Negroes were all excited at having so
many white folks around. It was the Missus' birthday. There
were great doings at Big House Plantation.

The first evening, the party went on until late in the night.
Some people left at dawn. Others slept awhile and left in the
afternoon. Some were house guests, and on the second night
there was a party again. But that night everybody was pretty
tired. And got pretty drunk, too, mostly. The Colonel was very

gay and very drunk; but his little wife cried, and went to bed.
She was mighty touchy, all the Negroes knew. Always poutin'
and spattin' and actin' funny with the Colonel.

Wonder why? Wonder why?

There was a party in the Quarters among the Negroes, too,
that second night. Livonia was there, dancing fit to kill. And the
music was wild. In the heat of the night, Cora went out of the
barn where the party was, out into the moonlight, and looked
up at the lights of the Big House on the rise. She stretched, and
breathed in the warm night air, and walked through the trees
toward the road that ran to town. She made a big circle about
the Big House, wondering a little what was going on there.
When she got to the road, she sat down under a huge live oak
tree. She could hear the laughter and clapping of the Negroes
down on the edge of the cotton fields. But in the Big House,
where it should have been gay, too, it was mighty quiet. Sometimes a loud and quarrelsome voice could be heard. Probably
the men were gambling, and the ladies gone to bed.

The trees cast great shadows across the road in the warm
light of the moon. Cora stretched, breathed deeply again, and
got up to go, when she saw very near her a figure walking in
the silvery dusk, a tall thin young white man walking in the
cotton. Suddenly he called her.

"Who're you?" It was young Norwood's speaking.

"I's Coralee Lewis, Aunt Tobie Lewis' daughter."

The white man came up to her, took her brown face in his
hands and lifted it at the moon. "You're out mighty late," he
said.

Cora's body trembled. Her mouth opened. In the shadow of
the live oak tree there by the road, thirty years ago, in a night
of moon. . . .

When the first child, Willie, was in her, she told her mother
all about it. The old woman was glad. "It's better'n slavin' in the
cotton fields," she said. "I's known colored women what's wore
silk dresses and lived like queens on plantations right here in
Georgy. . . ."

Even before the young Mrs. Norwood died (she did die—and childless), Cora was working in the Big House. And after Mrs. Norwood's death, Cora came there to sleep.

Now the water where the plums were felt cool to her hands this spring afternoon many years later as the Colonel went into the house, leaving their youngest boy dazed in front of her; and the nigger-voices all around her humming and chattering into loudness and laughter.

"Listen hyar," brother Willie said to Bert on the way from the Junction to the plantation that morning his brother arrived. "Listen hyar, I hopes you don't expect to go around all dressed up like you is now after you gets out to de place, 'cause de Colonel won't 'low it. He made Sis put away all them fine clothes she brought hyar last year—till she left."

"Tell him to kiss my behind," Bert said.

Willie bucked his eyes, stuttered, then kept quiet. His brother was the same Bert as he had been as a child. Crazy! Trouble coming. William made up his mind not to be in it, himself, one way or another. Though he was eight years older, he had always been afraid of Bert, with a fear worse than physical, afraid of the things that happened around Bert.

From the new Ford, Bert looked out at the straggling streets of the village of the Junction, at the Negroes lounging in front of stores, at the red-necked crackers, at the unkempt women. He heard the departing train whistle as it went deeper into Georgia, into Alabama. As they rode, he looked at the wide fields of young cotton stretching on either side, at the cabins of the share-croppers, at the occasional house of a white owner or overseer. Then he saw the gradual rise of the Norwood plantation, the famous Big House, surrounded by its live oaks and magnolias and maples, and its many acres of cotton. And he knew he was nearing home.

Six years away. Kid of fourteen when he left, wearing his first long trousers bought in the commissary store, feeling funny out of overalls, feeling very proud going away to school. Only the Lewis niggers (old man Norwood's kids by Cora) went away to

school in these parts. And with the going of Sallie, the youngest,
the little county school at Norwood's Crossroads closed up, and
didn't open any more. Sallie was the *Colonel's* last child—no
other niggers needed a school.

Old Aunt Tobie, the grandma, before she died, used to keep
on saying that the Lewis young 'uns ought to appreciate what
the Colonel was doing for 'em. No white man she ever heard of
cared anything 'bout educatin' his tar-brush chillun. But the
Colonel did. Somehow 'nother Cora was able to put it in the
Colonel's mind and keep it there until the last child, Sallie, got
sent off to Atlanta.

In Atlanta, Bert had entered the same Negro boarding school,
the Institute, that brother Willie and his oldest sister, Bertha, had
attended. But Willie, several years before, hadn't stayed there
long, being a dumb boy who liked the plantation better. Bertha
had gone up North once with the Spiritual Jubilee Singers, and
liked it so well that she remained to work in Chicago. Now, little
sister Sallie, seventeen, went to the Institute also, but had come
home this spring ahead of Bert, who fooled around Atlanta a
week or so before leaving, not wanting to come home really.

"Home, hell!"

Bert didn't want to come home. He felt he had no home. A
brown mother, and a white father; bed for him in a nigger cabin
down on the edge of the cotton fields. Soon as Cora's kids stopped
nursing, they went to live outside the Big House. Aunt Tobie,
the grandmother, had really raised them, until she died. Then
a cousin of Cora's brought up Sallie.

"Hell of a way to live," Bert thought, the night before his arrival, sitting in the Jim Crow car bound for south Georgia. During the long ride he had turned over in his mind incidents of his
childhood on the Big House Plantation. Sitting in the smoky
half-coach allotted to Negroes (the other half being a baggage
car), he thought of what it meant growing up as one of Colonel
Norwood's yard-niggers (a term used by field hands for the mulatto children of a white planter).

"It's hell," Bert thought.

Not that Cora's other kids had found it hell. Only he had

found it so, strangely enough. "The rest of 'em are too dumb, except little Sallie, and she don't say nothing—but it's hell to her, too, I reckon," the boy thought to himself as the train rocked and rumbled over the road. "Willie don't give a damn so long as his belly's full. And Bertha's got up North away from it all. I don't know what she really thought. . . . But I wish it hadn't happened to me."

With the self-pity of bewildered youth, he began to think about himself. Always, he had known the Colonel was his father, from the earliest he could remember. For one thing, Bert had been lighter than any of the other colored children on the plantation—a sort of ivory white. And as a small child, his hair had been straight and brown, his eyes gray, like Norwood's. His grandma, old Aunt Tobie, used to refer to them all, Willie and Bertha and Bert and Sallie, not without pride, as Colonel Tom's children. (There had been another brother who died.) Bert noticed early in life that all the other kids in the Quarters were named after their fathers, whereas he and his brother and sisters bore the mother's name, Lewis. He was Bert Lewis—not Bert Norwood. His mother slept in the Big House—but the children lived outside with Aunt Tobie or Cousin Betty. Those things puzzled little Bert.

As he grew up, he used to hear folks remarking on how much he looked like Colonel Tom, and how little like Cora. Nearly light enough to pass for white, folks said, spittin' image of his father, too. Bert had a temper and ways like white folks, too. Indeed, "You needn't act so much like quality with me," was one of Aune Tobie's favorite ways of reprimanding him when she wanted to take him down a peg or two.

He was always getting into mischief, playing pranks and worrying his mother at the back door of the Big House. There was a time once when the Colonel seemed to get pleasure out of letting little Bert trail around at his heels, but that period didn't last very long, for young Bert sassed the Colonel, too, just as though he were colored. And somehow, he had acquired that way of referring to Norwood as Papa. The Colonel told him, sternly and seriously, "Boy, don't *you* use that word to me." But

still, forgetful little devil that he was, he had come running up
to the Colonel that day in the stables yelling, "Papa, dinner's
ready."

The slap that he received made him see stars and darkness,
Bert remembered. As though he were brushing a fly out of the
way, the Colonel had knocked him down under the feet of the
horses, and went on talking to his guests. After the guests had
gone, he switched Bert mercilessly.

"Can't nobody teach you nothin' but a switch, nohow," said
old Aunt Tobie afterwards. "I tole you 'bout gittin' familiar wid
that white man."

"But he didn't need to scar him all up," Bert remembered
Cora's saying when she saw the black and blue marks on his
back. "I ain't bearin' him children for to beat 'em to death. . . .
You stay way from him, son, you hear?"

From that time on, between Bert and the Colonel, there had
been a barrier of fear—a fear that held a certain mysterious
fascination for Bert's sense of defiance, a fear that Bert from afar
was continually taunting and baiting. For instance, the Colonel
had a complex, Bert recalled, that all the Negroes knew, about
the front door of the Big House. His orders were that no Negroes
go in and out of that door, or cross his front porch. When the old
houseman, Sam, wanted to sweep off the porch, he would have
to go out the back and come all the way around. It was as absurd
as that. Yet Bert, as a child, in the Big House visiting or helping
Cora, would often dart out the front way when he thought the
Colonel was in town or down in the South Field, or asleep in his
library. Cora used to spank him for it, but it was a habit he kept
up until he went away, a big boy, to Atlanta.

Bert, home-bound now, smiled to himself in the stuffy Jim
Crow car, and wondered if the Colonel were still as tall and stern
and stiff-fronted as he used to be. No wonder his young white
wife had died years ago—having to live with him—although, according to Aunt Tobie's version, the Colonel had humored her
in every way. He really loved her, folks said, and had sworn after
her death that he would never marry again. He hadn't—he had
taken Cora.

And here Bert's mind balked and veered away from speculating about the intimate life of this old man and his mother. Bert knew that in a sense the white man had been kind to her. He remembered as a child the extra little delicacies that came down to Aunt Tobie and Cousin Betty and Cora's other relatives in the Quarters, especially at Christmas. He remembered how he had always known that the little colored school had not been there before Cora's children were born, and that it was no longer at the crossroads now. (For the Colonel and Mr. Higgins, being political powers in the county, were in charge of education, and their policy was to let Negroes remain unlettered. They worked better.) Bert knew, too, that it was his mother's influence that had got her children sent off to the Institute in Atlanta. But it was the *Colonel's* dislike of Bert that had kept him there, summer and winter, until now. Not that Bert minded. Summer school was fun, too. And tennis. And the pleasures of the town. And he was never homesick for the plantation—but he did wish sometimes that he had a home, and that the Colonel would treat him like a son.

Tall and light and good-looking, as Bert was now at twenty, he could have a very good time in Atlanta. Colored society had taken him up. He went around with the sons and daughters of Negro doctors and dentists and insurance brokers and professors. He had his hands full of pretty girls. Lots of cream-colored girls, chocolate brown girls, velvet-soft night-shade girls all liked Bert. And already he had been involved in a scandal with a doctor's wife.

To add to his good looks, Bert was an excellent athlete. He had been as far north as Washington with Institute teams, and had seen colored people at the Capitol riding in street cars where there had been no Jim Crow signs, and getting on trains that had no coaches especially for Negroes. Bert made up his mind to come North to live as soon as he finished school. He had one more year. And this last summer Cora wanted him to spend with her—because she sensed he might never come back to the plantation again.

Sallie, his sister, three classes behind him at the Institute, was frankly worried about his going home. She was afraid. "Colonel Tom's getting old. He ain't nice a-tall like he kinder used to be. He's getting more and more touchy," Sallie said to her brother. "And I know he ain't gonna like the looks of you. You don't look a bit like a Georgia boy any more."

"To hell with him," said Bert.

"I wouldn't even know you and Willie were brothers," Sallie said. For Sallie went home every summer and worked in the Big House with her mother, and saw Willie, and knew how things were on the plantation. Willie and the Colonel got along fine, because Willie was docile and good-natured, bowing and scraping and treating white folks like they expected to be treated. "But Bert, you ain't a bit like that."

"Why should I be?" Bert asked. "I'm the old man's son, ain't I? Got white blood in me, too."

"Yes, but . . ."

"But what?" Bert said. "Let Willie go on being a white-folks' nigger if he wants to, I won't!"

And that's the way it was when he came home.

There are people (you've probably noted it also) who have the unconscious faculty of making the world spin around themselves, throb and expand, contract and go dizzy. Then, when they are gone away, you feel sick and lonesome and meaningless.

In the chemistry lab at school, did you ever hold a test tube, pouring in liquids and powders and seeing nothing happen until a *certain* liquid or a *certain* powder is poured in, and then everything begins to smoke and fume, bubble and boil, hiss to foam, and sometimes even explode? The tube is suddenly full of action and movement and life. Well, there are people like those certain liquids or powders; at a given moment they come into a room, or into a town, even into a country—and the place is never the same again. Things bubble, boil, change. Sometimes the whole world is changed. Alexander came. Christ. Gandhi. A Russian named Lenin.

Not that there is any comparing Bert to Christ or Lenin. But after he returned to the Big House Plantation that summer, life was never the same. From Bert's very first day on the place something was broken, something went dizzy. The world began to spin, to ferment, and move into a new action.

Not to be a *white-folks' nigger*—Bert had come home with that idea in his head.

The Colonel sensed it in his outstretched hand and his tall young body—and had turned his back and walked into the house. Cora, with her hands in the cool water where the plums were, suddenly knew in her innermost soul a period of time had closed for her. That first night she prayed, cried in her room, asked the Lord why she had ever let her son come home. In his cabin Willie prayed, too, humble, Lord, humble. The Colonel rocked alone on his front porch, sucking a black cigar and cussing bitterly at he knew not what. The hum and laughter of the Negro voices went on as usual on the vast plantation, down to the last share-cropper's cabin, but not quite, not *quite* the same as they had been in the morning. And never to be the same again.

"Is you heard about Bert?"

Not to be a *white-folks' nigger!*

Bow down and pray in fear and trembling, go way back in the dark afraid; or work harder and harder; or stumble and learn; or raise up your fist and strike—but once the idea comes into your head, you'll never be the same again. Oh, test tube of life! Crucible of the South, find the right powder and you'll never be the same again—the cotton will blaze and the cabins will burn and the chains will be broken and men, all of a sudden, will shake hands, black men and white men, like steel meeting steel!

"The bastard," Bert said. "Why couldn't he shake hands with me? I'm a Norwood, too."

"Hush, son," said Cora, with the cool water from the plums on her hands.

And the hum of the black voices that afternoon spread to the cabins, to the cotton fields, to the dark streets of the Junction, what Bert had said—Bert with the ivory-yellow skin and the tall, proud young body, Bert come home not to be a white-folks' nigger.

"Lawd, chile, Bert's come home. . . ."
"Lawd, chile, and he said . . ."
"Lawd, chile, he said . . ."
"Lawd, chile . . ."
"Lawd . . ."

July passed, and August. The hot summer sun marched across
the skies. The Colonel ordered Bert to work in the fields. Bert
had not done so. Talbot, the white foreman, washed his hands
of it, saying that if he had his way, "that nigger would be run off
the place."

For the Colonel, the summer was hectic enough, what with
cotton prices dropping on the market; share-croppers restless
and moving; one black fieldhand beaten half to death by Talbot
and the storekeeper because he "talked high" to a neighboring
white planter; news of the Scottsboro trials and the Camp Hill
shootings exciting black labor.

Colonel Norwood ordered the colored rural Baptist minister
to start a revival and keep it going until he said stop. Let the
Negroes sing and shout their troubles away, as in the past. White
folks had always found revivals a useful outlet for sullen overworked darkies. As long as they were singing and praying, they
forgot about the troubles of this world. In a frenzy of rhythm
and religion, they laid their cross at the feet of Jesus.

Poor overworked Jesus! Somehow since the war, he hadn't
borne that cross so well. Too heavy, it's too heavy! Lately, Negroes seem to sense that it's not Jesus' cross, anyhow, it's their
own. Only old people praise King Jesus any more. On the Norwood plantation Bert's done told the young people to stop being
white-folks' niggers. More and more, the Colonel felt it was Bert
who brought trouble into the Georgia summer. The revival was
a failure.

One day he met the boy coming back from the river where he
had been swimming. The Colonel lit into him with all the cuss
words at his command. He told him in no uncertain language to
get down in the South Field to work. He told him there would

be no more school at Atlanta for him; that he would show him that just because Cora happened to be his mother, he was no more than any other nigger on the place. God damn him!

Bert stood silent and red in front of his father, looking as the Colonel must have looked forty years ago—except that he was a shade darker. He did not go down to the South Field to work. And all Cora's pleadings could not make him go. Yet nothing happened. That was the strange thing about it. The Colonel did nothing—to Bert. But he lit into Cora, nagged and scolded her for days, told her she'd better get some sense into her boy's head if she wanted any skin left on his body.

So the summer passed. Sallie, having worked faithfully in the house throughout the hottest months, went away to school again. Bert remained sullenly behind.

The day that ends our story began like this:

The sun rose burning and blazing, flooding the earth with the heat of early autumn, making even the morning oppressive. Folks got out of bed feeling like overripe fruit. The air of the morning shimmered with heat and ill humor. The night before, Colonel Norwood had been drinking. He got up trembling and shaky, yelling for Cora to bring him something clean to put on. He went downstairs cussing.

The Colonel did not want to eat. He drank black coffee, and walked out on the tall-pillared porch to get a breath of air. He was standing there looking through the trees at his cotton when the Ford swept by in a cloud of dust, past the front of the house and down the highway to town. Bert was driving.

The Colonel cussed out loud, bit his cigar, turned and went into the house, slamming the door, storming to Cora, calling up the stairs where she was working, "What the hell does he think he is, driving off to town in the middle of the morning? Didn't I tell Bert not to touch that Ford, to stay down yonder in the fields and work?"

"Yes, suh, Colonel Tom," Cora said. "You sure did."

"Tell him I want to see him soon as he comes back here. Send

him in here. And tell him I'll skin his yellow hide for him." The
Colonel spoke of Bert as though he were still a child.

"Yes, suh, Colonel Tom."

The day grew hotter and hotter. Heat waves rose from the
fields. Sweat dampened the Colonel's body. Sweat dampened
the black bodies of the Negroes in the cotton fields, too, the hard
black bodies that had built the Colonel's fortune out of earth
and sun and barehanded labor. Yet the Colonel, in spite of the
fact that he lived on this labor, sat in his shaded house fanning
that morning and wondering what made niggers so contrary—
he was thinking of Bert—as the telephone rang. The fat and
testy voice of his old friend Mr. Higgins trembled at the other
end of the wire. He was calling from the Junction.

Accustomed as he was to his friend's voice on the phone, at
first the Colonel could not make out what he was saying. When
he did understand, his neck bulged and the palms of the hands
that held the phone were wet with sweat. Anger and shame
made his tall body stoop and bend like an animal about to spring.
Mr. Higgins was talking about Bert.

"That yellow nigger . . ." Mr. Higgins said. "One of your
yard-niggers sassed . . ." Mr. Higgins said. "I thought I'd better tell you . . ." Mr. Higgins said. "Everybody . . ." Mr. Higgins said.

The whole town was excited about Bert. In the heat of this
overwarm autumn day, the hotheads of the white citizens of
the town had suddenly become inflamed about Bert. Mr. Higgins, county politician and postmaster at the Junction, was well
qualified to know. His office had been the center of the news.

It seemed that Bert had insulted the young white woman who
sold stamps and made out money orders at the Post Office. And
Mr. Higgins was telling the Colonel about it on the phone,
warning him to get rid of Bert, that people around the Junction
were getting sick and tired of seeing him.

At the post office this is what happened: a simple argument
over change. But the young woman who sold the stamps was
not used to arguing with Negroes, or being corrected by them

when she made a mistake. Bert said, "I gave you a dollar," holding out the incorrect change. "You gave me back only sixty-four cents."

The young woman said, counting the change, "Yes, but you have eight three-cent stamps. Move on now, there're others waiting." Several white people were in line.

Bert said, "Yes, but eight times three is not thirty-six. You owe me twelve cents more."

The girl looked at the change and realized she was wrong. She looked at Bert—light near-white nigger with gray-blue eyes. You gotta be harder on those kind than you have on the black ones. An educated nigger, too! Besides it was hot and she wasn't feeling well. A light near-white nigger with gray eyes! Instead of correcting the change, she screamed, and let her head fall forward in front of the window.

Two or three white men waiting to buy stamps seized Bert and attempted to throw him out of the post office. Bert remembered he'd been a football player—and Colonel Norwood's son —so he fought back. One of the white men got a bloody mouth. Women screamed. Bert walked out of the post office, got in the Ford and drove away. By that time, the girl who sold stamps had recovered. She was telling everyone how Bert had insulted her.

"Oh, my God! It was terrible," she said.

"That's one nigger don't know his place, Tom," Mr. Higgins roared over the phone. "And it's your fault he don't—sendin' 'em off to school to be educated." The Colonel listened to his friend at the other end of the wire. "Why that yellow buck comes to my store, and if he ain't waited on quick as the white folks are, he walks out. He said last week, standin' out on my corner, he wasn't *all* nigger no how; said his name was Norwood—not Lewis, like the rest of Cora's family; said your plantation would be his when you passed out—and all that kind o' stuff, boasting to the niggers listening about you being his father." The Colonel almost dropped the phone. "Now, Tom, you know that stuff don't go 'round these parts o' Georgia. Ruinous to other niggers hearing that sort of talk, too. There ain't been no race trouble in our county for three years—since the Deekins lynching—but

I'm telling you, Norwood, folks ain't gonna stand for this. I'm speaking on the quiet, but I see ahead. What happened this morning in the post office ain't none too good."

"When I get through with him," said the Colonel hoarsely, "you won't need to worry. Good-by."

The white man came out of the library, yelled for Sam, shouted for Cora, ordered whisky. Drank and screamed.

"God damn that son of yours! I'm gonna kill him," he said to Cora. "Get out of here," he shouted at Sam, who came back with cigars.

Cora wept. The Colonel raved. A car shot down the road. The Colonel rushed out, brandishing a cane to stop it. It was Bert. He paid no attention to the old man standing on the steps of the pillared porch, waving his stick. Ashen with fury, the Colonel came back into the house and fumbled with his keys at an old chest. Finally, a drawer opened and he took out a pistol. He went toward the door as Cora began to howl, but on the porch he became suddenly strengthless and limp. Shaking, the old man sank into a chair holding the gun. He would not speak to Cora.

Late in the afternoon, Colonel Norwood sent Cora for their son. The gun had been put away. At least Cora did not see it.

"I want to talk to that boy," the Colonel said. "Fetch him here." Damned young fool . . . bastard . . . of a nigger . . .

"What's he gonna do to my boy?" Cora thought. "Son, be careful," as she went across the yard and down toward Willie's cabin to find Bert. "Son, you be careful. I didn't bear you for no white man to kill. Son, you be careful. You ain't white, don't you know that? You be careful. O Lord God Jesus in heaven! Son, be careful!" Cora was crying when she reached Willie's door, crying all the way back to the Big House with her son.

"To hell with the old man," Bert said. "He ain't no trouble! Old as he is, what can he do to me?"

"Lord have mercy, son, is you crazy? Why don't you be like Willie? He ain't never had no fusses with de Colonel."

"White-folks' nigger," Bert said.

"Why don't you talk sense?" Cora begged.

"Why didn't he keep his promise, then, and let me go back to school in Atlanta, like my sister? You said if I came home this summer, he'd lemme go back to the Institute, didn't you? Then why didn't he?"

"Why didn't you act right, son? Oh-o-o!" Cora moaned. "You can't get nothin' from white folks if you don't act right."

"Act like Willie, you mean, and the rest of these cotton pickers? Then I don't want anything."

They had reached the back door now. It was nearly dark in the kitchen where Livonia was making biscuits.

"Don't rile him, Bert, child," Cora said as she took him through the house. "I don't know what he might do to you. He's got a gun."

"Don't worry 'bout me," Bert answered.

The setting sun made long paths of golden light across the parlor floor through the tall windows opening on the west. The air was thick and sultry with autumn heat. The Colonel sat, bent and old, near a table where there were whisky and cigars and a half-open drawer. When Bert entered he suddenly straightened up, and the old commanding look came into his eyes. He told Cora to go upstairs to her room.

Of course, he never asked Bert to sit down.

The tall mulatto boy stood before his father, the Colonel. The old white man felt the steel of him standing there, like the steel of himself forty years ago. Steel of the Norwoods darkened now by Africa, yet shared in common. The old man got up, straight and tall, too, and suddenly shook his fist in the face of the boy. "You listen to me," he said, trembling with quiet. "I don't want to have to whip you again like I did when you were a child." He was almost hissing. "The next time I might kill you. I been running this plantation thirty-five years and never had to beat a nigger old as you are. Never had any trouble out of none of Cora's children before either, but you." The old man sat down. "I don't have trouble with my colored folks. They do what I say or what Talbot says, and that's all there is to it. If they turn in crops, they get a living. If they work for wages, they

get paid. If they spend their money on licker, or old cars, or fixing up their cabins—they can do what they choose, long as they
know their places and it don't hinder their work. To Cora's
young ones—you hear me, boy?—I gave all the chances any
nigger ever had in these parts. More'n many a white child's had,
too. I sent you off to school. I gave your brother, Willie, that
house he's living in when he got married, pay him for his work,
help him out if he needs it. None of my darkies suffer. You went
off to school. Could have kept on, would have sent you back
this fall, but I don't intend to pay for no nigger, or white boy,
either, if I had one, that acts the way you been acting." Colonel
Norwood got up again, angrily. "And certainly not for no black
fool! I'm talking to *you* like this only because you're Cora's child
—but you know damn well it's my habit to *tell* people what to
do, not discuss it with them. I just want to know what's the matter with you, though—whether you're crazy or not? And if
you're not, you'd better change your ways a damn sight or it
won't be safe for you here, and you know it—venting your impudence on white women, ruining my niggers, driving like mad
through the Junction, carrying on just as you please. I'm
warning you, boy, God damn it! . . . Now I want you to answer me, and talk right." The old man sat down in his chair
again by the whisky bottle and the partly opened drawer. He
took a drink.

"What do you mean, talk right?" Bert said.

"I mean talk like a nigger should to a white man," the Colonel
snapped.

"Oh, but I'm not a nigger, Colonel Norwood," Bert said,
"I'm your son."

The old man frowned at the boy in front of him. "Cora's son,"
he said.

"Fatherless?" Bert asked.

"Bastard," the old man said.

Bert's hands closed into fists, so the Colonel opened the drawer
where the pistol was. He took it out and laid it on the table.

"You black bastard," he said.

"I've heard that before." Bert just stood there. "You're talking about my mother."

"Well," the Colonel answered, his fingers playing over the surface of the gun, "what can you do about it?"

The boy felt his whole body suddenly tighten and pull. The muscles of his forearms rippled.

"Niggers like you are hung to trees," the old man went on.

"I'm not a nigger," Bert said. "Ain't you my father? And a hell of a father you are, too, holding a gun on me."

"I'll break your black neck for you," the Colonel shouted. "Don't talk to me like that!" He jumped up.

"You'll break my neck?" The boy stood his ground as the father came toward him.

"Get out of here!" The Colonel shook with rage. "Get out! Or I'll do more than that if I ever lay eyes on you again." The old man picked up the pistol from the table, yet the boy did not move. "I'll fill you full of bullets if you come back here. Get off this place! Get to hell out of this county! Now, tonight. Go on!" The Colonel motioned with his pistol toward the door that led to the kitchen and the back of the house.

"Not that way," Bert said. "I'm not your servant. You must think I'm scared. Well, you can't drive me out the back way like a dog. You're not going to run me off, like a field hand you can't use any more. I'll go," the boy said, starting toward the front door, "but not out the back—from my own father's house."

"You nigger bastard!" Norwood screamed, springing between his son and the door, but the boy kept calmly on. The steel of the gun was between them, but that didn't matter. Rather, it seemed to pull them together like a magnet.

"Don't you . . ." Norwood began, for suddenly Bert's hand grasped the Colonel's arm, "dare put your . . ." and his old bones began to crack, "black hands on . . ."

"Why don't you shoot?" Bert interrupted him, slowly turning his wrist.

". . . me!"

"Why don't you shoot, then?"

The old man twisted and bent in fury and pain, but the gun fell to the floor.

"Why don't you shoot?" Bert said again as his hands sought his father's throat. With furious sureness they took the old white neck in their strong young fingers. "Why don't you shoot then, Papa?"

Colonel Norwood clawed the air, breathing hoarsely and loud, his tongue growing stiff and dry, his eyes beginning to burn.

"Shoot—why don't you, then? Huh? Why?"

The chemicals of their two lives exploded. Everything was very black around them. The white man's hands stopped clawing the air. His heart stood still. His blood no longer flowed. He wasn't breathing.

"Why don't you shoot?" Bert said, but there was no answer.

When the boy's eyes cleared, he saw his mother standing at the foot of the stairs, so he let the body drop. It fell with a thud, old and white in a path of red from the setting sun.

"Why didn't he shoot, Mama? He didn't want me to live. He was white. Why didn't he shoot then?"

"Tom!" Cora cried, falling across his body. "Colonel Tom! Tom! Tom!"

"He's dead," Bert said. "I'm living, though."

"Tom!" Cora screamed, pulling at the dead man. "Colonel Tom!"

Bert bent down and picked up the pistol. "This is what my father wanted to use on me," he said. "He's dead. But I can use it on all the white men in Georgia—they'll be coming to get me now. They never wanted me before, but I know they'll want me now." He stuffed the pistol in his shirt. Cora saw what her son had done.

"Run," she said, rising and going to him. "Run, chile! Out the front way quick, so's they won't see you in the kitchen. Make fo' de swamp, honey. Cross de fields fo' de swamp. Go de crick way. In runnin' water, dogs can't smell no tracks. Hurry, son!"

"Yes, Mama," Bert said slowly. "But if I see they gonna get me before I reach the swamp, then I'm coming back here. Let them take me out of my father's house—if they can." He patted the gun inside his shirt, and smiled. "They'll never string me up to some roadside tree for the crackers to laugh at. Not me!"

"Hurry, chile." Cora opened the door and the sunset streamed in like a river of blood. "Hurry, chile."

Bert went out across the wide pillared porch and down the road. He saw Talbot and the storekeeper coming, so he turned off through the trees. And then, because he wanted to live, he began to run. The whole sky was a blaze of color as he ran. Then it began to get dark, and the glow went away.

In the house, Cora started to talk to the dead man on the floor, just as though he were not dead. She pushed and pulled at the body, trying to get him to get up himself. Then she heard the footsteps of Talbot and the storekeeper on the porch. She rose and stood as if petrified in the middle of the floor. A knock, and two men were peering through the screen door into the dusk-dark room. Then Talbot opened the door.

"Hello, Cora," he said. "What's the matter with you, why didn't you let us in? Where's that damn fool boy o' your'n goin', comin' out the front way liked he owned the place? What's the matter with you, woman? Can't you talk? Where's Colonel Norwood?"

"Let's have some light in here," said the storekeeper, turning a button beside the door.

"Great God!" Talbot cried. "Jim, look at this!" The Colonel's body lay huddled on the floor, old and purple-white, at Cora's feet.

"Why, he's blue in the face," the storekeeper said bending over the body. "Oh! Get that nigger we saw walking out the door! That nigger bastard of Cora's. Get that nigger! . . . Why, the Colonel's dead!"

Talbot rushed toward the door. "That nigger," he cried. "He must be running toward the swamps now. . . . We'll get him. Telephone town, Jim, there in the library. Telephone the sheriff. Telephone the Beale family down by the swamp. Get men, white men, after that nigger."

The storekeeper ran into the library and began to call on the phone. Talbot looked at Cora, standing in the center of the room.

"Where's Norwood's car? In the barn? Talk, you black wench, talk!"

But Cora didn't say a word. She watched the two white men rush out of the house into the yard. In a few minutes, she heard the roar of a motor hurtling down the road. It was dark outside. Night had come.

Cora turned toward the body on the floor. "My boy," she said, "he can't get to de swamp now. They telephoned the white folks down that way to head him off. He'll come back home." She called aloud, "Colonel Tom, why don't you get up from there and help me? You know they're after our boy. You know they got him out there runnin' from de white folks in de night. Runnin' from de hounds and de guns and de ropes and all what they uses to kill poor niggers with. . . . Ma boy's out there runnin'. Why don't you help him?" Cora bent over the body. "Colonel Tom, you hear me? You said he was ma boy, ma bastard boy. I heard you. But he's your'n, too—out yonder in de dark runnin' —from your people. Why don't you get up and stop 'em? You know you could. You's a power in Polk County. You's a big man, and yet our son's out there runnin'—runnin' from po' white trash what ain't worth de little finger o' nobody's got your blood in 'em, Tom." Cora shook the dead body fiercely. "Get up from there and stop 'em, Colonel Tom." But the white man did not move.

Gradually Cora stopped shaking him. Then she rose and backed away from this man she had known so long. "You's cruel, Tom," she whispered. "I might a-knowed it—you'd be like that, sendin' ma boy out to die. I might a-knowed it ever since you beat him that time under de feet of de horses. Well, you won't mistreat him no more now. That's finished." She went toward the steps. "I'm gonna make a place for him. Upstairs under ma bed. He's ma chile, and I'll look out for him. And don't you come in ma bedroom while he's up there. Don't you come to ma bed either no more a-tall. I calls for you to help me now, Tom, and you just lays there. I calls you to get up now, and you don't move. Whenever you called *me* in de night, I woke up. Whenever you wanted me to love you, I reached out ma arms to you.

I bored you five children and now," her voice rose hysterically, "one of 'em's out yonder runnin' from your people. Our youngest boy's out yonder in de dark, runnin'! I 'spects you's out there, too, with de rest of de white folks. Uh-um! Bert's runnin' from *you*, too. You said he warn't your'n—Cora's po' little yellow bastard. But he is your'n, Colonel Tom, and he's runnin' from you. Yes, out yonder in de dark, you, *you* runnin' our chile with a gun in yo' hand, and Talbot followin' behind you with a rope to hang Bert with." She leaned against the wall near the staircase, sobbing violently. Then she went back toward the man on the floor. Her sobs gradually ceased as she looked down at his crumpled body. Then she said slowly, "Listen, I been sleepin' with you too long not to know that this ain't you, Tom, layin' down here with yo' eyes shut on de floor. You can't fool me— you ain't never been so still like this before—you's out yonder runnin' ma boy! Colonel Thomas Norwood runnin' ma boy through de fields in de dark, runnin' ma po' little helpless Bert through de fields in de dark for to lynch him and to kill him. . . . God damn you, Tom Norwood!" Cora cried, "God damn you!"

She went upstairs. For a long time the body lay alone on the floor in the parlor. Later Cora heard Sam and Livonia weeping and shouting in the kitchen, and Negro voices outside in the dark, and feet going down the road. She thought she heard the baying of hounds afar off, too, as she prepared a hiding place for Bert in the attic. Then she came down to her room and put the most beautiful quilts she had on her bed. "Maybe he'll just want to rest here first," she thought. "Maybe he'll be awful tired and just want to rest."

Then she heard a loud knock at the door, and white voices talking, and Sam's frightened answers. The doctor and the undertakers had come to take the body away. In a little while she heard them lifting it up and putting it in the dead wagon. And all the time, they kept talking, talking.

". . . 'll be havin' his funeral in town . . . ain't nothin' but niggers left out here . . . didn't have no relatives, did he, Sam? . . . Too bad. . . . Nobody to look after his stuff tonight. Every white man's able to walk's out with the posse . . . that young nigger'll swing before midnight . . . what a necktie party! . . . Say, Sam!"

"Yes, sah! Yes, sah!"

". . . that black housekeeper, Cora? . . . murderin' bastard's mother?"

"She's upstairs, I reckon, sah."

". . . like to see how she looks. Get her down here."

"Yes, sah!" Sam's teeth were chattering.

"And how about a little drink before we start back to town?"

"Yes, sah! Cora's got de keys fo' de licker, sah."

"Well, get her down, double quick, then!"

"Yes, sah!" Cora heard Sam coming up for her.

Downstairs, the voices went on. They were talking about her. ". . . lived together . . . ain't been a white woman here overnight since the wife died when I was a kid . . . bad business, though, livin' with a," in drawling cracker tones, "nigger."

As Cora came down the steps, the undertakers looked at her, half-grinning. "So you're the black wench that's got these educated darkie children? Hum-m! Well I guess you'll see one of 'em swinging full o' bullet holes before you get up in the morning. . . . Or maybe they'll burn him. How'd you like a roasted darkie for breakfast, girlie?"

Cora stood quite still on the stairs. "Is that all you wanted to say to me?" she asked.

"Now, don't get smart," the doctor said. "Maybe you think there's nobody to boss you now. We're goin' to have a little drink before we go. Get out a bottle."

"I take my orders from Colonel Norwood, suh," Cora said.

"Well, you'll take no more orders from him," the undertaker declared. "He's outside in the dead wagon. Get along now and get out a bottle."

"He's out yonder with de mob," Cora said.

"I tell you he's in my wagon, dead as a doornail."

"I tell you he's runnin' with de mob," Cora said.

"I believe this black woman's done gone nuts," the doctor cried. "Sam, you get the licker."

"Yes, sah!" Sam sputtered with fright. "Co-r-r-ra, gimme . . ."

But Cora did not move.

"Ah-a-a-a, Lawd hab mercy!" Sam cried.

"To hell with the licker, Charlie," the undertaker said nervously. "Let's start back to town. We want to get in on some of that excitement, too. They should've found that nigger by now —and I want to see 'em drag him out here."

"All right, Jim," the other agreed. Then, to Cora, "But don't you darkies go to bed until you see the bonfire. You all are gettin' beside yourselves around Polk County. We'll burn a few more of you if you don't watch out."

The men left and the wheels of the wagon turned on the drive. Sam began to cry.

"Hab mercy! Lawd Jesus, hab mercy! Cora, is you a fool? *Is* you? Then why didn't you give de mens de licker, riled as these white folks is? In ma old age, is I gonna be burnt by de crackers? Lawd, is I sinned? Lawd, what has I done?" He looked at Cora. "I sho ain't gonna stay heah tonight. I's gwine."

"Go on," she said. "The Colonel can get his own drinks when he comes back."

"Lawd God Jesus!" Sam, his eyes bucking from their sockets, bolted from the room fast as his old legs could carry him. Cora heard him running blindly through the house, moaning.

She went to the kitchen where pots were still boiling on the stove, but Livonia had fled, the biscuits burnt in the oven. She looked out the back door, but no lights were visible anywhere. The cabins were quiet.

"I reckon they all gone," she said to herself. "Even ma boy, Willie. I reckon he gone, too. You see, Colonel Tom, everybody's scared o' you. They know you done gone with de mob again, like you did that time they hung Luke Jordan and you went to help 'em. Now you's out chasin' ma boy, too. I hears you hollerin'."

And sure enough, all around the Big House in the dark, in a wide far-off circle, men and dog cries and auto horns sounded in the night. Nearer they came, even as Cora stood at the back door, listening. She closed the door, bolted it, put out the light, and went back to the parlor. "He'll come in by de front," she said.

"Back from de swamp way. He won't let 'em stop him from gettin' home to me agin, just once. Po' little boy, he ain't got no
place to go, no how. Po' boy, what growed up with such pride in
his heart. Just like you, Colonel Tom. Spittin' image o' you.
. . . Proud! . . . And got no place to go."

Nearer and nearer the manhunt came, the cries and the horns
and the dogs. Headlights began to flash in the dark down the
road. Off through the trees, Cora heard men screaming. And suddenly feet running, running, running. Nearer, nearer. She knew
it was him. She knew they had seen him, too.

Then there were voices shouting very near the house.

"Don't shoot, men. We want to get him alive."

"Close in on him!"

"He must be in them bushes there by the porch."

"Look!"

And suddenly shots rang out. The door opened. Cora saw
flashes of fire spitting into the blackness, and Bert's tall body in
the doorway. He was shooting at the voices outside in the dark.
The door closed.

"Hello, Ma," he said. "One or two of 'em won't follow me no
further."

Cora locked the door as bullets splintered through the wood,
shattered the windowpanes. Then a great volley of shots struck
the house, blinding headlights focused on the porch. Shouts
and cries of, "Nigger! Nigger! Get the nigger!" filled the night.

"I was waitin' for you, honey," Cora said. "Quick! Your hid-
in' place's ready for you, upstairs in de attic. I sawed out a place
under de floor. Maybe they won't find you, chile. Hurry, 'fore
your father comes."

"No time to hide, Ma," Bert panted. "They're at the door
now. They'll be coming in the back way, too. They'll be coming
in the windows. They'll be coming in everywhere. I got one
bullet left, Ma. It's mine."

"Yes, son, it's your'n. Go upstairs in Mama's room and lay
down on ma bed and rest. I won't let 'em come up till you're
gone. God bless you, chile."

Quickly, they embraced. A moment his head rested on her shoulder.

"I'm awful tired running, Ma. I couldn't get to the swamp. Seems like they been chasing me for hours. Crawling through the cotton a long time; I got to rest now."

Cora pushed him toward the stairs. "Go on, son," she said gently.

At the top, Bert turned and looked back at this little brown woman standing there, waiting for the mob. Outside the noise was terrific. Men shouted and screamed, massing for action. All at once they seemed to rush in a great wave for the house. They broke the doors and windows in, and poured into the room—a savage crowd of white men, red and wild-eyed, with guns and knives, sticks and ropes, lanterns and flashlights. They paused at the foot of the stairs where Cora stood looking down at them silently.

"Keep still, men," one of the leaders said. "He's armed. Say where's that yellow bastard of yours, Cora—upstairs?"

"Yes," Cora said. "Wait."

"Wait, hell!" the men cried. "Come on, boys, let's go!"

A shot rang out upstairs, then Cora knew it was all right.

"Go on," she said, stepping aside for the mob.

The next morning when people saw a bloody and unrecognizable body hanging in the public square at the Junction, some said with a certain pleasure, "That's what we do to niggers down here," not realizing Bert had been taken dead, and that all the fun for the mob had been sort of stale at the end.

But others, aware of what had happened, thought, "It'd be a hell of a lot better lynching a live nigger. Say, ain't there nobody else mixed up in this here Norwood murder? Where's that boy's brother, Willie? Heh?"

So the evening papers carried this item in the late editions:

DOUBLE LYNCHING IN GEORGIA

A large mob late this afternoon wrecked vengeance on the second of two Negro field hands, the murderers of Colonel Thomas Nor-

*wood, wealthy planter found dead at Big House Plantation. Bert
Lewis was lynched last night, and his brother, Willie Lewis, today.
The sheriff of the county is unable to identify any members of the
mob. Colonel Norwood's funeral has not yet been held. The dead
man left no heirs.*

Professor

Promptly at seven a big car drew up in front of the Booker T.
Washington Hotel, and a white chauffeur in uniform got out
and went toward the door, intending to ask at the desk for a
colored professor named T. Walton Brown. But the professor
was already sitting in the lobby, a white scarf around his neck
and his black overcoat ready to button over his dinner clothes.

As soon as the chauffeur entered, the professor approached.
"Mr. Chandler's car?" he asked hesitantly.

"Yes, sir," said the white chauffeur to the neat little Negro.
"Are you Dr. Walton Brown?"

"I am," said the professor, smiling and bowing a little.

The chauffeur opened the street door for Dr. Brown, then ran
to the car and held the door open there, too. Inside the big car
and on the long black running board as well, the lights came on.
The professor stepped in among the soft cushions, the deep rug,
and the cut-glass vases holding flowers. With the greatest of
deference the chauffeur quickly tucked a covering of fur about
the professor's knees, closed the door, entered his own seat in
front beyond the glass partition, and the big car purred away.
Within the lobby of the cheap hotel a few ill-clad Negroes
watched the whole procedure in amazement.

"A big shot!" somebody said.

At the corner as the car passed, two or three ash-colored children ran across the street in front of the wheel, their skinny legs
and poor clothes plain in the glare of the headlights as the

chauffeur slowed down to let them pass. Then the car turned and
ran the whole length of a Negro street that was lined with pawn-
shops, beer joints, pig's knuckle stands, cheap movies, hairdress-
ing parlors, and other ramshackle places of business patronized
by the poor blacks of the district. Inside the big car the professor, Dr. Walton Brown, regretted that in all the large Midwestern cities where he had lectured on his present tour in be-
half of his college, the main Negro streets presented the same
sleazy and disagreeable appearance: pig's knuckle joints, pawn-
shops, beer parlors—and houses of vice, no doubt—save that
these latter, at least, did not hang out their signs.

The professor looked away from the unpleasant sight of this
typical Negro street, poor and unkempt. He looked ahead
through the glass at the dignified white neck of the uniformed
chauffeur in front of him. The professor in his dinner clothes,
his brown face even browner above the white silk scarf at his
neck, felt warm and comfortable under the fur rug. But he felt,
too, a little unsafe at being driven through the streets of this city
on the edge of the South in an expensive car, by a white chauffeur.

"But, then," he thought, "this is the wealthy Mr. Ralph P.
Chandler's car, and surely no harm can come to me here. The
Chandlers are a power in the Middle West, and in the South
as well. Theirs is one of the great fortunes of America. In phi-
lanthropy, nobody exceeds them in well-planned generosity on
a large and highly publicized scale. They are a power in Negro
education, too—as long as it remains *Negro* and does not get
tangled up in integration. That is why I am visiting them tonight at their invitation."

Just now the Chandlers were interested in the little Negro
college at which the professor taught. They wanted to make it
one of the major Negro colleges of America. And in particular
the Chandlers were interested in his Department of Sociology.
They were thinking of endowing a chair of research there and
employing a man of ability for it. A Ph.D. and a scholar. A man
of some prestige, like the professor. For his *The Sociology of
Prejudice* (that restrained and conservative study of Dr. T. Wal-

ton Brown's) had recently come to the attention of the Chandler
Committee. And a representative of their philanthropies, visiting
the campus, had conversed with the professor at some length
about his book and his views. This representative of the committee found Dr. Brown highly gratifying, because in almost
every case the professor's views agreed with the white man's own.

"A fine, sane, dependable young Negro," was the description
that came to the Chandler Committee from their traveling representative.

So now the power himself, Mr. Ralph P. Chandler, and Mrs.
Chandler, learning that he was lecturing at one of the colored
churches of the town, had invited him to dinner at their mansion
in this city on the edge of the South. Their car had come to
call for him at the colored Booker T. Washington Hotel—where
the hot water was always cold, the dresser drawers stuck, and the
professor shivered as he got into his dinner clothes; and the bell-
boys, anxious for a tip, had asked him twice that evening if he
needed a half-pint or a woman.

But now he was in this big warm car and they were moving
swiftly down a fine boulevard, the black slums far behind them.
The professor was glad. He had been very much distressed at
having the white chauffeur call for him at this cheap hotel in
what really amounted to the red-light district of the town. But,
then, none of the white hotels in this American city would house
Negroes, no matter how cultured they might be. Marian Anderson herself had been unable to find decent accommodations
there, so the colored papers said, on the day of her concert.

Sighing, the professor looked out of the car at the wide lawns
and fine homes that lined the beautiful well-lighted boulevard
where white people lived. After a time the car turned into a
fashionable suburban road and he saw no more houses, but only
ivy-hung walls, neat shrubs, and boxwoods that indicated not
merely homes beyond but vast estates. Shortly the car whirled
into a paved driveway, past a small lodge, through a park full of
fountains and trees, and up to a private house as large as a hotel.
From a tall portico a great hanging lantern cast a soft glow on

the black and chrome body of the big car. The white chauffeur
jumped out and deferentially opened the door for the colored
professor. An English butler welcomed him at the entrance and
took his coat, hat, and scarf. Then he led the professor into a
large drawing room where two men and a woman were standing
chatting near the fireplace.

The professor hesitated, not knowing who was who; but Mr.
and Mrs. Chandler came forward, introduced themselves, shook
hands, and in turn presented their other guest of the evening,
Dr. Bulwick of the local Municipal College—a college that Dr.
Brown recalled did *not* admit Negroes.

"I am happy to know you," said Dr. Bulwick. "I am also a
sociologist."

"I have heard of you," said Dr. Brown graciously.

The butler came with sherry in a silver pitcher. They sat
down, and the whites began to talk politely, to ask Dr. Brown
about his lecture tour, if his audiences were good, if they were
mostly Negro or mixed, and if there was much interest in his
college, much money being given.

Then Dr. Bulwick began to ask about his book, *The Sociology of Prejudice,* where he got his material, under whom he
had studied, and if he thought the Negro Problem would ever
be solved.

Dr. Brown said genially, "We are making progress," which
was what he always said, though he often felt he was lying.

"Yes," said Dr. Bulwick, "that is very true. Why, at our city
college here we've been conducting some fine interracial ex-
periments. I have had several colored ministers and high-school
teachers visit my classes. We found them most intelligent people."

In spite of himself Dr. Brown had to say, "But you have no
colored students at your college, have you?"

"No," said Dr. Bulwick, "and that is too bad! But that is one
of our difficulties here. There is no college for Negroes—although nearly forty per cent of our population is colored. Some
of us have thought it might be wise to establish a separate junior

college for our Negroes, but the politicians opposed it on the score of no funds. And we cannot take them as students on our campus. That, at present, is impossible. It's too bad."

"But do you not think, Dr. Brown," interposed Mrs. Chandler, who wore diamonds on her wrists and smiled every time she spoke, "do you not think *your* people are happier in schools of their own—that it is really better for both groups not to mix them?"

In spite of himself Dr. Brown replied, "That depends, Mrs. Chandler. I could not have gotten my degree in any schools of our own."

"True, true," said Mr. Chandler. "Advanced studies, of course, cannot be gotten. But when your colleges are developed—as we hope they will be, and our committee plans to aid in their development—when their departments are headed by men like yourself, for instance, then you can no longer say, 'That depends.' "

"You are right," Dr. Brown agreed diplomatically, coming to himself and thinking of his mission in that house. "You are right," Dr. Brown said, thinking, too, of that endowed chair of sociology and himself in the chair, the ten thousand dollars a year that he would probably be paid, the surveys he might make and the books he could publish. "You are right," said Dr. Brown diplomatically to Ralph P. Chandler. But in the back of his head was that ghetto street full of sleazy misery he had just driven through, and the segregated hotel where the hot water was always cold, and the colored churches where he lectured, and the Jim Crow schools where Negroes always had less equipment and far less money than white institutions; and that separate justice of the South where his people sat on trial but the whites were judge and jury forever; and all the segregated Jim Crow things that America gave Negroes and that were never equal to the things she gave the whites. But Dr. Brown said, "You are right, Mr. Chandler," for, after all, Mr. Chandler had the money!

So he began to talk earnestly to the Chandlers there in the warm drawing room about the need for bigger and better black colleges, for more and more surveys of *Negro* life, and a well-developed department of sociology at his own little institution.

"Dinner is served," said the butler.

They rose and went into a dining room where there were flowers on the table and candles, white linen and silver, and where Dr. Brown was seated at the right of the hostess and the talk was light over the soup, but serious and sociological again by the time the meat was served.

"The American Negro must not be taken in by communism," Dr. Bulwick was saying with great positiveness as the butler passed the peas.

"He won't," agreed Dr. Brown. "I assure you, our leadership stands squarely against it." He looked at the Chandlers and bowed. "All the best people stand against it."

"America has done too much for the Negro," said Mr. Chandler, "for him to seek to destroy it."

Dr. Brown bobbed and bowed.

"In your *Sociology of Prejudice*," said Dr. Bulwick, "I highly approve of the closing note, your magnificent appeal to the old standards of Christian morality and the simple concepts of justice by which America functions."

"Yes," said Dr. Brown, nodding his dark head and thinking suddenly how on ten thousand dollars a year he might take his family to South America in the summer where for three months they wouldn't feel like Negroes. "Yes, Dr. Bulwick," he nodded, "I firmly believe as you do that if the best elements of both races came together in Christian fellowship, we would solve this problem of ours."

"How beautiful," said Mrs. Chandler.

"And practical, too," said her husband. "But now to come back to your college—university, I believe you call it—to bring that institution up to really first-class standards you would need . . . ?"

"We would need . . ." said Dr. Brown, speaking as a mouthpiece of the administration, and speaking, too, as mouthpiece for the Negro students of his section of the South, and speaking for himself as a once ragged youth who had attended the college

when its rating was lower than that of a Northern high school
so that he had to study two years in Boston before he could enter
a white college, when he had worked nights as redcap in the station and then as a waiter for seven years until he got his Ph.D.,
and then couldn't get a job in the North but had to go back down
South to the work where he was now—but which might develop
into a glorious opportunity at ten thousand dollars a year to
make surveys and put down figures that other scholars might
study to get their Ph.D.'s, and that would bring him in enough
to just once take his family on a vacation to South America
where they wouldn't feel that they were Negroes. "We would
need, Mr. Chandler, . . ."

And the things Dr. Brown's little college needed were small
enough in the eyes of the Chandlers. The sane and conservative
way in which Dr. Brown presented his case delighted the phil-
anthropic heart of the Chandlers. And Mr. Chandler and Dr.
Bulwick both felt that instead of building a junior college for
Negroes in their own town, they could rightfully advise local
colored students to go down South to that fine little campus
where they had a professor of their own race like Dr. Brown.

Over the coffee, in the drawing room, they talked about the
coming theatrical season. And Mrs. Chandler spoke of how she
loved Negro singers, and smiled and smiled.

In due time the professor rose to go. The car was called and
he shook hands with Dr. Bulwick and the Chandlers. The
white people were delighted with Dr. Brown. He could see it
in their faces, just as in the past he could always tell as a waiter
when he had pleased a table full of whites by tender steaks and
good service.

"Tell the president of your college he shall hear from us
shortly," said the Chandlers. "We'll probably send a man down
again soon to talk to him about his expansion program." And
they bowed farewell.

As the car sped him back toward town, Dr. Brown sat under
its soft fur rug among the deep cushions and thought how with
ten thousand dollars a year earned by dancing properly to the

tune of Jim Crow education, he could carry his whole family to South America for a summer where they wouldn't need to feel like Negroes.

Sorrow for a Midget

No grown man works in a hospital if he can help it—the pay is too low. But I was broke, jobs hard to find, and the employment office sent me there that winter.

Right in the middle of Harlem.

Work wasn't hard, just cleaning up the wards, serving meals off a rolling table, bulling around, pushing a mop. I didn't mind. I got plenty to eat.

It was a little special kind of hospital; there was three private rooms on my floor, and in one of them was a female midget. Miss Midget—a little lady who looked like a dried-up child to me. But they told me (so I wouldn't get scared of her) that she was a midget. She had a pocketbook bigger than she was. It laid on a chair beside her bed. Generous, too—nice, that little midget lady. She gave me a tip the first day I was there.

But she was dying.

The nurses told me Countess Midget was booked to die. And I had never seen nobody die. Anyhow, I hung around her. It was profitable.

"Take care of me good," she said. "I pay as I go, I always did know how to get service." She opened her big fat pocketbook, as big as she was, and showed me a thick wad of bills. "This gets it anytime, anywhere," she said.

It got it with me, all right. I stuck by. Tips count up. That's how I know so much about what happened in them few days she was in that hospital room, game as she could be, but booked to die.

"Not even penicillin can save her," the day nurse said, "not her." That was when penicillin was new.

Of course, the undertakers that year was all complaining about penicillin. They used to come to the hospital looking for corpses.

"Business is bad," one undertaker told me. "People don't die like they used to since this penicillin come in. Un-huh! Spring-time, in the old days, you could always count on plenty of folks dying of pneumonia and such, going outdoors catching cold before it was warm enough, and all. Funerals every other day then. Not no more. The doctors stick 'em with penicillin now—and they get well. Damn if they don't! Business is bad for morticians."

But that midget did not have pneumonia, neither a cold. She had went without an operation she needed too long. Now operations could do her no good. And what they put in the needle for her arm was not penicillin. It was something that did her no good either, just eased down the pain. It were kept locked up so young orderlies like me would not steal it and sell it to junkies. The nurses would not even tell me where it was locked up at.

You know, I did not look too straight when I come in that hospital. Short-handed—not having much help—they would hire almost anybody for an orderly in a hospital in Harlem, even me. So I got the job.

Right off, after that first day, I loved that midget. I said, "Little Bits, you're a game kiddie. I admire your spunk."

Midget said, "I dig this hospital jive. Them nurses ain't understandable. Nice, but don't understand. You're the only one in here, boy, I would ask to do me a favor. Find my son."

"You look like a baby to me, Countess. Where and when on earth did you get a son?" I asked.

"Don't worry about that," said Countess Midget. "I got him —and he's mine. I want him *right now*. He do not know I am in here sick—if he did, he would come—even were he ashamed of the way he looked. You find my son." She gave me twenty bucks for subway fare and taxi to go looking.

I went and searched and found her son. Just like she had said he might be, he were ashamed to come to the hospital. He was not doing so well. Fact is, her son was ragged as a buzzard feed-

ing on a Lenox Avenue carcass. But when I told him his mama
was sick in the Maggie Butler Pavilion of the Sadie Henderson
Hospital, he come. He got right up out of bed and left his old
lady and come.

"My mama has not called for me for a long, long time," he
said. "If she calls me now, like this boy says," he told his girl,
"wild horses could not hold me. Baby, I am going to see my
mama," he said.

"I did not even know you had a mama," whined the sleepy
old broad in the bed, looking as if she did not much care.

"Lots of things you do not know about this Joe," said the cat
to the broad. He got up and dressed and went with me, quick.

"That little bitty woman," I asked him in the street, "she is
your mama?"

"Damn right she's my mama," said the guy, who was near six
feet, big, heavy-set, black, and ragged. No warm coat on. I
thought I was beat, but he was the most. I could tell he had *been*
gone to the dogs, long gone. Still, he was a young man. From
him I took a lesson.

"I will never get this far down," to myself I said. "No, *not
never!*"

"Is she very low sick?" he asked about his mama. "Real sick?"

"Man, I don't know," I said. "She is sunk way down in bed.
And the sign on the door says NO VISITORS."

"Then how am I gonna get in?"

"Relatives is not visitors," I said. "Besides, I know the nurses.
Right now is not even visiting hours. Too early. But come with
me. You'll get in."

I felt sorry for a guy with a mama who was a midget who was
dying. A midget laying dying! Had she been my mama, I guess
I would have wanted to be there, though, in spite of the fact she
was a midget. I couldn't help wondering how could she be so
small and have this great big son? Who were his papa? And
how could his papa have had her?

Well, anyhow, I took him in to see the little Countess in that
big high hospital bed, so dark and small, in that white, white
room, in that white bed.

They had just given his mama a needle, so she were not right bright. But when she saw her son, her little old wrinkled face lighted up. Her little old tiny matchstick arms went almost around his neck. And she hollered, "My baby!" real loud. "My precious baby son!"

"Mama," he almost cried, "I have not been a good son to you."

"You have been my *only* son," she said.

The nurse hipped me, "Let's get out of here and leave 'em alone." So we went. And we left them alone for a long time, until he left.

That afternoon that midget died. Her son couldn't hardly have more than gotten home when I had to go after him again. I asked him on the way back to the hospital was he honest-to-God sure enough her son.

He shook his head. "No."

That is when I felt most sorry for that midget, when I heard him say No. He explained to me that he was just a took-in son, one she had sort of adopted when he was near-about a baby—because he had no father and no mother and she had no son. But she wanted people to *think* she had a son.

She was just his midget mama, that's all. He never had no real mama that he knew. But this little tiny midget raised him as best she could. Being mostly off in sideshows and carnivals the biggest part of the time, she boarded him out somewhere in school in the country. When he got teen-age and came back to Harlem, he went right straight to the dogs. But she loved him and he loved her.

When he found out, about 5:30 P.M., that she had died, that big old ragged no-good make-believe son of hers cried like a child.

Powder-White Faces

It was good to feel the sea spray on his face again, to look up at the stars rocking in the sky, to breathe the great clean rush of wind from the open ocean as the deck swayed beneath his feet.

The little old freighter had slipped down the East River, past the lights of New York like a glittering wall to starboard. Charlie Lee, mess boy, lit a cigarette, inhaled once, and threw it into the water.

"We're off, heh, mate?" said a white seaman, leaning on the rail beside the Oriental.

"Yep," Charlie Lee said. "Long gone this time."

The Statue of Liberty, holding its light, moved back into the darkness. Staten Island sliding by, Brooklyn on the other side, starry with lights, moved back into darkness.

"Good night," said the seaman, "I'm turnin' in."

"Night," said Charlie Lee. He lit another cigarette, and listened to the heavy beat of the engines settle into an even rhythm of full steam ahead, a beat that would not be silent for several weeks to come. In a certain steady way the waves hit the boatside, the masts rocked against the sky, the weight of the rail pressed on Charlie's chest and then fell away. All this sea movement would go on for many days. Charlie was glad his next port would be Cape Town, thousands of miles from Manhattan— for that morning Charlie had killed a woman.

As Charlie Lee stood by the ship's side looking out into the watery darkness of the Atlantic, he tried to think why he had done it. But he could not think why, he could only *feel* why. He could feel again, standing by the rail, all the hatred and anger of a lifetime that had suddenly that morning collected in his heart and gathered in his fingers at the sight of a white face and a red mouth on the pillow beneath him.

Charlie Lee had killed a *white* woman just twelve hours ago.

147

Charlie Lee. That wasn't his real name. Charlie had almost forgotten his real name. But Charlie Lee was a good name, he thought. It didn't sound Oriental like the names of most of the people on the little American possession in the Pacific from which he had come. It was better than a name like Ah Woo or Kakawali or Chung Sing.

But the name didn't really matter. What mattered was that Charlie's face was brown, his eyes slanted, and his hair heavy and black like a Chinese. Because of his color and perhaps his eyes, American ships wouldn't hire him for any work but a steward's or a kitchen boy's. American or English officers on his own island wouldn't give him a clerk's job if they could find a white person to fill it. And no white woman would marry him unless she were down and out.

But a white man, very long ago, had taken his youngest sister for a mistress, and she had borne him four children.

That was before Charlie grew up, changed his name, and went away to sea as a cabin boy on a tramp steamer bound for Frisco. For nearly ten years Charlie had never been back home. Sailing all the world. The Pacific, the Atlantic, the Mediterranean. Many cities, many people. White, brown, and yellow people. Stopping awhile to work ashore in California vineyards; one winter as a Santa Barbara houseboy: another winter in a New York elevator on Riverside Drive, up and down, up and down. And between times, the sea, the great clean old sea rocking beneath his feet—like tonight.

Now, Charlie Lee stood at the tramp's rail with the wind blowing in his face, wondering why he had killed that white woman this morning. He had never killed anybody in his life before. And this woman had really done nothing to him. Not *this* woman. Then why did he kill *her*? But when he tried to figure it out, he kept remembering other white women (not the one he had killed, but *other* women), port-town women, taxi-dance-hall women, women with powder-white faces who took all they could get from him and then let him go, called him names, kicked him out, or had him beaten up.

It began with the girls in Mollie's Tropical Beer Garden,

where he had worked at home out in the Pacific before he grew up and changed his name. There he ran errands for the white hostesses and the American Marines. There he often heard the girls declare they couldn't have anything to do with a native because if they did, Uncle Sam's boys wouldn't have anything to do with them. So the policy of Mollie's Beer Garden was WHITE ONLY insofar as her customers went. (There was a sign over the bar to that effect.) And although the waiters were native brown boys, the bartender—the only one who got a salary—was Irish. The brown boys worked for tips alone.

When Charlie went away to sea, the next foreign women he knew were White Russians under the carnival lights of Shanghai, rapacious females, hungry and diseased, who haunted the bars, dives, and dance halls, sleeping with anyone who could pay them, and picking pockets in the bargain. They cleaned Charlie out of all his money while his ship was in dock. And the doctors put him in the Marine Hospital when he reached San Francisco ill.

When he got better, he found a job in the grape orchards on the coast and experienced all the prejudices of white California toward the brown people from across the Pacific. Even if you were from an *American* island, it didn't seem to make any difference.

After two years in California Charlie went to sea again as a cabin boy on a freighter, San Diego, Colón, Havana, the Gulf ports. Then he got in jail, for the first time, at New Orleans.

All the mess boys went out together their first night in port, to a wineshop on St. Louis Street. Along the street the shutters kept clicking and white women kept looking out at the little Orientals in their broad-shouldered suits and highly polished shoes. Sometimes the women whispered, "Come in, baby." But the boys kept on to a place where they were sure they were welcome, for in this wineshop there were women, too. Rather faded women, it's true, a little old or a little ugly or a little droopy— but the best the Italian proprietor could get for a bar that catered to yellow-brown boys from the ships, for seldom did white sailors come there, and almost never men of the city.

But tonight, by chance, a group of white men did come—not sailors, but young Southern rowdies about town looking for fun. They were already half drunk, and they weren't used to seeing (as sailors would have been) brown men and white women mixing. They felt hurt about it as they stood drinking at the bar. They felt insulted. They got mad. They wanted to protect white womanhood.

"Let's clean out the spicks," one of them whispered.

A big guy turned on Charlie.

"Take your eyes off that white woman, coon," he said, hitting him across the mouth, *wham!* without warning.

Charlie staggered to his feet. His friends drew knives. The girls screamed and gathered behind the white men. Fists flew. A fight was on.

The next thing Charlie knew, he regained consciousness in a cell. Alone, his face battered, his clothes torn, his money and watch gone, he felt sick and his head whirled. There were iron bars all around him like a cage. His body hurt. And his soul hurt, too.

The last thing he remembered before the big white fellow knocked him out was that the girl whom he had just treated to a drink suddenly spat in his face. Charlie never forgot that. The judge gave him ten days in jail for disturbing the peace, and he missed his boat. For nearly a month he went hungry in New Orleans, but finally he managed to ship out on a coastwise steamer to New York. The salt of the sea healed the purple bruises on his face.

In Manhattan he got a job as elevator boy in a busy house on the Drive. Nights he spent in the taxi-dance halls above Columbus Circle frequented by sleek-haired little brown fellows, Filipinos, Hawaiians, and Chinese, dancing and dancing to rhumbas that were like the palm trees swaying in his native islands.

There were lots of white girls, powdered pink and blonde, who worked in these dance halls and lived on the boys who went to dance there. Once Charlie was in love with one of these hostesses. He kept bringing her all his money every week, until she said one night, "Darling, you don't make enough for me. Why don't you gamble or something and get some real dough?"

So Charlie began to lose all his wages trying to win more for her. Every week he lost. He worried about her, kept stopping the elevator at the wrong floors with her on his mind, and finally got fired from his job. Of course she left him.

When he found work again, it was as houseboy for a rich young man named Richards who had an apartment on lower Fifth Avenue.

He had plenty to do, but he was well paid. He liked the boss, and the boss liked him. But Charlie didn't like Mr. Richards's mistress. He found her too much like the girls in the taxi-dance halls, or in St. Louis Street in New Orleans, hard, rapacious, and crude. But sometimes, for days, he wouldn't see Mr. Richards—only this woman. And, as time went on, she became more and more familiar with Charlie, said things to him that she shouldn't say to a servant, kidded him, walked around before him in pink silk things that were only shadows, smiling. Charlie hated her. Even when she put all her jewels on—blonde as a beauty shop and sprinkled with perfume—she still made him think of Shanghai during the war and the hungry little Russian girls of Avenue Joffre who had stolen his money and left him ill years ago, and the white woman who spat in his face in New Orleans, and the dance-hall girl who left him when he went broke and had no job.

"Why can't Mr. Richards see what she's like?" Charlie wondered. "Me see."

Yet she was always nice to Charlie. Bold and invitingly nice. Even when she asked him to go out and buy dope for her and he refused, she didn't really mind. She only purred, "Don't tell Richie, will you?" as she went to the phone to order the white powder from a druggist she knew.

Now, Charlie recalled as he stood by the ship's rail, she and Mr. Richards kept talking about the dog races last night at the table during dinner. Later they went out and returned long after midnight. Charlie didn't hear them come in, but early in the morning the telephone rang. Long distance, Chicago calling. He woke Mr. Richards, who got all excited as he listened to the voice at the other end of the line. He kept talking about a merger, merger, merger. Finally he said, "I'll be there today." Then he called Charlie to pack his bag. "Flying to Chicago right away," he said. "Call a cab."

He kissed his blonde woman lying drowsy on the silken bed, and without eating, rushed out at dawn. Charlie didn't see him any more. In a few minutes the tragedy happened.

The blonde woman said, "Come here, Charlie." When Charlie came near the bed, she took him by his silky hair and pulled him down close to her breast.

"You're a cute China boy!" she said. "Kiss me."

But Charlie drew away. A sudden combination of anger and loathing came into his eyes. Fear and hatred. Distrust, suspicion, contempt for her lack of loyalty. What do you want with me? What's your game? What are you trying to gyp me out of? What do you want to do? I'm not your color! I know you too well— you and all your kind! You never played square by me, just like you don't play square by Mr. Richards. You white women, you cheats!

"Charlie," she said.

His brown hands gently sought her face, her chin. And *suddenly* closed on her throat. She did not even scream. Her mouth opened, but was silent. No breath, no sound. And Charlie didn't know why he did it.

Charlie suddenly remembered three Americans who killed a brown man in Honolulu over a white woman. He remembered the iron bars around him in New Orleans. And the powder-white faces of the Russian girls in Shanghai. And the hostesses in Mollie's Beer Garden, FOR WHITE ONLY. All the hidden resentment of years seemed to collect in his heart and gather in his fingers as the red mouth slowly opened on the pillow beneath him.

He did not want her. He only wanted to kill her—this woman who became suddenly *all* white women to him.

As he locked the apartment and went out into the early morning air, he smelled the sea again—the sea into which you can pour all the filth of the world, but the water never gets dirty.

Rouge High

Two streetwalkers came in and began to powder their faces. The waiter slid a couple of glasses of water along the counter and was about to take their order when a tall young fellow entered and knocked one of the girls plumb off the stool with a blow in the face.

"Here, honey! Take it! Here it is!" she began to yell.

Before she got up off the floor, she took a wrinkled bill from somewhere down in her bosom and gave it to him.

"Tryin' to hold out on me," said the fellow as he turned on his heel and left.

The girl got back up on the stool and went on powdering her face. She didn't shed a single tear.

"Ham and eggs, scrambled," said her companion.

"Nothin' but coffee for me," said the one who had been hit. "Them shots the doc gave me this mornin' made me sick. I can't eat a thing."

"Shots are hell," said the other one. "But, say, girlie, listen. What made Bunny think you was holdin' out on him?"

"He didn't think it, he knew it! He's pretty smart at figgerin' out what a John'll pay—that's why he's always on the corner lookin' 'em over when they come along. Bunny's an old hand at gettin' his."

"Then why didn't you give it to him then?"

"Aw, he ain't so wise as he thinks he is," said the girl as the waiter put her cup of coffee down in front of her. "Listen, I stole that last customer's pocketbook, too. And, believe me, I ain't splittin' these extra bucks with nobody!"

From somewhere under her clothes she pulled out a man's brown wallet, took out the money, and tossed the pocketbook across the counter to the waiter.

"Hey, kid," she said, "put that way down in the garbage can, underneath the coffee grounds. Get me?"

"I got you," the waiter said.

"What you gonna do, buy a new dress?" asked the other girl enviously.

"Naw, I got to pay the doctor for them shots."

She drank her coffee. When they went out, she gave the waiter a good tip.

"Honey," said the other girl as she opened the door, "your eye's gettin' black where Bunny hit you. Put a little more powder on it—or else rouge high."

The Gun

Picture yourself a lone bird in a cage with monkeys, or the sole cat in a kennel full of dogs. Even if the dogs became accustomed to you, they wouldn't make the best of playmates; nor could you, being a cat, mate with them, being dogs. Although, in the little town of Tall Rock, Montana, the barriers were less natural than artificial (entirely man-made barriers, in fact), nevertheless, to be the only Negro child in this small white city made you a stranger in a strange world; an outcast in the house where you lived; a part of it all by necessity, and yet no part at all.

Flora Belle Yates, as a child, used to shield herself from the frequent hurts and insults of white children with tears, blows, and sometimes curses. Even with only one Negro family, the Yateses, in Tall Rock, race relations were not too good. Her father and mother had come up from Texas years ago. Flora Belle had heard them tell about the night they left Texarkana, looking back to see their hut in flames and a mob shouting in the darkness. The mob wanted to lynch Flora Belle's father. It seemed that, in an argument about wages, he had beaten up a white man. Through some miracle, her mother said, they had gotten away in the face of the mob, escaping in a rickety Ford, crossing the state line and driving for three days, somehow making it to the Northwest. Her father had an idea of getting to Canada, fleeing like the slaves in slave days clean out of the United States, but gas and money ran out. He and his wife stopped to work along the way, and finally ended up by staying in Tall Rock. Flora's father had gotten a job there, tending to the horses and equipment of a big contractor. Her mother worked in the contractor's house as cook, maid, and washwoman. Shortly after their arrival, Flora Belle was born in a large room over the contractor's stable.

She was never a pretty baby, Flora Belle, for her parents were not beautiful people. Poor food and hard work had lined their faces and bent their bodies even before she was born. The fear and strain of their hegira, with the mother pregnant, did not help to produce a sweet and lovely child. Flora Belle's face, as she grew up, had a lugubrious expression about it that would make you laugh if you didn't know her—but would make you sorry for her if you did know her.

Then, too, from helping her mother with the white folks' washing and her father to tend the horses, Flora Belle grew up strong and heavy, with rough hands and a hard chest like a boy's. She had hard ways, as well. A more attractive colored girl might have appealed to the young white men of the town for illegitimate advances, but nobody so much as winked at Flora Belle. She graduated from high school without ever having had a beau of any kind. The only colored boys she had ever seen were the ones who came through Tall Rock once with a circus.

Just before her graduation, her mother laid down and died— quite simply—"worked to death," as she put it. Tired! A white preacher came to the house and preached her funeral with a few white neighbors present. After that Flora Belle lived with her aging father and cooked his meals for him—the two of them alone, dark souls in a white world. She did the contractor's family washing, as the new Irish maid refused to cook, clean—and then wash, too. Flora Belle made a few dollars a week washing and ironing.

One day, the second summer after she came out of high school, her father said, "I'm gonna leave here, Flora Belle." So they went to Butte. That was shortly after World War I ended, in the days of Prohibition. Things were kind of dead in Butte, and most of the Negroes there were having a hard time, or going into bootlegging. Flora Belle and her father lived in the house with a family who sold liquor. It was a loud and noisy house, with people coming and going way up in the night. There was gambling in the kitchen.

There were very few Negroes in Butte, and Flora Belle made friends with none of them. Their ways were exceedingly strange to her, since she had never known colored people before. And she to them was just a funny-looking stuck-up ugly old girl. They took her shyness to mean conceit, and her high-school English to mean superiority. Nobody paid any attention to Flora.

Her father soon took up with a stray woman around town. He began to drink a lot, too. Months went by and he found no steady work, but Flora Belle did occasional house cleaning. They still had a little money that they had saved, so one day Flora Belle said, "Pa, let's buy a ticket and leave this town. It's no good."

And the old man said, "I don't care if I do."

Flora Belle had set her mind on one of the big cities of the coast where there would be lots of nice colored people she could make friends with. So they went to Seattle, her and Pa. They got there one winter morning in the rain. They asked a porter in the station where colored people could stop, and he sent them to a street near the depot where Negroes, Filipinos, Japanese, and Chinese lived in boxlike buildings. The street had a busy downtown atmosphere. Flora Belle liked it very much, the moving people, the noise, the shops, the many races.

"I'm glad to get to a real city at last," she said.

"This rain is chillin' me to the bone," her father answered, walking along with their suitcases. "I wish I had a drink." He left Flora Belle as soon as their rooms were rented and went looking for a half-pint.

In Seattle it rained and rained. In the gray streets strange people of many shades and colors passed, all of them going places, having things to do. In the colored rooming house, as time went by, Flora Belle met a few of the roomers, but they all were busy, and they did not ask her to join them in their activities. Her father stayed out a good deal, looking for a job, he said —but when he came back, you could smell alcohol on his breath. Flora Belle looked for a job, also, but without success.

She was glad when Sunday came. At least she could go to church, to a colored church—for back in Tall Rock there had been no Negro church, and the white temples were not friendly to a black face.

"I'm A.M.E., myself," the landlady said. "The Baptists do too much shoutin' for me. You go to my church."

So Flora Belle went to the African Methodist Episcopal Church—alone, because the landlady was too busy to take her. That first day at services quite a few members shook hands with her. This made Flora Belle very happy. She went back that evening and joined the church. She felt warm and glad at just meeting people. She was invited to attend prayer meeting and to become a member of the Young Women's Club, dues ten cents a week. She in turn asked some of the sisters, with fumbling incoherence, if they knew where she could get a job. The churchwomen took her phone number and promised to call her if they heard of anything. Flora Belle walked home through the rain that night feeling as if she had at last come to a welcome place.

Sure enough, during the week, a woman did call up to let her know about a job. "It's a kinder hard place," the woman said over the phone, "but I reckon you can stand it awhile. She wants a maid to sleep in, and they don't pay much. But since you ain't workin', it might beat a blank."

Flora Belle got the job. She was given the servant's room. It was damp and cold; the work was hard, and the lady exacting; the meager pay came once a month, but Flora Belle was thankful to have work.

"Now," she thought to herself, "I can get some nice clothes and meet nice people, 'cause I'm way behind, growing up in a town where there wasn't none of my color to be friends with. I want to meet some boys and girls and have a good time."

But she had only one night off a week, Sunday evening to go to church. Then Flora Belle would fix herself up as nice as she knew how and bow and bow in her friendliest fashion, fighting against shyness and strangeness, but never making much of an impression on folks. At church everybody was nice enough, to be sure, but nobody took up more time with her than brotherly love required. None of the young men noticed her at all, what with dozens of pretty girls around, talkative and gay—for Flora Belle stood like she was tongue-tied when she was introduced to anybody. Just stood staring, trying to smile. She didn't know the easy slang of the young people, nor was she good at a smart comeback if someone made a bright remark. She was just a big, homely silent woman whose desire for friends never got past that lugubrious look in her wistful eyes and that silence that frightened folks away.

A crippled man after Sunday services tried to make up to her once or twice. He talked and talked, but Flora Belle could manage to say nothing more than "Yes, sir," or, "No, sir," to everything he said, like a dumb young girl—although she was now twenty-five, and too unattractive to play coy.

Even the sporting men—to whom women give money—used to laugh about Flora Belle. "Man, I wouldn't be seen on the streets with that truck horse," was their comment in the pool halls.

So a year went by and Flora Belle had no more friends than she had had back in Butte or Tall Rock. "I think I'll go away from here," she said to herself. "Try another town. I reckon all cities ain't like Seattle, where folks is so cold and it rains all the time."

So she went away. She left Pa living in sin with some old

Indian woman and shining shoes in a white barber shop for a living. He had begun to look mighty bowed and wrinkled, and he drank increasingly.

Flora Belle went to San Francisco. She had a hard time finding work, a hard time meeting people, a hard time trying to get a boy friend. But in California she didn't take up so much time with the church. She met, instead, some lively railroad porters and maids who gave parties and lived a sort of fast life. Flora Belle managed to get in good with the porters' crowd, mostly by handing out money freely to pay for food and drinks when parties were being arranged.

She was usually an odd number, though, having no man. Nevertheless, she would come by herself to the parties and try her best to be a good sport, to drink and be vulgar. But even when she was drunk, she was still silent and couldn't think of anything much to say. She fell in love with a stevedore and used to give him her pay regularly and buy him fine shirts, but he never gave her any matrimonial encouragement, although he would take whatever she offered him. Then she found out that he was married already and had four children. He told her he didn't want her, anyway.

"I'm gonna leave this town," Flora Belle said to herself, "if the bus station still sells tickets."

So the years went on. The cities on the coast, the fog cities of fruit trees and vineyards, passed in procession—full of hard work and loneliness. Cook in a roadhouse, maid for a madam, ironer in a laundry, servant for rich Mexicans—Monterrey—Berkeley—San Diego—Marysville—San Jose. At last she came to Fresno. She was well past thirty. She felt tired. She wanted sometimes to die. She had worked so long for white folks, she had cooked so many dinners, made so many beds.

Working for a Fresno ranch owner, looking after his kids, trying to clean his house and keep things as his wife desired, passing lonely nights in her room over the garage, she felt awful tired, awful tired.

"I wish I could die," she said to herself. By now she often talked out loud. "I wish I could die."

And one day, she asked, "Why not?"

The idea struck her all of a sudden, "Why not?"

So on her Thursday afternoon off from work, she bought a pistol. She bought a box of bullets. She took them home—and somehow she felt better just carrying the heavy package under one arm along the street.

That night in her room over the garage she unwrapped the gun and looked at it a long time. It was black, cold, steel-like, heavy and hard, dependable and certain. She felt sure it could take her far away—whenever she wanted to go. She felt sure it would not disappoint her—if she chose to leave Fresno. She was sure that with the gun, she would never again come to an empty town.

She put in all the bullets it would hold, six, and pressed its muzzle to her head. "Maybe the heart would be better," she thought, putting its cold nose against her breast. Thus she amused herself in her room until late in the night. Then she put the pistol down, undressed, and went to bed. Somehow she felt better, as though she could go off anytime now to some sweet good place, as though she were no longer a prisoner in the world, or in herself.

She slept with the pistol under her pillow.

The following morning she locked it in her trunk and went down to work. That day her big ugly body moved about the house with a new lightness. And she was very kind to the white lady's children. She kept thinking that in the tray of her trunk there was something that meant her good, and would be kind to her. So the days passed.

Every night in her little room, over the garage, after she had combed her hair for bed, she would open the trunk and take the pistol from its resting place. Sometimes she would hold it in her lap. Other nights she would press the steel-black weapon to her heart and put her finger on the trigger, standing still quite a long time. She never pulled the trigger, but she knew that she could pull it whenever she wished.

Sometimes, in bed in the dark, she would press the gun between her breasts and talk to it like a lover. She would tell it all the things that had gone on in her mind in the past. She would tell it all that she had wanted to do, and how, now, she didn't want to do anything, only hold this gun, and be sure—*sure* that she could go away if she wanted to go—anytime. She was sure!

Each night the gun was there—like she imagined a lover might be. Each night it came to bed with her, to lie under the pillow near her head or to rest in her hand. Sometimes she would touch that long black pistol in the dark and murmur in her sleep, "I love . . . you."

Of course, she told nobody. But everybody knew that something had happened to Flora Belle Yates. She knew what. Her life became surer and happier because of this friend in the night. She began to attend church regularly on Sunday, to sing, shout, and take a more active part in the week-night meetings. She began to play with her employer's children, and to laugh with his wife over the little happenings in the house. The white lady began to say to her neighbors, "I've got the best maid in the world. She was awfully grouchy when she first came, but now that she's gotten to like the place, she's simply wonderful!"

As the months went by, Flora Belle began to take on weight, to look plump and jolly, and to resemble one of those lovable big dark-skinned mammies in the picture books. It was the gun. As some people find assurance in the Bible or in alcohol, Flora Belle found assurance in the sure cold steel of the gun.

She is still living alone over the white folks' garage in Fresno —but now she can go away anytime she wants to.

Fine Accommodations

In two seconds they'd be pulling out of Atlanta, going North. The long platform was busy with people, redcaps, baggage trucks, travelers, and relatives waving farewell. The New York Limited had a heavy load. Peter Johnson, porter, stood beside the Pullman steps. He looked down toward the engine and saw the last mail bags being thrown into a coach ahead. " 'Bout to be hitting it," he thought, when a hurrying redcap, bending under the weight of three big brown bags that seemed, from the way he was panting, to be loaded with iron, cried, "Here we are, buddy!"

Behind the redcap came a large elderly well-dressed Negro, followed by a young colored man with a portable typewriter and two brief cases. Porter Peter Johnson smiled as he took one of the heavy bags from the redcap, reaching at the same time for the two brief cases which the young man carried.

"Never mind," said the young fellow, "these are very valuable. Here, you take the typewriter."

"Drawing room A," said the redcap.

"Rich colored folks," thought Peter Johnson, and a thrill of pride ran through him that two members of his own race were riding the crack New York Limited—in an expensive drawing room at that!

Peter Johnson knew that in the South the railroad people sometimes gave Negroes the drawing room for the price of an ordinary berth, just to have them out of sight, but that would never happen on a crowded extra-fare train where space was booked a week ahead. No, these Negroes had obviously paid good money for a de-luxe trip north in such fine accommodations.

"They ain't sporting people," Peter Johnson said to himself, noting the quiet attire and beribboned spectacles of the elderly man, and the nervous college-boy face of the younger passenger. "He must be some big shot, the old fellow, professor, or a bishop, or a race leader. I'll find out directly."

But before Peter Johnson could ask the sweating redcap who the man was, he had pocketed his tip and gone. The train was pulling out. The porter hurried down the corridor to close the car doors.

By and by, as the train hit the suburbs and gathered speed, and the porter had changed into his white jacket, he came back to drawing room A and knocked on the door.

"Come," said a heavy voice inside.

The porter entered and smiled, bowed, and began to put the huge bags up out of the way. The elderly brownskin man was sitting by the window, his hands full of papers covered with notes and figures. The young man was not in the room.

"Going all the way?" asked the porter as he busied himself with the bags.

"Washington," said the elderly man, "to the White House."

"Oh," said the porter, with admiration. "It's a honor to be carrying you on this train." He must be a *big* Negro, Peter Johnson thought. I'm glad we've got race men like him.

"I am called to see the President," went on the elderly man pompously, "concerning Negro labor."

"They're gonna raise wages, ain't they?" asked the porter.

"In some instances, yes," replied the man, studying his papers.

"I thought for everybody," said the porter.

"We are hoping to adjust that," answered the man. The race leader said no more. He seemed intensely occupied with his papers, so the porter went out.

That night when Peter Johnson came to make up the berths, the elderly Negro was in the club car. The young man closed his portable typewriter to exchange a few friendly words with the porter.

"I used to work on the road, too," he said, "dining car, on the Central."

"Where did you run?" the porter asked.

"New York to Buffalo mostly," the young man said.

"Nice run," said the porter. "What's your business now, might I ask? You look like a educated fellow."

"I graduated from Columbia," said the young man, sorting out the carbons of something he had been copying. "Now I'm assistant secretary to Dr. Jenkins here, president of Attucks Institute, perhaps the most important Negro school in the South."

"I'd like to send my son there when he's big enough," said the porter. "I got a boy twelve years old."

"Where do you live?" the young man asked.

"Harlem," the porter replied.

"Well, I'd send him to a Northern school then," advised the secretary. "I work down South, but I don't like it. It's still full of prejudice."

"Something in that," said the porter, making down the berths. "But Dr. Jenkins is a great leader, ain't he? I want my boy to know some of the big men of his own color."

"I guess you're right," said the young man a little uncertainly, "but . . ."

"Anybody the President calls to Washington must be a fine man," declared the porter simply.

"Not always," the young man said with a sudden bitter intenseness—then he looked as though he wished he hadn't said it. "I guess I'd better shut up."

"Listen, I don't talk," said the porter.

"It's your saying you'd like to send your son to that school that gets me," said the young man slowly. "Don't send him there!"

"What's the matter?" asked the porter. "You don't like the school or your boss, or what?"

"It's not that," said the young man. "Personally, he's fine to work for, but I—" he hesitated again, and then blurted out, "I don't like what he's doing."

"I thought he was a fine man," said the porter.

"My father was a better man," said the young fellow, "and he was a porter."

"Your father was a porter, too, you say? Where'd he run?"

"On the Pennsy to Pittsburgh the last two years before he died. Jim Palmer was his name."

"Jim Palmer?" said the porter. "Why, I knew him! Big tall fellow? Why, me and him used to run together on Number Nine years ago. We used to pal around together."

"Well, you know what he was like then," said the young man. "He was a real man, wasn't he?"

"He sure was," cried the porter. "Why, he helped to form our union."

"Yes," said the young fellow. "He wanted colored people to stand up and be somebody, didn't he? To fight for their rights! To organize. If you knew my father, you know that. He worked like hell to put me and my brothers through school. And he wouldn't like what I'm doing now, not by a damn sight."

"What do you mean, son, he wouldn't like it?" asked the porter. "I can call you *son* if you're Jim Palmer's boy."

"And I can talk to you like a father," said the young man. "I got to talk to somebody. I'm going to give this job up—even if it does pay a good salary, even if it is a 'position.' Dr. Jenkins is a big man, I know, and a famous Negro—but the way he keeps *big* is by *not playing square*. Don't send your boy to his school."

"What do you mean?" asked the porter.

"Well, take this labor relations thing," said the young man. "He's *not* going to Washington to help Negroes get higher wages, nor the same wages the whites get, nor what the code promises them down South. Do you know why he's going to Washington?"

"No," said the porter.

"To get the authorities to except from the code those industries in the South where Negroes are employed, to get them to allow white factory owners to pay Negroes less than they pay white workers—to permit them to do that *with Government sanction!*" He rose and stood looking at the porter. "Why? Because the white trustees of that Southern school of his are men who employ Negroes, who make their money off of Negroes, and who don't want to pay us a living wage. You see, that's the way he keeps on being a *big* man—bowing to Southern white customs. That's how much Dr. Jenkins cares about his race! His people! He never opened his mouth about the boy who was beaten to death by the police near his campus last month. I'm fed up. It makes me feel guilty just typing out these polite surveys and reports, toned down, conciliatory, understated, for him to take to Washington. They look scholarly as hell, but are intended to help keep poor black people just where we've been all the time—poor and black! You understand me! I don't want to be secretary to that kind of man. I can't be!"

"I thought he was a *real* leader," said the porter sadly.

Just then the door opened and Dr. Jenkins entered, the butt of a nearly smoked-out cigar in his mouth.

"Did you finish copying the survey?" he asked his secretary.

"Yes," said the young man, "but I didn't agree with it."

"It's not necessary that you agree," snapped Dr. Jenkins as the porter went out. The rest of his words were lost as the door closed and the train roared through the night.

For a moment the porter stood thinking in the corridor. "The last Negro passenger I had in that drawing room was a pimp from Birmingham. Now I got a professor. I guess both of them have to have ways of paying for such fine accommodations."

No Place to Make Love

We had no place to make love. We could kiss in doorways, or hold hands in the movies, or somebody might lend us a car. But most of the time we had no place at all to make love. I tell you all that, Mister, so you'll understand how come we're here, me and Mary, and not looking for charity, either.

Poor and young. But old enough to work, old enough for our parents to make us bring home the bacon every week. But never old enough for anybody to worry about our love life, Mister. Kids in our kind of families have to worry about that themselves. The old folks are all loved out, so they don't care how we get along—just so we don't get hitched too soon and take their pay checks away.

Me and Mary wasn't hardly making enough to get married. I had my mother to take care of and two kid sisters. Pa died on us last year. Both of us had to quit school in our teens. Mary had a big family, too, house full of sisters and brothers. Being the oldest, she had to bring home every cent she made in the hosiery mill. Even white like me and Mary, it's no fun growing up down South in a poor family, I tell you, Mister.

Though poor, our parents were awful religious. They liked revivals, liked to put money in the church and help support the Bible school. If me and Mary went to the movies on Sunday, they'd kick because we didn't go to church, too. Her parents didn't like me worth a damn, nohow. They knew I wanted to marry her—and they thought they'd lose a paying boarder if Mary left.

Me, I wanted to take her away. Sure! Come up North somewhere. But there was Ma on my hands, sufferin' and complainin' all the time. Mister, you know, sometimes I think kids ought to be born without parents.

The old folks knew we didn't have no place even to make love. They didn't care. A small town ain't like a big one where you can find a place. When you're too poor to own even an old Ford, what can you do—with your house full of family all the time?

Well, last summer we went out in the woods. And we found a hill. And we pretended we was in the Garden of Eden—only we could always hear the cars and busses passing in the road below.

Then one night coming home about dusk-dark, with the sun gone down and the first stars coming out, Mary said, "Honey, I guess I ought to tell you. I drunk that stuff again twice last week, but it didn't do no good—and it's almost two months now."

I said, "Listen! I don't care if it don't work. Let's get married. I like kids, don't you?"

So I found out how much a license costs—and the next Sunday when we went out on our hill, we was man and wife. I took her home to sleep on the davenport in the parlor with me—and Ma raised hell. Said we'd starve to death getting married, young as we was—and she'd be glad of it. Said what right did we have getting married anyhow, and she not knowing about it? What business did we have birthing a child with no money? My mother got sick and went to bed. All our folks like to died. Yet

and still, Mary's parents told everybody they was glad to have
her out of the house, glad to get rid of her, pregnant as she was.
But they did everything they could to break us up. For the first
time in history her mother got friendly with my mother, and
they would spend hours talking about how foolish we was, and
how ungrateful for all their raising.

My mother was as nasty to Mary as she could be. So was my
sisters. Before we'd get home from work, they'd have their dinner all fixed and et. Mary would have to go cook another dinner
for ourselves—and me buying all the food for them, too. Relatives sure can be mean when they want to!

Ma kept saying she was going to tell the authorities how we'd
put our ages up to get married without telling our parents, and
she'd have the whole thing annulled. But then there was our
baby on the road. She knew when it came, I'd have to take care
of the kid anyhow—so she didn't do nothing but talk.

"Hardly dry behind the ears yet, and a baby coming," she'd
say.

I'd grin, but it made me mad. She didn't mean it in fun. Old
folks are fierce. Between the lot of 'em, they made us so tired,
Mary and me, that we just got on the evening train one night
and come to New York. We both want our kid to be born in a
friendly place, that's why, away from relatives.

Of course, I didn't know it was so hard to get a job in New
York, or so cold up here. You see, Mister, I ain't never been
away from home before. With the kid coming and all, I got to
have something to do, recession or not. Mary ain't able to work,
and they won't even let me shovel snow for the city. You got to
be a registered voter, the man says.

You're the second welfare investigator what's been here. The
first one, the white man, said he couldn't do a thing. We don't
come under his jurisdiction. Maybe you can tell us what jurisdiction we do come under? What about young folks like us who
want a decent place for our kid to be born in? I'm getting des-
perate, Mister! Mary is, too. We got rent to pay. We don't want
our kid to be born out in the cold, maybe growing up like we

did—without even a place to make love. I don't want relief, Mister, but I do want a job. I know you understand. You niggers have a hard time, too, don't you?

On the Way Home

Carl was not what you would call a drinking man. Not that he had any moral scruples about drinking, for he prided himself on being broad-minded. But he had always been told that his father (whom he couldn't remember) was a drunkard. So in the back of his head, he didn't really feel it right to get drunk. Except for perhaps a glass of wine on holidays, or a bottle of beer if he was out with a party and didn't want to be conspicuous, he was a teetotaler.

Carl had promised his mother not to drink *at all*. He was an only child, fond of his mother. But she had raised him with almost too much kindness. To adjust himself to people who were less kind had been hard. But since there were no good jobs in Sommerville, he came away to Chicago to work. Every month, for a Sunday, he went back home, taking the four o'clock bus Saturday afternoon, which put him off in front of his boyhood door in time for supper—with country butter, fresh milk, and home-made bread.

After supper he would go uptown with his mother in the cool of evening, if it was summer, to do her Saturday night shopping. Or if it was winter, they might go over to a neighbor's house and pop corn or drink cider. Or friends might come to their home and sit around the parlor talking and playing old records on an old victrola—Sousa's marches, Nora Bayes, Bert Williams, Caruso—records that most other people had long ago thrown away or forgotten. It was fun, old-fashioned, and very

different from the rum parties most of his office friends indulged
in in Chicago.

Carl had definitely promised his mother and himself not to
drink. But this particular afternoon he stood in front of a long
counter in a liquor store on Clark Street and heard himself say,
strangely enough, "A bottle of wine."

"What kind of wine?" the clerk asked brusquely.

"That kind," Carl answered, pointing to a row of tall yellow
bottles on the middle shelf. It just happened that his finger
stopped at the yellow bottles. He did not know the names or
brands of wines.

"That's sweet wine," the clerk said.

"That's all right," Carl affirmed, for he wanted to get the
wine quickly and go.

The clerk wrapped the bottle, made change, and turned to
another customer. Carl took the bottle and went out. He walked
slowly, yet he could hardly wait to get to his room. He had never
been so anxious to drink before. He might have stopped at a
bar, since he passed many, but he was not used to drinking at
bars. So he went to his room.

It was quiet in the big dark old rooming house. There was
no one in the hall as he went up the wide, creaking staircase.
All the roomers were at work. It was Tuesday. He would have
been at work, too, had he not received at the office about noon
a wire that his mother was suddenly very ill, and he had better
come home. He knew there was no bus until four o'clock. It
was one now. He would get ready to go soon. But he needed a
drink. Did not men sometimes drink to steady their nerves? In
novels they took a swig of brandy—but brandy made Carl sick.
Wine would be better—milder.

In his room he tore open the package and uncorked the bottle
even before he hung his hat in the closet. He took his tooth-
brush out of a glass on his dresser and poured the glass a third
full of the amber-yellow wine. He tried to keep himself from
wondering if his mother was going to die.

"Please, no!" he prayed. He drank the wine.

He sat down on the bed to get his breath back. That climb

up the steps had never taken his breath before, but now his heart was beating fast, and sweat had come out on his brow, so he took off his coat, tie, shirt, and got ready to wash his face.

He had better pack his bag first. Then, he suddenly thought, he had no present for his mother—but he caught himself in the middle of the thought. This was not Saturday, not one of his monthly Saturdays when he went home. This was Tuesday, and there was this telegram from the Rossiters in his pocket that had suddenly broken the whole rhythm of his life:

YOUR MOTHER GRAVELY ILL STOP COME HOME AT ONCE.

John and Nellie Rossiter had been neighbors since childhood. They would not frighten him needlessly. His mother must be very ill indeed, so he need not think of taking her a present. He went to the closet door to pull out the suitcase, but his hands did not move. The wine, amber-yellow in its tall bottle, stood on the dresser beside him. Warm, sweet, forbidden.

There was no one in the room. Nobody in the whole house perhaps except the landlady. Nobody really in all Chicago to talk to in his trouble. With a mother to take care of on a small salary, room rent, a class at business college, books to buy, there's not much time left to make friends or take girls out. In a big city it's hard for a strange young man to know people.

Carl poured the glass full of wine again—drank it. Then he opened the top drawer, took out his toilet articles and put them on the bed. From the second drawer he took a couple of shirts. Maybe three would be better, or four. This was not a weekend. Perhaps he had better take some extra clothing—in case his mother was ill long, and he had to stay a week or more. Perhaps he'd better take his dark suit in case she . . .

It hit him in the stomach like a fist. A pang of fear spread over his whole body. He sat down trembling on the bed.

"Buck up, old man!" The sound of his own voice comforted him. He smiled weakly at his face in the mirror.

"Be a man!"

He filled the glass full this time and drank it without stopping. He had never drunk so much wine before, and this was warm, sweet, and palatable. He stood, threw his shoulders back, and felt suddenly tall as though his head were touching the ceiling. Then, for no reason at all, he looked at himself in the mirror and began to sing. He made up a song out of nowhere that repeated itself over and over:

> *"In the spring the roses*
> *In the spring begin to sing*
> *Roses in the spring*
> *Begin to sing . . ."*

He took off his clothes, put on his bathrobe, carefully drained the bottle, then went down the hall to the bathroom, still singing. He ran a tub full of water, climbed in, and sat down. The water in the tub was warm like the wine. He felt good remembering a dark grassy slope in a corner of his mother's yard where he played with a little girl when he was very young at home. His mother came out, separated them, and sent the little girl away because she wasn't of a decent family. But now his mother would never dismiss another little girl be——

Carl sat up quickly in the tub, splashed water over his back and over his head. Drunk? What's the matter? What's the matter with you? Thinking of your mother that way and maybe she's dy—— Say! Listen, don't you know you have to catch a four o'clock bus? And here he was getting drunk before he even started on the way home. He trembled. His heart beat fast, so fast that he lay down in the tub to catch his breath, all but his head covered with the warm water.

To lie quiet that way was fine. Still and quiet. Tuesday. Everybody working at the office. And here he was, Carl Anderson, lying quiet in a deep tub of warm water. Maybe someday in a few years with a little money saved up, and no expenses at home, and a car to take girls out in the spring,

> *"When the roses sing*
> *In the spring . . ."*

He had a good voice and the song that he had made up himself about roses sounded good with wine on his breath as he
sang, so he stood up in the tub, grabbed a towel, and began to
sing quite lustily. Suddenly there was a knock at the door.

"What's going on in there?"

It was the landlady's voice in the hall outside. She must have
heard him singing downstairs.

"Nothing, Mrs. Dyer! Nothing! I just feel like singing."

"Mr. Anderson? Is that you? What're you doing in the house
this time of day?"

"I'm on the way home to see my mother. She . . ."

"You sound happier than a lark about it. I couldn't imagine . . ."

He heard the landlady's feet shuffling off down the stairs,
back to her ironing.

"She's . . ." His head began to go round and round. "My
mother's . . ." His eyes suddenly burned. To step out of the
tub, he held tightly to the sides. Drunk, that's what he was!
Drunk!

He lurched down the hall, fell across the bed in his room,
and buried his head in the pillows. He stretched his arms above
his head to the rods of the bedstand. He felt ashamed. With his
head in the pillows all was dark. His mother dying? No! No!
But he was drunk.

In the dark he seemed to feel his mother's hand on his head
when he was a little boy, and her voice saying, "Be sweet, Carl.
Be a good boy. Keep clean. Mother loves you. She'll look out for
you. Be sweet—and remember what you're taught at home."

Then the roses in the song he had made up and the wine he
had drunk began to go around and around in his head and he
felt as if he had betrayed his mother and home singing about
roses and spring and dreaming of cars and pretty girls with that
yellow telegram in his coat pocket on the back of the chair beside the bed that suddenly seemed to go around and around.

But when he closed his eyes, it stopped. He held his breath.
He buried his head deeper in the pillows. He lay very still. It

was dark and warm. And quiet, and darker than ever. A long time passed, a very long time, dark, and quiet, and peaceful, and still.

"Mr. Anderson! Hey, Mr. Anderson!"
In the darkness far off, somebody called, then nearer—but still very far away—then knocking on a distant door.
"Mr. Anderson!"
The voice was quite near now, sharper. The door opened, light streamed in. A hand shook his shoulder. He opened his eyes. Mrs. Dyer stood there, looking down at him in indignant amazement.
"Mr. Anderson, are you drunk?"
"No, Mrs. Dyer," he said in a daze, blinking at the landlady standing above him. The electric light bulb she had switched on hurt his eyes.
"Mr. Anderson, they's a long-distance call for you on the phone down in the hall. Get up. Tie up that bathrobe. Hurry on down there and get it, will you? I've been yelling for you for five minutes."
"What time is it?" Carl sat bolt upright. The landlady stopped in the door.
"It's after dinnertime," she said. "Must be six-thirty, seven o'clock."
"Seven o'clock?" Carl gasped. "I've missed my bus!"
"What bus?"
"The four o'clock bus."
"I guess you have," said the landlady. "Alcohol and time-tables don't mix, young man. That must be your mother on the phone now." Disgusted, she went downstairs, leaving his door open.
The phone! Carl felt sick and unsteady on his legs. He pulled his bathrobe together and stumbled down the stairs. The phone! A kind of weakness rushed through his veins. The telephone! He had promised his mother not to drink. She said his father . . . He couldn't remember his father. He died long ago. Now his mother was . . . Anyhow, he should have been home by

seven o'clock, at her bedside, holding her hand. He could have been home an hour ago. Now, maybe she . . .

He picked up the receiver. His voice was hoarse, frightened. "Hello. Yes, this is Carl . . . Yes, Mrs. Rossiter . . ."

"Carl, honey, we kept looking for you on that six o'clock bus. My husband went out on the road a piece to meet you in his car. We thought it might be quicker. Carl, honey . . ."

"Yes, Mrs. Rossiter . . ."

"Your mother . . ."

"Yes, Mrs. Rossiter . . ."

"Your mother just passed away. I thought maybe you ought to know in case you hadn't already started. I thought maybe . . ."

For a moment he couldn't hear what she said. Then he knew that she was asking him a question—that she was repeating it.

"I could have Jerry drive to Chicago and get you tonight. Would you like to have me do that, since there's no bus now until morning?"

"I wish you would, Mrs. Rossiter. But then, no—listen! Never mind! There's two or three things I ought to do before I come home. I ought to go to the bank. I must. But I'll catch that first bus home in the morning. First thing in the morning, Mrs. Rossiter, I'll be home."

"We're your neighbors and your friends. You know *this* is your home, too, so come right here."

"Yes, Mrs. Rossiter, I know. I will. I'll be home."

He ran back upstairs and jumped into his clothes, feeling that he had to get out. Had to get out! His body burned. His throat was dry. He picked up the wine bottle and looked at the label. Good wine! Warm and easy to the throat! Hurry before perhaps the landlady came. Hurry! She wouldn't understand this haste.

Did she die alone?

Quickly he put on his coat and plunged down the steps. Outside it was dark. The street lights seemed dimmer than usual.

Did she die alone?

At the corner there was a bar, palely lighted. He had never stopped there before, but this time he went in. He could drink all he wanted to now.

Alone, at home, alone! Did she die alone?

The bar was big and dismal, like a barn. A juke box played a raucous hit song. A woman stood near the machine singing to herself.

Carl went up to the bar.

"What'll it be?" The bartender passed his towel over the counter in front of him.

"A drink," Carl said.

"Whisky?"

"Yes."

"Can you make it two?" asked the woman in a warm low voice.

"Sure," Carl said. "Make it two."

"What's the matter? You're shivering!" she exclaimed.

"Cold," Carl said.

"You've been drinking?" the woman said. "But it don't smell like whisky."

"Wasn't," Carl said. "Was wine."

"Oh! I guess you can mix up your drinks, heh? O.K. Try it. But if that wine along with this whisky knocks you out," she purred, "I'll have to take you home to my house, little boy."

"Home?" Carl asked.

"Yes," the woman said, "home with me. You and me—home."

She put her arm around his shoulders.

"Home?" Carl said.

"Home, sure, baby! Home to my house."

"Home?" Carl was about to repeat when suddenly a volley of uncontrolled sobs shook his body, choking the word "home." He leaned forward with his head in his arms and wept like a kid.

"Home . . . home . . . home . . ."

The bartender and the woman looked at him in amazement. The juke box stopped.

The woman said gently, "You're drunk, fellow. Come on, buck up! I'll take you home. It don't have to be to my house either—if you don't want to go. Where do you live? I'll see that you get home."

Mysterious Madame Shanghai

We other roomers occasionally met her in the entrance hall, coming in or going out. She was a tall old woman. Her olive skin was leathery and seared, heavily lined, with the lines of her face and neck well filled with a covering of rice powder. She spoke pleasantly enough, in a deep, almost masculine voice, a simple, "Good day." That was all. But she never tried to make friends with any of the other roomers in the house. She was Mrs. Dyer's woman of mystery. Because she occasionally went down the second-floor hall to the bathroom in an amazing Chinese kimono of blue silk heavily brocaded with golden dragons, somebody had nicknamed her Madame Shanghai. The name stuck.

Mrs. Dyer, the landlady, certainly did not like her, and would wonder about her in a series of constantly varying and uncomplimentary suppositions—for nobody in the house really *knew* anything about Madame Shanghai. She looked like a gypsy, a fair East Indian, or a mulatto. But since she was no trouble and paid her rent on time, Mrs. Dyer had no good cause to ask her to move. Indeed, Mrs. Dyer did not honestly want her to move until she had wormed out of her who she was, had been, and why. Simply to know that her current name was Ethel Cunningham and that she worked now in the stock room of a downtown department store was really to know nothing at all—since it was written all over the woman that she had had a past.

Mrs. Dyer had great curiosity about her roomers' pasts. If they didn't have one, or failed to reveal it, our landlady usually

made one up for them out of her own imagination, nourished
by the novels she had read and the movies she had seen. The
past which Mrs. Dyer created for Ethel Cunningham hardly
became a lady.

"No woman could be so quiet today," Mrs. Dyer said to me
one evening, "except that her morals've been loose in the past!"

I laughed, because I really didn't care about Madame Shanghai's morals, past or present. She was old enough to be
my mother. So was Mrs. Dyer.

"Furthermore, no old woman would wear so much powder if
she hadn't been used to wearing more when she was young!"

"Mrs. Dyer, could I have one of those big bath towels this
week?"

"And forty years ago no nice girl covered up her complexion
with rouge. . . . A big bath towel, you say? Them big towels
is for my front rooms, young man. You don't occupy no walnut
suite. How would them little towels of yours look hanging on a
towel rack in them big rooms?"

"But I'm a big man, Mrs. Dyer, and I need a big towel to wipe
myself on."

"Well, here—since it's to be drying yourself. Fact is, you are
a pretty big fellow. But mind you don't go putting your pal in
the back room up to wanting a big towel, too. I haven't got but
a dozen and they're for the front rooms, like I'm telling you."

"Yes, Mrs. Dyer. Thank you."

She waddled off down the hall. I gave her the polite raspber-
ries—after I shut the door. Then I got out of my clothes and
started for the bathroom, but somebody was in there, so I came
back, laid out a clean shirt on the bed and wiped off my tan
shoes. When I finally got washed and dressed, it was almost
eight o'clock, a blue summer dusk, cool and pleasant. To take
the girl to a show, or for a walk in the park? The park would be
better, I thought as I started down the dimly lighted steps in
Mrs. Dyer's hall. At the curve of the stairs I almost ran over
Ethel Cunningham. She was coming up very slowly, breathing
heavily.

"Why, Madame Shang—Miss Cunningham," I stammered. She frightened me. "Are you sick?"

"I'm not sick—but—but—could you come upstairs with me, please a minute, Mr. Shields?"

"Let me help you."

I took her arm to the top of the steps and walked with her down the hall to her room. She fumbled nervously for her key, then opened the door. I had never been in her room before. It was a small room, not of the type to which Mrs. Dyer gave big towels. On the dresser were a number of photographs of a man—all the same man. In most of the pictures he wore a riding habit and carried a whip. He had a mustache. The pictures were faded, as though taken many years ago.

"That's him," Madame Shanghai gasped. "And he's waiting downstairs to kill me!"

"What?" I cried, astonished, envisioning a man rushing into the room that very moment with drawn pistol.

"On the sidewalk," she said. "He hasn't seen me yet. But I saw him just as I started out."

I felt relieved that he had not seen her, but puzzled. Was she crazy?

"Go downstairs and tell him I love him," Madame Shanghai said, her eyes wide and anxious, her voice full of pleading. "Go tell him that God has punished me enough all these years."

"But what is it all about? I don't know what you mean. Who is he, Miss Cunningham?"

"My husband."

"Your husband?"

"Come back from the grave! I thought he was dead. I haven't seen him for twenty years—and then—now—oh, my God!" She sat on the bed and covered her face with her hands. "He was covered with blood."

"What?"

"I had tried to kill him. I let Tamaris tear the skin from his body and didn't even stop her."

"Tamaris?"

"The biggest cat in the world!"

"Cat?" I wanted to laugh because I thought she was talking about another woman.

"A tiger, Mr. Shields. I told Tamaris myself to claw him to death."

"But where did you get a tiger?"

She sat up and looked at me in surprise.

"Why, we were the greatest wild-animal act in the business —before you were born, I guess. They billed us as the Daring Darnells. We played every circus and hippodrome in the world. But I was in love with him—too much in love—and jealous. He was in love with me, too—but cruel. Oh, so cruel! He thought I was an animal that needed to be tamed. So we fought all the time—with our fists, with whips, with our fingernails, with ropes. That was because we loved each other, I know now. I still love him. I want you to go downstairs and tell him I didn't mean to kill him. I'd go, but I'm afraid he'll shoot me before I get a chance to speak. Shoot me, or knife me, or slap my head off, I don't know which. He's a jealous man about women, Mr. Shields."

Again I wanted to laugh. Madame Shanghai was so wrinkled, ugly, and old, what man would want to knock her head off now?

"You tried to kill him once?"

"I thought I *had* killed him. I certainly wanted to. I sic'ed the wildest of the cats on him one night in the center of the big top before five thousand people. I thought he was dead when they dragged him out in front of a crowd sick with horror."

"Why did you try to kill him?"

"Over a ring, a ring my mother gave me, an old old ring with a hundred years of circus life behind it in Bohemia. That night, just as we went into the cage, Marie, the French bareback rider, passed on her white horse leaving the arena, blowing kisses in answer to the applause—and there on her finger was my ring! I turned green with rage, jealousy, anger, hate. I knew my husband must have taken it from our trunk and given it to her to wear. She was beautiful and blonde—and he had a weakness for blonde women. I was dark as a gypsy. After I saw that ring on her finger, I said to him while we got the lions snarling into place on their stools, 'So you've stolen my ring and given it to that French hussy?'

" 'Shut up and take care of these cats,' was his answer. 'We're giving a performance.'

" 'I'll not shut up,' I said, 'you double-crossing no-good . . .'

"Just then the tigers leaped into the cage.

" 'My fist'll make you shut up as soon as I get out of this cage,' he said.

" 'You'll never get out,' I answered. 'Tamaris!'

"Tamaris was the largest and most beautiful of tigers, a tiger I had raised from a cub who obeyed me like a dog. I pointed my whip at the man in the ring whom I loved and hated more than anybody else in the world—my husband—whom I permitted to beat me, curse me, but whom I could not let give *my ring* to Marie.

" 'Tamaris!' I said, giving her the signal to spring.

"All the blood left my husband's face. Like lightning the sleek young animal crouched, then swept through the air. He screamed. Her great paws ripped into his flesh from the skull down. She bore him to the ground, mangled him with her tiger's teeth. The crowd gasped, sat tense, held its breath, then let loose a mighty groan of fright and horror as people saw the blood.

"From outside, the guards shot Tamaris. They opened the doors of the cage and took Jim out, a mass of bloody pulp. The show went on. They rushed him to the hospital. I walked back to the dressing tent. A dozen circus women crowded around to comfort me. But I wanted one thing only—that was my ring.

"The women were all astonished that I didn't cry. 'I can't cry,' I said. I was too humiliated, hurt, and angry. Just then Marie, that Frenchwoman, came in. I grabbed her hand, she thought for comfort, but really to see if my ring was there.

"Suddenly my heart stopped. It was *not* my ring, after all, on her finger! Merely one that looked like it! I could see it plainly now. The stone wasn't even the same kind of stone in her ring. It was paste.

"My blood turned to water. I stumbled across the tent to my

trunk. I almost broke the lock. I could hardly wait to get it open. There, inside, safe as always, was my ring—the old gypsy ring of my mother's.

"Then I began to sob. I had deceived myself about my husband. I began to shriek. I howled like a mad woman. I tore my hair and rolled on the ground. Life can never hold another hour as bitter as that hour was for me.

"It was six weeks before Jim regained consciousness. The show went on across the country, but I remained behind by his side. When he opened his eyes at last and recognized me, the first words he said were, 'Get away! Ethel, get away! Before I kill you.'

"The doctors would not allow me in the room with him after that. The sight of me sent him into a fury that endangered his life. The sound of my name caused him to burn with fever. I was forbidden to come into the hospital. So I went back to the circus. Always a great drawing card, as an animal tamer I was famous. I continued to make a great deal of money. I spent it all on my husband, trying to bring him back to life and health—though he cursed me with every breath he drew into his slowly healing body. I knew that now for me from his scarred lips came nothing but hate. Still I sent him all the delicacies I could find that I thought he might like. I sent him champagne. I sent him money. I paid the hospital bills promptly. All he ever sent back was a curse or a threat, if he could persuade the doctors or nurses to write the profane words for him.

"Finally, without my knowledge, he was released from the hospital. I had wanted to see him to tell him I loved him, to beg his forgiveness on my knees, to devote the rest of my life to making him happy. I had hoped he would let me. Instead there came a wire from the head doctor at the hospital saying, 'Beware! He threatens to kill you.'

"And in a letter from his nurse that followed, I was told that he had spoken often of his intention to buy a gun, to trail the circus, to sit there in the audience someday and shoot me down as I stood in the center cage among my beautiful animals.

"Don't think, Mr. Shields, that I minded dying. It wasn't that.

I simply did not want to die without a chance to speak to him, without a word of sorrow and love and apology for his ears. I wanted a chance to fall on my knees in front of him and say, 'Jim, forgive me.' Even though his gun was ready to blow my brains out.

"But to be shot without knowing when or where, without seeing Jim's face that I loved—even though mangled by tiger's claws and distorted with hate for me—to die without touching his hand even though it held my death! No! I couldn't bear that! Daily I went through hell after that letter came. Every time I entered the ring I expected a bullet to whistle out of the crowd. I lost control of my beasts. I went to pieces. I spent all my time in the cage peering into the crowd trying to see if he was there —my husband. Before my act I haunted the front of the big tent from noon on, looking to see if he entered the grounds. The managers thought I was going crazy. Though they liked freaks in the circus, they didn't like fools, so I gave up. I had to quit.

"I hid in a little town whose name I've forgotten now and let the circus go on without me. I let them have my animals. I changed my name. I worked as a cook, a maid, traveling everywhere looking for him, but I couldn't find him. Finally, I thought perhaps he had died. Then I came here to Chicago. Now, thank God, he's found me. But, oh, please, Mr. Shields, help me! Prepare him! Go downstairs and tell him not to kill me until I have a chance to say, 'Forgive me! Just forgive me. Jim, forgive me!' "

"I'll go," I said, still doubting, "and tell him—if he's still there."

"He'll never leave," the woman declared.

I went down the steps and out of Mrs. Dyer's rooming house, half smiling, for I expected to see nobody on the sidewalk. I thought it was all just some crazy dream in Madame Shanghai's rice-powdered old head—but I was mistaken. Sure enough, in the half dark of the street lights just outside a man limped back and forth, a man bent sidewise as though by some old wound, an elderly man whose leather-colored face was crisscrossed by scars. His mouth was twisted. Now I was afraid, too.

"Pardon me," I said timidly, "but I've been told you are looking for a woman who lives in this house?"

"I am," he said, "since you seem to know. I'm looking for my wife."

"To—to—kill her?" I asked.

He said nothing.

"She wants to speak to you before you do," I said.

"Then tell her to come to me," he answered.

"You'll give her a chance?"

"Tell her to come and see."

I went back into the house and told her what he had said.

"I'll go," she answered. I was trembling, but she was not.

Madame Shanghai went bravely down the steps, walking like a woman used to going into a cage with wild animals. I followed her to the door, cold sweat on my forehead. Already, as if in anticipation of drama, three or four people had gathered on the sidewalk. Mrs. Dyer had raised her window.

The man in the street waited quite still for his wife to come toward him beneath the street light. She went, holding out her arms in a gesture of the greatest love I have ever seen. But then she swayed, put her hands to her mouth, called weakly, "Jim!" and fell in a faint at his feet.

The man with the crooked body hesitated, then bent down swiftly and lifted her in his arms. He came up the steps into the house.

"Where is her room?" he asked.

I pointed upward. He went ahead and I followed, trailed now by a half-dozen roomers. He burst in through the half-open door and laid her on the bed. As he bent over, a pistol fell from his pocket. But he did not pick it up.

"You are not going to kill her?" I said.

"No," he answered tensely, "I'm just going to slap the life back into her . . . then I'm going to kiss her."

He began to slap her face soundly on one cheek, then the other, and a dusty haze of rice powder floated upward.

Madame Shanghai opened her eyes. "Jim!" she cried, "you

love me—or you wouldn't be slapping me like this. You love me! You love me!"

They kissed, crushed in each other's arms. We closed their door, but it was hard to get our landlady out of the hall.

Patron of the Arts

Although it was only four o'clock of an autumn afternoon, the lights were on in the corners of Darby's little fifth-floor studio apartment, those soft rose-colored lights that make even an ugly woman look charming—particularly if she is as smartly groomed as many New York women of color are. Through the windows with their *tête de negre* drapes, one saw a wind-blown, autumn-leafed view of aristocratic Sugar Hill, and southward, the less well-kept regions of Harlem, through which, in spite of poverty, fame had stalked to carry off a Josephine Baker or an Eartha Kitt.

Darby looked out, puffing impatiently on a cigarette and waiting for the lady to arrive. She was thirty-five and, according to the poets, there is no woman so charming as the woman of thirty-five. Darby had read this somewhere. He was twenty-one, fresh out of college. Today he had everything in readiness—the little anchovies, the ice in the bowl, the Bacardi, and the limes. He knew what she liked, this green-eyed brownskin Mrs. Oldham who had been one of his first friends in New York. Back home in Oklahoma over his drawing board in art class in high school, Darby had dreamed of women like Cornelia Oldham. There were none in the Southwest that a Negro boy might meet.

Now that he knew her—and had known her—there was a little creole girl at the Art Students League downtown he liked much better—a struggling young artist like himself in a strange city. He wished he could marry her.

Standing in reverie, Darby heard the elevator door close. He straightened his tie—despite the fact that he might shortly take it off. You see, he was only twenty-one, and he wanted to look his best at first.

The bell rang. He went to his door, and there was Cornelia. Taller than Darby, sleek in black and white, green-eyed and wise and old. Oh, so charming—a brownskin woman with sea-green eyes! He took her in his arms, but the very first words she said caused him to jump halfway across the room.

"Darling," she whispered, panting, looking at him with her great green eyes like a cat's, "I have told . . . my husband . . . all."

Something stopped beating in Darby's breast. It was his heart. "What?" he cried.

"Yes, dear, I have told him I love you!"

Darby stood behind the sofa. He stared at her with wide young eyes. He knew she had a husband, to be sure, a large dark man, a solid figure in the Negro community. But that personage had always seemed quite remote, far away at home in St. Albans, or working at his Seventh Avenue office. This was Darby's first experience with a married woman. And he never dreamed that they told their husbands all.

"What—what," stuttered the young man as soon as he could talk, "what—did—your husband say?"

"He rose," Cornelia panted, "and stalked out of the room."

Her green eyes in her *café-au-lait* face were full of tragedy. At once Darby had visions of an irate spouse still stalking—right on up to his apartment with a pistol in his hand.

"Lord!" Darby cried. "Cornelia, why did you do that?"

"I love you," she said, "that's why."

"But—but maybe he'll come here and shoot up the place!"

"Let him," she cried. "First we'll mix a cocktail." She took off her wraps and sat down. The youth stood behind the sofa, shaking his head.

"I—I will not fix a cocktail," he said. She leaned her head

back for a kiss. "Suppose he were tailing you! Why, he'd find us in a—a compromising position!" Darby retreated toward the wall.

"Darling!" Cornelia cried, rising to come swiftly toward him, her green eyes gleaming, her dark hair done by Rose Meta. "Don't worry . . ."

Just then there was a ring at the door. Darby stood as if petrified while Cornelia returned to the sofa. Finally he managed to move his legs, close his mouth, and turn the doorknob.

The janitor stood in the hall.

"I'll take them socks, Mr. Middlefield, you said you wanted my wife to mend."

"Could you come back later, *please?*" said Darby.

"Yes, suh," said the man.

"Let's get out of here," Darby said as he closed the door. "Your husband might come at any moment, Cornelia."

"He's still in his office, darling."

"I don't care," said Darby, "let's go."

Thinking how his mother back home in Tulsa would feel if she read in the papers that he was killed over a *married* woman, Darby opened the closet and took out his coat.

"If you leave me," Cornelia said, "I will shoot myself."

"There's nothing here for you to shoot yourself with," said Darby, putting on his coat.

"Then I'll grind up glass and eat it."

"Don't be a fool!" cried Darby.

"I am," said Cornelia, "about you!"

"I want *you* to go home," Darby begged desperately.

"I won't," answered Cornelia.

"Then I'm going out to a phone and call your husband and explain everything to him. After all, you're just my patron, Mrs. Oldham. You paid me well to paint your portrait."

"Is that all I am to you?" cried Cornelia. She poured herself a huge drink, not bothering to mix it.

"That's all I'll ever admit," said the young man. "I'm going to explain fully to your husband *now*—our relationship. After that, please take your portrait home. It's finished." He pointed toward the easel where rested the oil painting he had made of her.

"You coward!" said Mrs. Oldham. "Afraid of my husband! Why, you and I could go to Paris and be free."

"I don't want to go to Paris," said Darby, "I'm going to a phone."

He left Cornelia in front of the cocktail shaker as he rushed out. From the pay station in the drugstore at the corner, Darby finally got Dr. Oldham on the phone.

"I am Darby Middlefield," said the young man nervously.

"Who?" asked Dr. Oldham.

"Middlefield, the artist."

"The artist?"

"I'm calling you about your wife."

"My wife? Why about *my* wife?"

"Because I want to make it plain to you, Dr. Oldham, we are nothing to each other."

"What? But why?"

Darby repeated what he had just said.

"My dear boy," said Dr. Oldham, "my wife and I have lived apart for years. Our divorce is pending."

"But—but——"

"Whoever you are," said Dr. Oldham, "from the sound of your voice, you must be very young. You need not worry about me."

"But I thought she had told you all?" said Darby plaintively.

"She probably did," explained Dr. Oldham. "But I am so bored at Cornelia's frequent affairs with young men immature enough to be her sons that I usually walk out of the room when she begins her confidences. I've heard them for years, so I am no longer amused, damn it!"

"You mean you don't care?"

"I certainly don't," said Dr. Oldham. "Cornelia's a woman of forty-seven who can take care of herself."

"Forty-seven?" said Darby. "She told me she was thirty-five!"

"I can smell your youth!" said Dr. Oldham. He hung up the phone.

"Thirty-five! *Forty-seven!*" Darby murmured to himself as he left the booth. "Thirty-five! That lying chick!"

When he got back to his apartment Cornelia had gone. Without partaking of any ground glass, she had drunk *half* of his bottle of Bacardi instead.

Resting on the tray beside the bottle was a little note:

Dearest Darby:
Please keep the picture you painted of me to take with you when you go back to Oklahoma. Perhaps, when you are older, you might like to remember how your patron looked.

Love,
CORNELIA

Early Autumn

When Bill was very young, they had been in love. Many nights they had spent walking, talking together. Then something not very important had come between them, and they didn't speak. Impulsively, she had married a man she thought she loved. Bill went away, bitter about women.

Yesterday, walking across Washington Square, she saw him for the first time in years.

"Bill Walker," she said.

He stopped. At first he did not recognize her, to him she looked so old.

"Mary! Where did you come from?"

Unconsciously, she lifted her face as though wanting a kiss, but he held out his hand. She took it.

"I live in New York now," she said.

"Oh"—smiling politely. Then a little frown came quickly between his eyes.

"Always wondered what happened to you, Bill."

"I'm a lawyer. Nice firm, way downtown."

"Married yet?"

"Sure. Two kids."

"Oh," she said.

A great many people went past them through the park. People they didn't know. It was late afternoon. Nearly sunset. Cold.

"And your husband?" he asked her.

"We have three children. I work in the bursar's office at Columbia."

"You're looking very . . ." (he wanted to say *old*) ". . . well," he said.

She understood. Under the trees in Washington Square, she found herself desperately reaching back into the past. She had been older than he then in Ohio. Now she was not young at all. Bill was still young.

"We live on Central Park West," she said. "Come and see us sometime."

"Sure," he replied. "You and your husband must have dinner with my family some night. Any night. Lucille and I'd love to have you."

The leaves fell slowly from the trees in the Square. Fell without wind. Autumn dusk. She felt a little sick.

"We'd love it," she answered.

"You ought to see my kids." He grinned.

Suddenly the lights came on up the whole length of Fifth Avenue, chains of misty brilliance in the blue air.

"There's my bus," she said.

He held out his hand, "Good-by."

"When . . ." she wanted to say, but the bus was ready to pull off. The lights on the avenue blurred, twinkled, blurred. And she was afraid to open her mouth as she entered the bus. Afraid it would be impossible to utter a word.

Suddenly she shrieked very loudly, "Good-by!" But the bus door had closed.

The bus started. People came between them outside, people crossing the street, people they didn't know. Space and people. She lost sight of Bill. Then she remembered she had forgotten to give him her address—or to ask him for his—or tell him that her youngest boy was named Bill, too.

Never Room with a Couple

Even if they don't pay very much, you can have lots of fun working in a summer camp and you meet plenty of funny people. Last summer at a big camp in upstate New York I was head chief dishwasher and bottlewiper, with plenty else to do besides. For one thing, I had to help the cook get all the vegetables ready. I peeled so many potatoes that if you'd put all them spuds eye to eye, they'd reach from Waycross to Jalapy and back. But who's gonna worry 'bout that? Summer's gone now.

One afternoon me and the second cook was sitting out in the shade behind the cook shack, peeling spuds, when up from the lake comes a Jewish couple quarreling to beat the band. They was in bathing suits, a man and his wife, and they was both kinda fat and old. When they quarreled, their stomachs wobbled up and down. I wanted to laugh, but I didn't.

"You see that?" said the second cook. "I bet she's been flirtin' underwater with some other man."

"Might be the other way round," I said. "Maybe it was him and another woman."

"Which ever way it was," said the cook, "some woman is to blame."

"What makes you figger that?" I asked.

"It's always a woman is to blame," said the cook as he grabbed a potato I had just peeled, and looked at me. "Pick out them eyes good, boy," he said, although I knew perfectly well how to peel potatoes and *was* picking out the eyes good. But then I was only eighteen and Allie was an old guy about forty, always giving me advice. He sort of took it upon himself to look out for me, so he was always telling me stories with morals, like I was a kid.

"I never will forget that last family quarrel I was mixed up

191

in," Allie went on as we peeled and cut. "Who was to blame?
A woman! Son, they's terrible! That hussy like to ruint me!"

"Who?" I said. "Where? When?"

"Never room with a couple," Allie counseled gravely. He
paused to let this warning sink in. "Son, as long as you away
from your mother's home, no matter where you may be, never
room with a married couple. It's dangerous!" He looked me
solemnly in the eye over our bucket of potatoes. "You are young
and you don't know! But, boy, I'm tellin' you, if you rent a room
when you go back to Harlem, rent from a widow or an orphan, a
West Indian or a Geechee, but never room with a couple! A
man and his wife, plus a roomer—son, that's poison!"

"Why?" I said, to keep the tale going and get the potatoes
peeled so I could take a swim before supper.

"Why?" Allie answered, looking at me as if I was a child.
"I'm gonna tell you why. Look at me, here peeling potatoes!
Well, I used to be a first-class captain-waiter who could carry
more orders on one tray than any waiter in New York—and
look at me now! All from roomin' with a couple."

"What!" I said in astonishment.

"Sure, just look at me!" Allie said. "Their name was Wilkins.
A nice young couple, Joe and his wife, Fannie. I used to run on
the road with Joe before I quit the dining cars. So when he told
me one day, 'Me and my wife's got a nice little apartment in a
Hundred Forty-third. Why don't you come on up and room
with us, fellow? Quiet and homelike—and only three bucks a
week,' I said, 'I believe I will.' Which I did, cause I knowed they
needed the rent. So long about this time last year I moved in and
paid my rent. They gimme the rear back room. They had a nice
apartment on the third floor, with my window looking across
the alley at more third floors. Nighttime, all them radios goin',
it was swell! Harlem just full o' music—not like up here in these
woods where all you can hear is yourself snorin'."

"Then what happened?" I said.

"Funny thing, son," Allie went on. "Before I went there to
room, Joe's wife ain't never appealed to me a-tall. I like 'em
three-quarters pink, and she were just a ordinary light brown-

skin. But seemed like to me Fannie blossomed out and got prettier after I moved in. Or maybe seein' her every day at close range got me used to overlookin' her fizziogomy. Anyhow, one Sunday morning when Joe's train was out and I was goin' to the bath to shave, I met her trippin' down the hall on her way to church. I said, 'Baby, I could go for you!' When Fannie flashed them pearly teeth o' her'n in my face, I said, 'When do Joe come home?'

"She said, 'Not till twelve o'clock tonight.'

"I said, 'That'll do!' And, son, don't you know that woman got crazy about me?"

"Naturally," I answered, sarcastic-like, because in every tale he told, the women were always crazy about him.

Allie went on, "Fannie wanted to give me a diamond ring, but I wouldn't take it. I said, 'No, honey, your husband's just a working man.'

"She said, 'That don't make no difference, Allie. I'd take Joe's money and buy *you* a diamond—just to see you smile.'

"But I said, 'No, baby, I really don't need nary diamond. Just let me wear somethin' o' your'n. Any old thing—to think of you by!'

"She said, 'What?'

"I said, 'How about that little old horseshoe ring you got on your finger there?'

"She said, 'Aw, no, sugar! That belongs to Joe. He lets me wear it, but it ain't no good.'

"So I said, 'You thinks more of Joe than you does of me?'

" 'No, I don't, honey!' she said real quick. 'You can have it if you want it. Here!' And she gimme Joe's ring. 'But don't wear it around the house,' she said.

" 'Do you think I'm a fool?' I told her.

"I really didn't want the ring nohow, but I knowed it was Joe's—and I just wanted to see would she give it to me. Well, sir, to make a long story short, it wasn't no time till Joe found out that that ring was gone. Then it was that I should've moved, but I didn't have the sense—not thinkin' he'd suspicion *me*. We was always such good friends on the road.

"But one night I come home from the hotel where I was workin' and I'd no more than put my key in the latch when I heard 'em quarrelin'. I tipped down the hall real easy past their bedroom door, but when I went to unlock my own door, since I had done left my window open in the morning, the wind blew the door back with a bang. I heard Joe open his door and say, 'There's that so-and-so now!' So I knew they was quarrelin' 'bout me!

" 'Baby,' Fannie said to Joe, 'come in here and shut the door. Can't you see I ain't got no clothes on?'

" 'Shut up!' said Joe, and he called her out of her name.

" 'Don't call me that,' said Fannie, ' 'cause I'm a pure woman.'

" 'You don't say!' said Joe.

" '*Say*, nothin', Joe Wilkins,' she hollered, 'you know I am,' said Fannie.

" 'Yes, until that roomer come here,' yelled Joe. 'Right up till last August when Allie King showed up?'

" 'Till now, as far as Allie is concerned,' yelled Fannie.

" 'Then where is my horseshoe ring?'

" 'In the drawer,' she lied.

" 'Lemme see!'

"I could hear Fannie lookin' through the drawers for that ring she knew wasn't there—'cause I had it in my pocket. Then she begins to cry—and I was sweatin' blood! I ain't even turned on the light yet in my room. Just holdin' my hat in my hand *sweatin' blood*—'cause there wasn't but one way to get out of my room without passin' their door, and that was to jump. The third floor is pretty high—but Joe's a fightin' man.

" 'Fannie,' he said, 'who's got my ring?'

" 'What do you mean, who?' cried Fannie.

" 'You know what *who* means,' said Joe.

" 'Somebody musta stole it,' said Fannie.

" 'Who'd steal a no-good horseshoe ring?' said Joe. 'You give it to Allie King.'

" 'Ow-o-o-o-o-o!' cried Fannie. I knowed he'd raised his hand to hit her—so I put on my hat to go.

" 'And you ain't the only one I'm gonna hit,' yelled Joe. 'I'm goin' in there and beat that no-good son-of-a-so-and-so to death right now.' He started down the hall for me.

" 'Aw-ooo-oo-o!' Fannie yelled as I heard Joe chargin' towards my door—but before he could put his hand on the knob, I was gone!"

"Gone where?" I asked, dropping a potato.

"Gone out," said Allie. "I stepped right through that third-floor window down into the yard."

"Three stories down?"

"I didn't miss it," said Allie. "I like to took that window with me, too—I was in such a hurry. Don't think I lingered in the back yard neither. No, sir! I crawled right on up to Lenox and grabbed me a taxi."

"Crawled?" I said.

"Sure, *crawled!* I'd done broke both my ankles! That's why I'm peelin' spuds out here in this lonesome camp today. I can't wait table no mo' with these crippled-up feet—and all from roomin' with a couple!"

Allie looked at me with a warning eye over our bucket of potatoes.

"*Never* room with a couple, son," he said solemnly, "less'n they are over eighty."

Tragedy at the Baths

"That it should happen in my Baths!" was all she could say. "That it should happen in my Baths!" And try as they would, nobody could console her. Señora Rueda was quite hysterical. Being a big strong woman, her screams alarmed the neighborhood.

She and her now-deceased husband had owned the Baths for years—the Esmeralda Baths—among the cleanest and most respectable in Mexico City, family baths where only decent people came for their weekly tub or shower or *baño de vapor*. Indeed, her establishment, with its tiled courtyard and splashing fountain, was a monument to the neighborhood, a middle-class section of flats and shops near the Loreto. Now this had happened!

Why! Señora Rueda had known the young man for years—that is, he had been a customer of the Esmeralda Baths since his youth, coming there for his weekly shower and swim in the little tiled tank. Sometimes, when he was flush, he took a private tub, and a good steaming out—which cost a peso. Juan Maldonado was the young man's name. He was a tall nice-looking boy.

That Sunday morning when he presented himself at the wicket and asked for a private tub for two—himself and his wife—Señora Rueda was not especially surprised. Even by reading the papers, one can't keep up with all the marriages that take place—and young men will eventually get married.

As she handed Juan his change, she looked up to see beside him a vibrant black-haired girl with the soft Indian-brown complexion of a Mexican mestiza. Señora Rueda smiled. "A nice couple," she thought as the attendant showed them to their room and their tub. "Two beautiful youths," she thought, and sighed.

Some bathhouses, she knew, did not allow the sexes to mingle within their walls, but Señora Rueda did not mind when they were legally married. Being respectable neighborhood baths, nothing but decent people were her patrons, anyway. She had no reason to suspect young Maldonado.

But an hour later there was another tale to tell! Not even smelling salts then could calm poor Señora Rueda. Oh, why did it have to happen in her Baths? *Por Dios*, why?

This is the story as it came to me. It may not be wholly true, for in the patios and courtyards of Loreto romantic and colorful additions have probably been added by those who know Juan and his family. The Mexicans love sad romantic tales with many embroidered touches of sentimental heartbreak and ironic frustration. But, although versions of what led up to that strange Sunday morning in the Esmeralda Baths may vary in the telling, what actually happened therein—everybody knows. And it was awful!

In the first place, they were not married, Juan and that woman!

He met her in a very strange way, anyhow. The mounted police were charging a demonstration against the government. The Zocalo was filled with people trampling the grass and the flowers. Juan crossed the square on the way to the shop where he worked, giving the demonstrators a wide berth—as his particular politics were not involved that day. But just as he got midway across the Zocalo, the police began to charge on horses and the crowd began to run, so Juan was forced to run, too.

Everyone was trying to reach the shelter of the *portales* opposite the Palace, or the gates of the Cathedral, or the safety of a side street. Juan was heading toward Avenida Madero, the clatter of the horses' hoofs behind him, when, just in front of him, a woman stumbled and fell.

Juan stopped running and picked her up, lifted her in his arms and went on. Once out of the square, in the quiet of a side street, he put her down on her feet and offered her his handkerchief to wipe the dust and tears from her face. Then he saw that she was young and very beautiful, with the soft Indian-brown complexion of a Mexican mestiza.

"Ay, *Señor*," she said to the tall young man in front of her, "how can I ever thank you?"

But just at that moment a man approached, hatless and wild-eyed. He, too, had been caught in the spinning crowd, had seen his wife fall, but could not get to her—and then she had disappeared! For a while the husband was frantic, but finally he caught sight of her around the corner, faced by a tall young man who was offering her his handkerchief and gazing deep into her lovely eyes.

"You don't need to thank me," the young man was saying,

"just let me look at you," as the girl caught sight of her approaching husband.

"Sunday at the Maximo," she whispered. "I want to thank you alone."

"At your service," said the young man as the panting husband arrived.

Now, the husband was also a fairly young man, but neither as tall nor as handsome as Maldonado. He was much too short and frail to be married to so charming a woman. He kept an *escritorio*, a writing room, in the Portal of Santo Domingo on the little square, where letters were written for peasants who had no education, and where people could get legal documents copied on the typewriter, or have their names penned with decorative flourishes on a hundred calling cards.

The husband, too, there in the side street that day, thanked young Maldonado for having rescued his wife from the feet of the crowd and the hoofs of the police horses. Then they all shook hands and went their way, the tall young man going south, the pretty girl and her prosaic husband, north.

But the following Sunday Maldonado waited at the entrance of the Cinema Maximo, where a Bogart film was being shown, and about five o'clock, sure enough, she appeared, alone. She was even prettier than the day he had picked her up in the Zocalo, and very shy, as if ashamed of what she was doing.

They took seats way up in the balcony, where lovers sit and hold hands in the dark. And soon they were holding hands, too.

"There was something about the strength of your arms the other day," she said, "even before I looked into your eyes, that made me want to stay with you forever."

"Stop!" yelled a cop, firing across the screen.

"And there was something in the feel of your body lying in my arms that made me never want to put you down," said Juan.

"My name is Consuelo Aguilar," the girl said softly. "You have met my husband."

"Tell me about him," said Juan.

"He is crazy about me," Consuelo answered, "and ter-

ribly jealous! He wants to be a writer, but all he writes is letters
for peasants."

"And if he knew you were here . . . ?"

"But he won't know. He stays home on Sundays and writes
poems! When I tell him they're no good, he says I don't love
him and threatens to commit suicide. He is very emotional, my
little husband."

"And where does he think you are now?"

"At my aunt's."

It was really love, and at first sight, so they say in the patios
of Loreto. But they also say that Juan was a little dumb, and a
little inexperienced in the ways of women.

They kept on meeting in *cines* and dance halls, and things
began to be more and more dangerous for both of them, for husbands very often kill lovers in Mexico—and go free. It is the
thing to do! But what this husband did was even worse! At least,
Señora Rueda thought so.

But what his wife did was terrible, too. In Catholic lands
where divorces are practically impossible, and where women are
never supposed to leave their husbands, anyhow—this wife
planned to run away with Maldonado! But, being young and
foolish (or so they say in Loreto), for some strange reason or
other, on the Sunday of their elopement they planned to take a
bath first. And that is how the couple happened to be in Señora
Rueda's quiet Esmeralda Baths.

There the husband came and caught them! Or, rather, he
deliberately followed them there. The miracle was that he did
not kill them both! Instead, he bought a season's ticket for a
whole year of baths (probably not realizing what he was doing),
then went into the corridor outside the room where Juan and
Consuelo were bathing—and shot *himself!*

Then it was that the uproar began, and such an uproar! People commenced to emerge from their tubs, clad and unclad, to
run and scream. Doors began to open, and steam escaped into the
courtyard. In the excitement, someone turned off the water

main and the fountain stopped running. Naturally, Consuelo and Maldonado came out to see what was going on—and stumbled over the bleeding body of Señor Aguilar at their feet.

"Oh, my God!" Consuelo cried. "He said he would kill himself if I ran away with you."

"How did he ever know you were coming away with *me?*" asked the young man in astonishment.

"I told him," said Consuelo. Her eyes were hard. "I wanted to see if he really would commit suicide. He threatened to so often. But now, darling," she turned softly toward Juan, "with him gone, we can get married."

"But suppose he had killed *us!*" said Maldonado, trembling in the doorway with only a towel about his body.

"That little coward," sneered Consuelo, "wasn't man enough!"

"But he did kill himself," said Maldonado slowly, turning back into the room, away from the body on the floor and the crowd that had gathered.

"Kiss me," purred Consuelo, lifting her pretty face toward Juan's as she closed their door.

"Get away from me!" cried Juan, suddenly sickened with horror. Flinging open the door, he gave her a terrific push into the hall.

Consuelo fell prone over the body of her husband, and beginning to realize that she was, after all, a widow, and that there were six good typewriters to be inherited from the *escritorio,* she commenced to sob in approved fashion on the floor, embracing the corpse of her late spouse, hysterically—as a good wife should.

When the police got through asking questions of them both, and of Señora Rueda, Juan went home alone and left Consuelo still crying at the Baths. It took him a long time to get over the fact that she had told her husband—and the sound of that single pistol shot echoed in his head for months.

But the saddest thing of all, so they say in Loreto, was that when the details of their tragic triangle appeared in the papers, Juan's employer read them with such scandalized interest that

he promptly dismissed him from his work. Consuelo lost only a
husband she didn't want. But young Maldonado lost his *job*.

As for Señora Rueda, she swore never to rent another tub
to a couple.

Trouble with the Angels

At every performance lots of white people wept. And almost
every Sunday while they were on tour, some white minister invited the Negro actor who played God to address his congregation and thus help improve race relations—because almost everywhere they needed improving. Although the play had been the
hit of the decade in New York, its Negro actors and singers were
paid much less than white actors and singers would have been
paid for performing it. And, although the white producer and his
backers made more than half a million dollars, the colored troup-
ers on tour lived in cheap hotels and often slept in beds that
were full of bugs. Only the actor who played God would sometimes, by the hardest, achieve accommodations in a white hotel,
or be put up by some nice white family, or be invited to the
home of the best Negroes in town. Thus God probably thought
that everything was lovely in the world. As an actor he really
got very good write-ups in the papers.

Then they were booked to play Washington, and that's where
the trouble began. Washington, the capital of the United States,
is, as every Negro knows, a town where no black man was allowed inside a downtown theater, not even in the gallery, until
very recently. The legitimate playhouses had no accommodations for colored people. Incredible as it may seem, until Ingrid
Bergman made her stand, Washington was worse than the Deep
South in that respect.

But God wasn't at all worried about playing Washington. He thought surely his coming would improve race relations. He thought it would be fine for the good white people of the capital to see him—a colored God—even if Negroes couldn't. Not even those Negroes who worked for the government. Not even the black Congressman.

But several weeks before the Washington appearance of the famous "Negro" play about charming darkies who drank eggnog at a fish fry in heaven, storm clouds began to rise. It seemed that the Negroes of Washington strangely enough had decided that they, too, wanted to see this play. But when they approached the theater management on the question, they got a cold shoulder. The management said they didn't have any seats to sell Negroes. They couldn't even allot a corner in the upper gallery —there was such a heavy ticket demand from white folks.

Now this made the Negroes of Washington mad, especially those who worked for the government and constituted the best society. The teachers at Howard got mad, too, and the ministers of the colored churches who wanted to see what a black heaven looked like on the stage.

But nothing doing! The theater management was adamant. They really couldn't sell seats to Negroes. Although they had no scruples about making a large profit on the week's work of Negro actors, they couldn't permit Negroes to occupy seats in the theater.

So the Washington Negroes wrote directly to God, this colored God who had been such a hit on Broadway. They thought surely he would help them. Several organizations, including the Negro Ministerial Alliance, got in touch with him when he was playing Philadelphia. What a shame, they said by letter, that the white folks will not allow us to come to see you perform in Washington. We are getting up a protest. We want you to help us. Will you?

Now God knew that for many years white folks had not allowed Negroes in Washington to see any shows—not even in the churches, let alone in theaters! So how come they suddenly

thought they ought to be allowed to see God in a white playhouse?

Besides, God was getting paid pretty well, and was pretty
well known. So he answered their letters and said that although
his ink was made of tears and his heart bled, he couldn't afford
to get into trouble with Equity. Also, it wasn't his place to go
around the country spreading dissension and hate, but rather
love and beauty. And it would surely do the white folks of the
District of Columbia a lot of good to see Him, and it would
soften their hearts to hear the beautiful Negro spirituals and
witness the lovely black angels in his play.

The black drama lovers of Washington couldn't get any real
satisfaction out of God by mail—their colored God. So when
the company played Baltimore, a delegation of the Washington
Negroes went over to the neighboring city to interview him. In
Baltimore, Negroes at least were allowed to sit in the galleries
of the theaters.

After the play, God received the delegation in his dressing
room and wept about his inability to do anything concerning the
situation. He had, of course, spoken to his management about it
and they thought it might be possible to arrange a special Sunday night performance for Negroes. God said it hurt him to his
soul to think how his people were mistreated, but the play must
go on.

The delegation left in a huff—but not before they had spread
their indignation to other members of the cast of the show. Then
among the angels there arose a great discussion as to what they
might do about the Washington situation. Although God was
the star, the angels, too, were a part of the play.

Now, among the angels there was a young Negro named
Johnny Logan who never really liked being an angel, but who,
because of his baritone voice and Negro features, had gotten the
job during the first rehearsals in New York. Now, since the play
had been running three years, he was an old hand at being an
angel.

Logan was from the South—but he hadn't stayed there long

after he grew up. The white folks wouldn't let him. He was the kind of young Negro most Southern white people hate. He believed in fighting prejudice, in bucking against the traces of discrimination and Jim Crow, and in trying to knock down any white man who insulted him. So he was only about eighteen when the whites ran him out of Augusta, Georgia.

He came to New York, married a waitress, got a job as a red-cap, and would have settled down forever in a little flat in Harlem, had not some of his friends discovered that he could sing. They persuaded him to join a Redcap Quartette. Out of that had come this work as a black angel in what turned out to be a Broadway success in the midst of the depression.

Just before the show went on the road, his wife had their first kid, so he needed to hold his job as a singing angel, even if it meant going on tour. But the more he thought about their forthcoming appearance in a Washington theater that wasn't even Jim Crow—but barred Negroes altogether—the madder Logan got. Finally he got so mad that he caused the rest of the cast to organize a strike!

At that distance from Washington, black angels—from tenors to basses, sopranos to blues singers—were up in arms. Everybody in the cast, except God, agreed to strike.

"The idea of a town where colored folks can't even sit in the gallery to see an all-colored show. I ain't gonna work there myself."

"We'll show them white folks we've got spunk for once. We'll pull off the biggest actors' strike you ever seen."

"We sure will."

That was in Philadelphia. In Baltimore their ardor had cooled down a bit, and it was all Logan could do to hold his temper as he felt his fellow angels weakening.

"Man, I got a wife to take care of. I can't lose no week's work!"

"I got a wife, too," said Logan, "and a kid besides, but I'm game."

"You ain't a trouper," said another as he sat in the dressing room putting on his make-up.

"Naw, if you was, you'd be used to playing all-white houses.

In the old days . . ." said the man who played Methuselah, powdering his gray wig.

"I know all about the old days," said Logan, "when black minstrels blacked up even blacker and made fun of themselves for the benefit of white folks. But who wants to go back to the old days?"

"Anyhow, let's let well enough alone," said Methuselah.

"You guys have got no guts—that's all I can say," said Logan.

"You's just one of them radicals, son, that's what you are," put in the old tenor who played Saul. "We know when we want to strike or don't."

"Listen, then," said Logan to the angels who were putting on their wings by now, as it was near curtain time, "if we can't make it a real strike, then let's make it a general walkout on the opening night. Strike for one performance anyhow. At least show folks that we won't take it lying down. Show those Washington Negroes we back them up—theoretically, anyhow."

"One day ain't so bad," said a skinny black angel. "I'm with you on a one-day strike."

"Me, too," several others agreed as they crowded into the corridor at curtain time. The actor who played God was standing in the wings in his frock coat.

"Shss-ss!" he said.

Monday in Washington. The opening of that famous white play about black life in a scenic heaven. Original New York cast. Songs as only Negroes can sing them. Uncle Tom come back as God.

Negro Washington wanted to picket the theater, but the police had an injunction against them. Cops were posted for blocks around the playhouse to prevent a riot. Nobody could see God. He was safely housed in the quiet home of a conservative Negro professor, guarded by two detectives. The papers said black radicals had threatened to kidnap him. To kidnap God!

Logan spent the whole day rallying the flagging spirits of his fellow actors, talking to them in their hotel rooms. They were solid for the one-day strike when he was around, and weak when he wasn't. No telling what Washington cops might do to them if they struck. They locked Negroes up for less than that in Washington. Besides, they might get canned, they might lose their pay, they might never get no more jobs on the stage. It was all right to talk about being a man and standing up for your race, and all that—but hell, even an actor has to eat. Besides, God was right. It was a great play, a famous play! They ought to hold up its reputation. It did white folks good to see Negroes in such a play. Logan must be crazy!

"Listen here, you might as well get wise. Ain't nobody gonna strike tonight," one of the men told him about six o'clock in the lobby of the colored Whitelaw Hotel. "You'd just as well give up. You're right. We ain't got no guts."

"I won't give up," said Logan.

When the actors reached the theater, they found it surrounded by cops, and the stage was full of detectives. In the lobby there was a long line of people—white, of course—waiting to buy standing room. God arrived with motorcycle cops in front of his car. He had come a little early to address the cast. With him was the white stage manager and a representative of the New York producing office.

They called everybody together on the stage. The Lord wept as he spoke of all his race had borne to get where Negroes are today. Of how they had struggled. Of how they sang. Of how they must keep on struggling and singing—until white folks see the light. A strike would do no good. A strike would only hurt their cause. With sorrow in his heart—but more noble because of it—he would go on with the play. He was sure his actors—his angels—his children—would continue, too.

The white men accompanying God were very solemn, as though hurt to their souls to think what their Negro employees were suffering, but far more hurt to think that Negroes had wanted to jeopardize a week's box-office receipts by a strike! That would really harm everybody!

Behind God and the white managers stood two big detectives.

Needless to say, the Negroes finally went downstairs to put on their wings and make-up. All but Logan. He went downstairs to drag the cast out by force, to make men of darkies, to carry through the strike. But he couldn't. Not alone. Nobody really wanted to strike. Nobody wanted to sacrifice anything for race pride, decency, or elementary human rights. The actors only wanted to keep on appearing in a naïve dialect play about a quaint, funny heaven full of niggers at which white people laughed and wept.

The management sent two detectives downstairs to get Logan. They were taking no chances. Just as the curtain rose they carted him off to jail—for disturbing the peace. The colored angels were all massed in the wings for the opening spiritual when the police took the black boy out, a line of tears running down his cheeks.

Most of the actors *wanted* to think Logan was crying because he was being arrested—but in their souls they knew that was not why he wept.

On the Road

He was not interested in the snow. When he got off the freight, one early evening during the depression, Sargeant never even noticed the snow. But he must have felt it seeping down his neck, cold, wet, sopping in his shoes. But if you had asked him, he wouldn't have known it was snowing. Sargeant didn't see the snow, not even under the bright lights of the main street, falling white and flaky against the night. He was too hungry, too sleepy, too tired.

The Reverend Mr. Dorset, however, saw the snow when he switched on his porch light, opened the front door of his parsonage, and found standing there before him a big black man with snow on his face, a human piece of night with snow on his face—obviously unemployed.

Said the Reverend Mr. Dorset before Sargeant even realized

he'd opened his mouth: "I'm sorry. No! Go right on down this street four blocks and turn to your left, walk up seven and you'll see the Relief Shelter. I'm sorry. No!" He shut the door.

Sargeant wanted to tell the holy man that he had already been to the Relief Shelter, been to hundreds of relief shelters during the depression years, the beds were always gone and supper was over, the place was full, and they drew the color line anyhow. But the minister said, "No," and shut the door. Evidently he didn't want to hear about it. And he *had* a door to shut.

The big black man turned away. And even yet he didn't see the snow, walking right into it. Maybe he sensed it, cold, wet, sticking to his jaws, wet on his black hands, sopping in his shoes. He stopped and stood on the sidewalk hunched over— hungry, sleepy, cold—looking up and down. Then he looked right where he was—in front of a church. Of course! A church! Sure, right next to a parsonage, certainly a church.

It had *two* doors.

Broad white steps in the night all snowy white. Two high arched doors with slender stone pillars on either side. And way up, a round lacy window with a stone crucifix in the middle and Christ on the crucifix in stone. All this was pale in the street lights, solid and stony pale in the snow.

Sargeant blinked. When he looked up, the snow fell into his eyes. For the first time that night he *saw* the snow. He shook his head. He shook the snow from his coat sleeves, felt hungry, felt lost, felt not lost, felt cold. He walked up the steps of the church. He knocked at the door. No answer. He tried the handle. Locked. He put his shoulder against the door and his long black body slanted like a ramrod. He pushed. With loud rhythmic grunts, like the grunts in a chain-gang song, he pushed against the door.

"I'm tired . . . Huh! . . . Hongry . . . Uh! . . . I'm sleepy . . . Huh! I'm cold . . . I got to sleep somewheres," Sargeant said. "This here is a church, ain't it? Well, uh!"

He pushed against the door.

Suddenly, with an undue cracking and screaking, the door

began to give way to the tall black Negro who pushed ferociously against it.

By now two or three white people had stopped in the street, and Sargeant was vaguely aware of some of them yelling at him concerning the door. Three or four more came running, yelling at him.

"Hey!" they said. "Hey!"

"Uh-huh," answered the big tall Negro, "I know it's a white folks' church, but I got to sleep somewhere." He gave another lunge at the door. "Huh!"

And the door broke open.

But just when the door gave way, two white cops arrived in a car, ran up the steps with their clubs, and grabbed Sargeant. But Sargeant for once had no intention of being pulled or pushed away from the door.

Sargeant grabbed, but not for anything so weak as a broken door. He grabbed for one of the tall stone pillars beside the door, grabbed at it and caught it. And held it. The cops pulled and Sargeant pulled. Most of the people in the street got behind the cops and helped them pull.

"A big black unemployed Negro holding onto our church!" thought the people. "The idea!"

The cops began to beat Sargeant over the head, and nobody protested. But he held on.

And then the church fell down.

Gradually, the big stone front of the church fell down, the walls and the rafters, the crucifix and the Christ. Then the whole thing fell down, covering the cops and the people with bricks and stones and debris. The whole church fell down in the snow.

Sargeant got out from under the church and went walking on up the street with the stone pillar on his shoulder. He was under the impression that he had buried the parsonage and the Reverend Mr. Dorset who said, "No!" So he laughed, and threw the pillar six blocks up the street and went on.

Sargeant thought he was alone, but listening to the *crunch,*

crunch, crunch on the snow of his own footsteps, he heard other footsteps, too, doubling his own. He looked around, and there was Christ walking along beside him, the same Christ that had been on the cross on the church—still stone with a rough stone surface, walking along beside him just like he was broken off the cross when the church fell down.

"Well, I'll be dogged," said Sargeant. "This here's the first time I ever seed you off the cross."

"Yes," said Christ, crunching his feet in the snow. "You had to pull the church down to get me off the cross."

"You glad?" said Sargeant.

"I sure am," said Christ.

They both laughed.

"I'm a hell of a fellow, ain't I?" said Sargeant. "Done pulled the church down!"

"You did a good job," said Christ. "They have kept me nailed on a cross for nearly two thousand years."

"Whee-ee-e!" said Sargeant. "I know you are glad to get off."

"I sure am," said Christ.

They walked on in the snow. Sargeant looked at the man of stone.

"And you have been up there two thousand years?"

"I sure have," Christ said.

"Well, if I had a little cash," said Sargeant, "I'd show you around a bit."

"I been around," said Christ.

"Yeah, but that was a long time ago."

"All the same," said Christ, "I've been around."

They walked on in the snow until they came to the railroad yards. Sargeant was tired, sweating and tired.

"Where you goin'?" Sargeant said, stopping by the tracks. He looked at Christ. Sargeant said, "I'm just a bum on the road. How about you? Where you goin'?"

"God knows," Christ said, "but I'm leavin' here."

They saw the red and green lights of the railroad yard half veiled by the snow that fell out of the night. Away down the track they saw a fire in a hobo jungle.

"I can go there and sleep," Sargeant said.

"You can?"

"Sure," said Sargeant. "That place ain't got no doors."

Outside the town, along the tracks, there were barren trees and bushes below the embankment, snow-gray in the dark. And down among the trees and bushes there were makeshift houses made out of boxes and tin and old pieces of wood and canvas. You couldn't see them in the dark, but you knew they were there if you'd ever been on the road, if you had ever lived with the homeless and hungry in a depression.

"I'm side-tracking," Sargeant said. "I'm tired."

"I'm gonna make it on to Kansas City," said Christ.

"O.K.," Sargeant said. "So long!"

He went down into the hobo jungle and found himself a place to sleep. He never did see Christ no more. About 6:00 A.M. a freight came by. Sargeant scrambled out of the jungle with a dozen or so more hobos and ran along the track, grabbing at the freight. It was dawn, early dawn, cold and gray.

"Wonder where Christ is by now?" Sargeant thought. "He musta gone on way on down the road. He didn't sleep in this jungle."

Sargeant grabbed the train and started to pull himself up into a moving coal car, over the edge of a wheeling coal car. But strangely enough, the car was full of cops. The nearest cop rapped Sargeant soundly across the knuckles with his night stick. Wham! Rapped his big black hands for clinging to the top of the car. Wham! But Sargeant did not turn loose. He clung on and tried to pull himself into the car. He hollered at the top of his voice, "Damn it, lemme in this car!"

"Shut up," barked the cop. "You crazy coon!" He rapped Sargeant across the knuckles and punched him in the stomach. "You ain't out in no jungle now. This ain't no train. You in jail."

Wham! across his bare black fingers clinging to the bars of his cell. Wham! between the steel bars low down against his shins.

Suddenly Sargeant realized that he really was in jail. He

wasn't on no train. The blood of the night before had dried on his face, his head hurt terribly, and a cop outside in the corridor was hitting him across the knuckles for holding onto the door, yelling and shaking the cell door.

"They musta took me to jail for breaking down the door last night," Sargeant thought, "that church door."

Sargeant went over and sat on a wooden bench against the cold stone wall. He was emptier than ever. His clothes were wet, clammy cold wet, and shoes sloppy with snow water. It was just about dawn. There he was, locked up behind a cell door, nursing his bruised fingers.

The bruised fingers were his, but not the *door*.

Not the *club*, but the fingers.

"You wait," mumbled Sargeant, black against the jail wall. "I'm gonna break down this door, too."

"Shut up—or I'll paste you one," said the cop.

"I'm gonna break down this door," yelled Sargeant as he stood up in his cell.

Then he must have been talking to himself because he said, "I wonder where Christ's gone? I wonder if he's gone to Kansas City?"

Big Meeting

The early stars had begun to twinkle in the August night as Bud and I neared the woods. A great many Negroes, old and young, were plodding down the dirt road on foot on their way to the Big Meeting. Long before we came near the lantern-lighted tent, we could hear early arrivals singing, clapping their hands lustily, and throwing out each word distinct like a drumbeat. Songs like "When the Saints Go Marching Home" and "That Old-Time Religion" filled the air.

In the road that ran past the woods, a number of automobiles and buggies belonging to white people had stopped near the tent so that their occupants might listen to the singing. The whites stared curiously through the hickory trees at the rocking figures in the tent. The canvas, except behind the pulpit, was rolled up on account of the heat, and the meeting could easily be seen from the road, so there beneath a tree Bud and I stopped, too. In our teens, we were young and wild and didn't believe much in revivals, so we stayed outside in the road where we could smoke and laugh like the white folks. But both Bud's mother and mine were under the tent singing, actively a part of the services. Had they known we were near, they would certainly have come out and dragged us in.

From frequent attendance since childhood at these Big Meetings held each summer in the South, we knew the services were divided into three parts. The testimonials and the song-service came first. This began as soon as two or three people were gathered together, continuing until the minister himself arrived. Then the sermon followed, with its accompanying songs and shouts from the audience. Then the climax came with the calling of the lost souls to the mourners' bench, and the prayers for sinners and backsliders. This was where Bud and I would leave. We were having too good a time being sinners, and we didn't want to be saved—not yet, anyway.

When we arrived, old Aunt Ibey Davis was just starting a familiar song:

> "Where shall I be when that first trumpet sound?
> Lawdy, where shall I be when it sound so loud?"

The rapidly increasing number of worshipers took up the tune in full volume, sending a great flood of melody billowing beneath the canvas roof. With heads back, feet and hands patting time, they repeated the chorus again and again. And each party of new arrivals swung into rhythm as they walked up the aisle by the light of the dim oil lanterns hanging from the tent poles.

Standing there at the edge of the road beneath a big tree, Bud and I watched the people as they came—keeping our eyes open for the girls. Scores of Negroes from the town and nearby vil-

lages and farms came, drawn by the music and the preaching.
Some were old and gray-headed; some in the prime of life; some
mere boys and girls; and many little barefooted children. It was
the twelfth night of the Big Meeting. They came from miles
around to bathe their souls in a sea of song, to shout and cry and
moan before the flow of Reverend Braswell's eloquence, and to
pray for all the sinners in the county who had not yet seen the
light. Although it was a colored folks' meeting, whites liked to
come and sit outside in the road in their cars and listen. Sometimes there would be as many as ten or twelve parties of whites
parked there in the dark, smoking and listening, and enjoying
themselves, like Bud and I, in a not very serious way.

Even while old Aunt Ibey Davis was singing, a big red Buick
drove up and parked right behind Bud and me beneath the tree.
It was full of white people, and we recognized the driver as Mr.
Parkes, the man who owned the drugstore in town where colored
people couldn't buy a glass of soda at the fountain.

> "It will sound so loud it will wake up the dead!
> Lawdy, where shall I be when it sound?"

"You'll hear some good singing out here," Mr. Parkes said to
a woman in the car with him.

"I always did love to hear darkies singing," she answered
from the back seat.

Bud nudged me in the ribs at the world "darkie."

"I hear 'em," I said, sitting down on one of the gnarled roots
of the tree and pulling out a cigarette.

The song ended as an old black woman inside the tent got up
to speak. "I rise to testify dis evenin' fo' Jesus!" she said. "Ma
Saviour an' ma Redeemer an' de chamber wherein I resusti-
cates ma soul. Pray fo' me, brothers and sisters. Let yo' mercies
bless me in all I do an' yo' prayers go with me on each travelin'
voyage through dis land."

"Amen! Hallelujah!" cried my mother.

Just in front of us, near the side of the tent, a woman's clear
soprano voice began to sing:

> *"I am a po' pilgrim of sorrow*
> *Out in this wide world alone . . ."*

Soon others joined with her and the whole tent was singing:

> *"Sometimes I am tossed and driven,*
> *Sometimes I don't know where to go . . ."*

"Real pretty, ain't it?" said the white woman in the car behind us.

> *"But I've heard of a city called heaven*
> *And I've started to make it my home."*

When the woman finished her song, she rose and told how her husband left her with six children, her mother died in a poorhouse, and the world had always been against her—but still she was going on!

"My, she's had a hard time," giggled the woman in the car.

"Sure has," laughed Mr. Parkes, "to hear her tell it."

And the way they talked made gooseflesh come out on my skin.

"Trials and tribulations surround me—but I'm goin' on," the woman in the tent cried. Shouts and exclamations of approval broke out all over the congregation.

"Praise God!"

"Bless His Holy Name!"

"That's right, sister!"

"Devils beset me—but I'm goin' on!" said the woman. "I ain't got no friends—but I'm goin' on!"

"Jesus yo' friend, sister! Jesus yo' friend!" came the answer.

"God bless Jesus! I'm goin 'on!"

"Dat's right!" cried Sister Mabry, Bud's mother, bouncing in her seat and flinging her arms outward. "Take all this world, but gimme Jesus!"

"Look at Mama," Bud said half amused, sitting there beside me smoking. "She's getting happy."

"Whoo-ooo-o-o! Great Gawd A'mighty!" yelled old man Walls

near the pulpit. "I can't hold it dis evenin'! Dis mawnin', dis evenin', dis mawnin', Lawd!"

"Pray for me—cause I'm goin' on!" said the woman. In the midst of the demonstration she had created, she sat down exhausted, her armpits wet with sweat and her face covered with tears.

"Did you hear her, Jehover?" someone asked.

"Yes! He heard her! Halleloo!" came the answer.

"Dis mawnin', dis evenin', dis mawnin', Lawd!"

Brother Nace Eubanks began to line a song:

> *"Must Jesus bear his cross alone*
> *An' all de world go free?"*

Slowly they sang it line by line. Then the old man rose and told of a vision that had come to him long ago on that day when he had been changed from a sinner to a just man.

"I was layin' in ma bed," he said, "at de midnight hour twenty-two years past at Seven hundred fourteen Pine Street in dis here city when a snow-white sheep come in ma room an' stood behind de washbowl. Dis here sheep, hit spoke to me wid tongues o' fiah an' hit said, 'Nace, git up! Git up, an' come wid me!' Yes, suh! He had a light round 'bout his head like a moon, an' wings like a dove, an' he walked on hoofs o' gold an' dis sheep hit said, 'I once were lost, but now I'm saved, an' you kin be like me!" Yes, suh! An' ever since dat night, brothers an' sisters, I's been a chile o' de Lamb! Pray fo' me!"

"Help him, Jesus!" Sister Mabry shouted.

"Amen!" chanted Deacon Laws. "Amen! Amen!"

> *"Glory! Hallelujah!*
> *Let de halleluian roll!*
> *I'll sing ma Saviour's praises far an' wide!"*

It was my mother's favorite song, and she sang it like a paean of triumph, rising from her seat.

"Look at Ma," I said to Bud, knowing that she was about to start her nightly shouting.

"Yah," Bud said. "I hope she don't see me while she's standing up there, or she'll come out here and make us go up to the mourners' bench."

"We'll leave before that," I said.

> *"I've opened up to heaven*
> *All de windows of ma soul,*
> *An' I'm livin' on de halleluian side!"*

Rocking proudly to and fro as the second chorus boomed and swelled beneath the canvas, Mama began to clap her hands, her lips silent now in this sea of song she had started, her head thrown back in joy—for my mother was a great shouter. Stepping gracefully to the beat of the music, she moved out toward the center aisle into a cleared space. Then she began to spring on her toes with little short rhythmical hops. All the way up the long aisle to the pulpit gently she leaped to the clap-clap of hands, the pat of feet, and the steady booming song of her fellow worshipers. Then Mama began to revolve in a dignified circle, slowly, as a great happiness swept her gleaming black features, and her lips curved into a smile.

> *"I've opened up to heaven*
> *All de windows of my soul . . ."*

Mama was dancing before the Lord with her eyes closed, her mouth smiling, and her head held high.

> *"I'm livin' on de halleluian side!"*

As she danced, she threw her hands upward away from her breasts, as though casting off all the cares of the world.

Just then the white woman in Mr. Parkes's car behind us laughed. "My Lord, John, it's better than a show!"

Something about the way she laughed made my blood boil. That was *my mother* dancing and shouting. Maybe it was better than a show, but nobody had any business laughing at her, least of all white people.

I looked at Bud, but he didn't say anything. Maybe he was thinking how often we, too, made fun of the shouters, laughing at our parents as though they were crazy—but deep down inside us we understood why they came to Big Meeting. Working all day all their lives for white folks, they *had* to believe there was a "halleluian side."

I looked at Mama standing there singing, and I thought about how many years she had prayed and shouted and praised the Lord at church meetings and revivals, then came home for a few hours' sleep before getting up at dawn to go cook and scrub and clean for others. And I didn't want any white folks, especially whites who wouldn't let a Negro drink a glass of soda in their drugstore or give one a job, sitting in a car laughing at Mama.

"Gimme a cigarette, Bud. If these dopes behind us say any more, I'm gonna get up and tell 'em something they won't like."

"To hell with 'em," Bud answered.

I leaned back against the gnarled roots of the tree by the road and inhaled deeply. The white people were silent again in their car, listening to the singing. In the dark I couldn't see their faces to tell if they were still amused or not. But that was mostly what they wanted out of Negroes—work and fun—without paying for it, I thought, work and fun.

To a great hand-clapping body-rocking foot-patting rhythm, Mama was repeating the chorus over and over. Sisters leaped and shouted and perspiring brothers walked the aisles, bowing left and right, beating time, shaking hands, laughing aloud for joy, and singing steadily when, at the back of the tent, the Reverend Duke Braswell arrived.

A tall, powerful jet-black man, he moved with long steps through the center of the tent, his iron-gray hair uncovered, his green-black coat jim-swinging to his knees, his fierce eyes looking straight toward the altar. Under his arm he carried a Bible.

Once on the platform, he stood silently wiping his brow with a large white handkerchief while the singing swirled around him. Then he sang, too, his voice roaring like a cyclone, his white teeth shining. Finally he held up his palms for silence and the song gradually lowered to a hum, hum, hum, hands and

feet patting, bodies still moving. At last, above the broken cries
of the shouters and the undertones of song, the minister was
able to make himself heard.

"Brother Garner, offer up a prayer."

Reverend Braswell sank on his knees and every back bowed.
Brother Garner, with his head in his hands, lifted his voice
against a background of moans:

"Oh, Lawd, we comes befo' you dis evenin' wid fear an' trem-
blin'—unworthy as we is to enter yo' house an' speak yo' name.
We comes befo' you, Lawd, 'cause we knows you is mighty
an' powerful in all de lands, an' great above de stars, an' bright
above de moon. Oh, Lawd, you is bigger den de world. You
holds de sun in yo' right hand an' de mornin' star in yo' left,
an' we po' sinners ain't nothin', not even so much as a grain o'
sand beneath yo' feet. Yet we calls on you dis evenin' to hear us,
Lawd, to send down yo' sweet Son Jesus to walk wid us in our
sorrows to comfort us on our weary road 'cause sometimes we
don't know which-a-way to turn! We pray you dis evenin', Lawd,
to look down at our wanderin' chilluns what's gone from home.
Look down in St. Louis, Lawd, an' look in Memphis, an' look
down in Chicago if they's usin' Thy name in vain dis evenin',
if they's gamblin' tonight, Lawd, if they's doin' any ways wrong
—reach down an' pull 'em up, Lawd, an' say, 'Come wid me,
cause I am de Vine an' de Husbandman an' de gate dat leads to
Glory!' "

Remembering sons in faraway cities, "Help him, Jesus!"
mothers cried.

"Whilst you's lookin' down on us dis evenin', keep a mighty
eye on de sick an' de 'flicked. Ease Sister Hightower, Lawd,
layin' in her bed at de pint o' death. An' bless Bro' Carpenter
what's come out to meetin' here dis evenin' in spite o' his
broken arm from fallin' off de roof. An' Lawd, aid de pastor dis
evenin' to fill dis tent wid yo' Spirit, an' to make de sinners
tremble an' backsliders shout, an' dem dat is without de church
to come to de moaners' bench an' find rest in Jesus! We ask Thee
all dese favors dis evenin'. Also to guide us an' bless us wid Thy

bread an' give us Thy wine to drink fo' Christ de Holy Saviour's sake, our Shelter an' our Rock. Amen!"

"There's not a friend like de lowly Jesus . . ."

Some sister began, high and clear after the passion of the prayer,

"No, not one! . . . No, not one!"

Then the preacher took his text from the open Bible. "Ye now therefore have sorrow: but I will see you again, and your hearts shall rejoice, and your joy no man taketh from you."

He slammed shut the Holy Book and walked to the edge of the platform. "That's what Jesus said befo' he went to the cross, children—'I will see you again, and yo' hearts shall rejoice!' "

"Yes, sir!" said the brothers and sisters. " 'Deed he did!"

Then the minister began to tell the familiar story of the death of Christ. Standing in the dim light of the smoking oil lanterns, he sketched the life of the man who had had power over multitudes.

"Power," the minister said. "Power! Without money and without titles, without position, he had power! And that power went out to the poor and afflicted. For Jesus said, 'The first shall be last, and the last shall be first.' "

"He sho did!" cried Bud's mother.

"Hallelujah!" Mama agreed loudly. "Glory be to God!"

"Then the big people of the land heard about Jesus," the preacher went on, "the chief priests and the scribes, the politicians, the bootleggers, and the bankers—and they begun to conspire against Jesus because *He had power!* This Jesus with His twelve disciples preachin' in Galilee. Then came that eve of the Passover, when he set down with His friends to eat and drink of the vine and the settin' sun fell behind the hills of Jerusalem. And Jesus knew that ere the cock crew, Judas would betray Him, and Peter would say, 'I know Him not,' and all alone by Hisself He would go to His death. Yes, sir, He knew! So He got up from the table and went into the garden to pray. In this hour of trouble, Jesus went to pray!"

Away at the back of the tent some old sister began to sing:

> *"Oh, watch with me one hour*
> *While I go yonder and pray . . ."*

And the crowd took up the song, swelled it, made its melody fill the hot tent while the minister stopped talking to wipe his face with his white handkerchief.

Then, to the humming undertone of the song, he continued, "They called it Gethsemane—that garden where Jesus fell down on His face in the grass and cried to the Father, 'Let this bitter hour pass from me! Oh, God, let this hour pass.' Because He was still a young man who did not want to die, He rose up and went back into the house—but His friends was all asleep. While Jesus prayed, His friends done gone to sleep! But, 'Sleep on,' he said, 'for the hour is at hand.' Jesus said, 'Sleep on.' "

"Sleep on, sleep on," chanted the crowd, repeating the words of the minister.

"He was not angry with them. But as Jesus looked out of the house, He saw that garden alive with men carryin' lanterns and swords and staves, and the mob was everywhere. So He went to the door. Then Judas come out from among the crowd, the traitor Judas, and kissed Him on the cheek—oh, bitter friendship! And the soldiers with handcuffs fell upon the Lord and took Him prisoner.

"The disciples was awake by now, oh yes! But they fled away because they was afraid. And the mob carried Jesus off.

"Peter followed Him from afar, followed Jesus in chains till they come to the palace of the high priest. There Peter went in, timid and afraid, to see the trial. He set in the back of the hall. Peter listened to the lies they told about Christ—and didn't dispute 'em. He watched the high priest spit in Christ's face— and made no move. He saw 'em smite Him with the palms of they hands—and Peter uttered not a word for his poor mistreated Jesus."

"Not a word! . . . Not a word! . . . Not a word!"

"And when the servants of the high priest asked Peter, 'Does you know this man?' he said, 'I do not!'

"And when they asked him a second time, he said, 'No!'

"And yet a third time, 'Do you know Jesus?'

"And Peter answered with an oath, 'I told you, no!'

"Then the cock crew."

"De cock crew!" cried Aunt Ibey Davis. "De cock crew! Oh, ma Lawd! De cock crew!"

"The next day the chief priests taken counsel against Jesus to put Him to death. They brought Him before Pilate, and Pilate said, 'What evil hath he done?'

"But the people cried, 'Crucify Him!' because they didn't care. So Pilate called for water and washed his hands.

"The soldiers made sport of Jesus where He stood in the Council Hall. They stripped Him naked, and put a crown of thorns on His head, a red robe about His body, and a reed from the river in His hands.

"They said, 'Ha! Ha! So you're the King! Ha! Ha!' And they bowed down in mockery before Him, makin' fun of Jesus.

"Some of the guards threw wine in His face. Some of the guards was drunk and called Him out o' His name—and nobody said, 'Stop! That's Jesus!' "

The Reverend Duke Braswell's face darkened with horror as he pictured the death of Christ. "Oh yes! Peter denied Him because he was afraid. Judas betrayed Him for thirty pieces of silver. Pilate said, 'I wash my hands—take Him and kill Him.'

"And His friends fled away! . . . Have mercy on Jesus! . . . His friends done fled away!"

"His friends!"

"His friends done fled away!"

The preacher chanted, half moaning his sentences, not speaking them. His breath came in quick, short gasps, with an indrawn "umn!" between each rapid phrase. Perspiration poured down his face as he strode across the platform, wrapped in this drama that he saw in the very air before his eyes. Peering over the heads of his audience out into the darkness, he began the ascent to Golgotha, describing the taunting crowd at Christ's heels and the heavy cross on His shoulders.

"Then a black man named Simon, blacker than me, come and took the cross and bore it for Him. Umn!

"Then Jesus were standin' alone on a high hill, in the broilin' sun, while they put the crosses in the ground. No water to cool His throat! No tree to shade His achin' head! Nobody to say a friendly word to Jesus! Umn!

"Alone, in that crowd on the hill of Golgotha, with two thieves bound and dyin', and the murmur of the mob all around. Umn!

"But Jesus never said a word! Umn!

"They laid they hands on Him, and they tore the clothes from His body—and then, and then"—loud as a thunderclap, the minister's voice broke through the little tent—"they raised Him to the cross!"

A great wail went up from the crowd. Bud and I sat entranced in spite of ourselves, forgetting to smoke. Aunt Ibey Davis wept. Sister Mabry moaned. In their car behind us the white people were silent as the minister went on:

> *"They brought four long iron nails*
> *And put one in the palm of His left hand.*
> *The hammer said . . . Bam!*
> *They put one in the palm of His right hand.*
> *The hammer said . . . Bam!*
> *They put one through His left foot . . . Bam!*
> *And one through His right foot . . . Bam!"*

"Don't drive it!" a woman screamed. "Don't drive them nails! For Christ's sake! Oh! Don't drive 'em!"

> *"And they left my Jesus on the cross!*
> *Nails in His hands! Nails in His feet!*
> *Sword in His side! Thorns circlin' His head!*
> *Mob cussin' and hootin' my Jesus! Umn!*
> *The spit of the mob in His face! Umn!*
> *His body hangin' on the cross! Umn!*
> *Gimme piece of His garment for a souvenir! Umn!*
> *Castin' lots for His garments! Umn!*
> *Blood from His wounded side! Umn!*
> *Streamin' down His naked legs! Umn!*

Droppin' in the dust—umn—
That's what they did to my Jesus!
They stoned Him first, they stoned Him!
Called Him everything but a child of God.
Then they lynched Him on the cross."

In song I heard my mother's voice cry:

"Were you there when they crucified my Lord?
Were you there when they nailed Him to the tree?"

The Reverend Duke Braswell stretched wide his arms against the white canvas of the tent. In the yellow light his body made a cross-like shadow on the canvas.

"Oh, it makes me to tremble, tremble!
Were you there when they crucified my Lord?"

"Let's go," said the white woman in the car behind us. "This is too much for me!" They started the motor and drove noisily away in a swirl of dust.

"Don't go," I cried from where I was sitting at the root of the tree. "Don't go," I shouted, jumping up. "They're about to call for sinners to come to the mourners' bench. Don't go!" But their car was already out of earshot.

I didn't realize I was crying until I tasted my tears in my mouth.

Breakfast in Virginia

Two colored boys during the war. For the first time in his life one of them, on furlough from a Southern training camp, was coming North. His best buddy was a New York lad, also on furlough, who had invited him to visit Harlem. Being colored, they had to travel in the Jim Crow car until the Florida Express reached Washington.

The train was crowded and people were standing in WHITE day coaches and in the COLORED coach—the single Jim Crow car. Corporal Ellis and Corporal Williams had, after much insistence, shared for a part of the night the seats of other kindly passengers in the coach marked COLORED. They took turns sleeping for a few hours. The rest of the time they sat on the arm of a seat or stood smoking in the vestibule. By morning they were very tired. And they were hungry.

No vendors came into the Jim Crow coach with food, so Corporal Ellis suggested to his friend that they go into the diner and have breakfast. Corporal Ellis was born in New York and grew up there. He had been a star track man with his college team, and had often eaten in diners on trips with his teammates. Corporal Williams had never eaten in a diner before, but he followed his friend. It was midmorning. The rush period was over, although the dining car was still fairly full. But, fortunately, just at the door as they entered there were three seats at a table for four persons. The sole occupant of the table was a tall, distinguished gray-haired man. A white man.

As the two brownskin soldiers stood at the door waiting for the steward to seat them, the white man looked up and said, "Won't you sit here and be my guests this morning? I have a son fighting in North Africa. Come, sit down."

"Thank you, sir," said Corporal Ellis, "this is kind of you. I am Corporal Ellis. This is Corporal Williams."

The elderly man rose, gave his name, shook hands with the two colored soldiers, and the three of them sat down at the table. The young men faced their host. Corporal Williams was silent, but Corporal Ellis carried on the conversation as they waited for the steward to bring the menus.

"How long have you been in the service, Corporal?" the white man was saying as the steward approached.

Corporal Ellis could not answer this question because the steward cut in brusquely, "You boys can't sit here."

"These men are my guests for breakfast, steward," said the white man.

"I am sorry, sir," said the white steward, "but Negroes cannot be served now. If there's time, we may have a fourth sitting before luncheon for them, if they want to come back."

"But these men are soldiers," said the white man.

"I am sorry, sir. We will take *your* order, but I cannot serve them in the state of Virginia."

The two Negro soldiers were silent. The white man rose. He looked at the steward a minute, then said, "I am embarrassed, steward, both for you and for my guests." To the soldiers he said, "If you gentlemen will come with me to my drawing room, we will have breakfast there. Steward, I would like a waiter immediately, Room E, the third car back."

The tall, distinguished man turned and led the way out of the diner. The two soldiers followed him. They passed through the club car, through the open Pullmans, and into a coach made up entirely of compartments. The white man led them along the blue-gray corridor, stopped at the last door, and opened it.

"Come in," he said. He waited for the soldiers to enter.

It was a roomy compartment with a large window and two long comfortable seats facing each other. The man indicated a place for the soldiers, who sat down together. He pressed a button.

"I will have the porter bring a table," he said. Then he went on with the conversation just as if nothing had happened. He told them of recent letters from his son overseas, and of his pride in all the men in the military services who were giving up the pleasures of civilian life to help bring an end to Hitlerism. Shortly the porter arrived with the table. Soon a waiter spread a cloth and took their order. In a little while the food was there.

All this time Corporal Williams from the South had said nothing. He sat, shy and bewildered, as the Virginia landscape passed outside the train window. Then he drank his orange juice with loud gulps. But when the eggs were brought, suddenly he spoke, "This here time, sir, is the first time I ever been invited to eat with a white man. I'm from Georgia."

"I hope it won't be the last time," the white man replied. "Breaking bread together is the oldest symbol of human friendship." He passed the silver tray. "Would you care for rolls or muffins, Corporal? I am sorry there is no butter this morning. guess we're on rations."

"I can eat without butter," said the corporal.

For the first time his eyes met those of his host. He smiled. Through the window of the speeding train, as it neared Washington, clear in the morning sunlight yet far off in the distance, they could see the dome of the Capitol. But the soldier from the Deep South was not looking out of the window. He was looking across the table at his fellow American.

"I thank you for this breakfast," said Corporal Williams.

Blessed Assurance

Unfortunately (and to John's distrust of God) it seemed his son was turning out to be a queer. He was a brilliant queer, on the Honor Roll in high school, and likely to be graduated in the spring at the head of the class. But the boy was colored. Since colored parents always like to put their best foot forward, John was more disturbed about his son's transition than if they had been white. Negroes have enough crosses to bear.

Delmar was his only son, Arletta, the younger child, being a girl. Perhaps John should not have permitted his son to be named Delmar—Delly for short—but the mother had insisted on it. Delmar was *her* father's name.

"And he is *my* son as well as yours," his wife informed John.

Did the queer strain come from *her* side? Maternal grandpa had seemed normal enough. He was known to have had several affairs with women outside his home—mostly sisters of Tried Stone Church of which he was a pillar.

God forbid! John, Delly's father thought, could he himself have had any deviate ancestors? None who had acted even remotely effeminate could John recall as being a part of his family. Anyhow, why didn't he name the boy at birth *John, Jr.*, after

himself? But his wife said, "Don't saddle him with Junior."
Yet she had saddled him with Delmar.

If only Delly were not such a sweet boy—no juvenile delin-
quency, no stealing cars, no smoking reefers ever. He did the
chores without complaint. He washed dishes too easily, with no
argument, when he might have left them to Arletta. He seldom,
even when at the teasing stage, pulled his sister's hair. They
played together, Delly with dolls almost as long as Arletta did.
Yet he was good at marbles, once fair at baseball, and a real
whizz at tennis. He could have made the track team had he not
preferred the French Club, the Dramatic Club, and Glee Club.
Football, his father's game in high school, Delly didn't like.
He couldn't keep his eye on the ball in scrimmage. At seventeen he had to have glasses. The style of rather exaggerated
rims he chose made him look like a girl rather than a boy.

"At least he didn't get rhinestone rims," thought John half-
thought didn't think felt faint and aloud said nothing. That
spring he asked, "Delmar, do you have to wear *white* Bermuda
shorts to school? Most of the other boys wear levis or just plain
pants, don't they? And why wash them out yourself every night,
all that ironing? I want you to be clean, son, but not *that* clean."

Another time, "Delmar, those school togs of yours don't have
to match so perfectly, do they? Colors *blended*, as you say, and
all like that. This school you're going to's no fashion school—
at least, it wasn't when I went there. The boys'll think you're
sissy."

Once again desperately, "If you're going to smoke, Delmar,
hold your cigarette between your *first* two fingers, not between
your thumb and finger—like a woman."

Then his son cried.

John remembered how it was before the boy's mother packed
up and left their house to live with another man who made
more money than any Negro in their church. He kept an
apartment in South Philly and another in Harlem. Owned
a Cadillac. Racket connections—politely called *politics*. A shame
for his children, for the church, and for him, John! His wife
gone with an uncouth rascal!

But although Arletta loathed him, Delly liked his not-yet-legal stepfather. Delly's mother and her burly lover had at least had the decency to leave Germantown and change their religious affiliations. They no longer attended John's family church where Delmar sang in the Junior Choir.

Delly had a sweet high tenor with overtones of Sam Cooke. The women at Tried Stone loved him. Although Tried Stone was a Baptist church, it tended toward the sedate—Northern Baptist in tone, not down-home. Yet it did have a Gospel Choir, scarlet robed, since a certain untutored segment of the membership demanded lively music. It had a Senior Choir, too, black robed, that specialized in anthems, sang *Jesu, Joy of Man's Desiring*, the Bach cantatas, and once a year presented *The Messiah*. The white robed Junior Choir, however, even went so far as to want to render a jazz recessional—Delly's idea—which was vetoed. This while he was trying to grow a beard like the beatniks he had seen when the Junior Choir sang in New York and the Minister of Music had taken Delly on a trip to the Village.

"God, don't let him put an earring in his ear like some," John prayed. He wondered vaguely with a sick feeling in his stomach should he think it through then then think it through right then through should he try then and think it through should without blacking through think blacking out then and there think it through?

John didn't. But one night he remembered his son had once told his mother that after he graduated from high school he would like to study at the Sorbonne. The Sorbonne in Paris! John had studied at Morgan in Baltimore. In possession of a diploma from that *fine* (in his mind) Negro institute he took pride. Normally John would have wanted his boy to go there, yet the day after the Spring Concert he asked Delmar, "Son, do you still want to study in France? If you do, maybe—er—I guess I could next fall—Sorbonne. Say, how much is a ticket to Paris?"

In October it would be John's turn to host his fraternity brothers at his house. Maybe by then Delmar would—is the

Sorbonne like Morgan? Does it have dormitories, a campus? In Paris he had heard they didn't care about such things. Care about such what things didn't care about what? At least no color lines.

Well, anyhow, what happened at the concert a good six months before October came was, well—think it through clearly now, get it right. Especially for that Spring Concert, Tried Stone's Minister of Music, Dr. Manley Jaxon, had written an original anthem, words and score his own, based on the story of Ruth:

> "Entreat me not to leave thee,
> Neither to go far from thee.
> Whither thou goeth, I will go.
> Always will I be near thee. . . ."

The work was dedicated to Delmar who received the first handwritten manuscript copy as a tribute from Dr. Jaxon. In spite of its dedication, one might have thought that in performance the solo lead—Ruth's part—would be assigned to a woman. Perversely enough, the composer allotted it to Delmar. Dr. Jaxon's explanation was, "No one else can do it justice." The Minister of Music declared, "The girls in the ensemble really have *no* projection."

So without respect for gender, on the Sunday afternoon of the program, Delmar sang the female lead. Dr. Jaxon, saffron robed, was at the organ. Until Delmar's father attended the concert that day, he had no inkling as to the casting of the anthem. But, when his son's solo began, all John could say was, "I'll be damned!"

John had hardly gotten the words out of his mouth when words became of no further value. The "Papa, what's happening?" of his daughter in the pew beside him made hot saliva rise in his throat—for what suddenly had happened was that as the organ wept and Delmar's voice soared above the Choir with all the sweetness of Sam Cooke's *tessitura,* backwards off the organ stool in a dead faint fell Dr. Manley Jaxon. Not only did Dr. Jaxon fall from the stool, but he rolled limply down the steps from the organ loft like a bag of meal and tumbled prone onto the rostrum, robes and all.

Amens and *Hallelujahs* drowned in the throats of various elderly sisters who were on the verge of shouting. Swooning teen-age maidens suddenly sat up in their pews to see the excitement. Springing from his chair on the rostrum, the pastor's mind deserted the pending collection to try to think what to say under the unusual circumstances.

"One down, one to go," was all that came to mind. After a series of pastorates in numerous sophisticated cities where Negroes did everything whites do, the Reverend Dr. Greene had seen other choir directors take the count in various ways with equal drama, though perhaps less physical immediacy.

When the organ went silent, the choir died, too—but Delmar never stopped singing. Over the limp figure of Dr. Jaxon lying on the rostrum, the "Entreat me not to leave thee" of his solo flooded the church as if it were on hi-fi.

The members of the congregation sat riveted in their pews as the deacons rushed to the rostrum to lift the Minister of Music to his feet. Several large ladies of the Altar Guild fanned him vigorously while others sprinkled him with water. But it was not until the church's nurse-in-uniform applied smelling salts to Dr. Jaxon's dark nostrils, did he lift his head. Finally, two ushers led him off to an anteroom while Delmar's voice soared to a high C such as Tried Stone Baptist Church had never heard.

"Bless God! Amen!" cried Reverend Greene. "Dr. Jaxon has only fainted, friends. We will continue our services by taking up collection directly after the anthem."

"Daddy, why did Dr. Jaxon have to faint just when brother started singing?" whispered John's daughter.

"I don't know," John said.

"Some of the girls say that when Delmar sings, they want to scream, they're so overcome," whispered Arletta. "But Dr. Jaxon didn't scream. He just fainted."

"Shut up," John said, staring straight ahead at the choir loft.

"Oh, God! Delmar, *shut up!*" John's hands gripped the back of the seat in front of him. "Shut up, son! *Shut up*," he cried. "Shut up!"

Silence. . . .

"We will now lift the offering," announced the minister. "Ushers, get the baskets." Reverend Greene stepped forward. "Deacons, raise a hymn. Bear us up, sisters, bear us up!"

His voice boomed:

> "Blessed assurance!"

He clapped his hands once.

> "Jesus is mine!"

"Yes! Yes! Yes!" he cried.

> "Oh, what a fortress
> Of glory divine!"

The congregation swung gently into song:

> "Heir of salvation,
> Purchase of God!"

"Hallelujah! Amen! Halle! Halle!"

> "Born of the Spirit"

"God damn it!" John cried. "God *damn* it!"

> "Washed in His blood. . . ."

Something in Common

Hong Kong. A hot day. A teeming street. A mélange of races. A pub, over the door the Union Jack.

The two men were not together. They came in from the street, complete strangers, through different doors, but they both

reached the bar at about the same time. The big British bartender looked at each of them with a wary, scornful eye. He
knew that, more than likely, neither had the price of more than
a couple of drinks. They were distinctly down at the heel, had
been drinking elsewhere, and were not customers of the bar.
He served them with a deliberation that was not even condescending—it was menacing.

"A beer," said the old Negro, rattling a handful of Chinese
and English coins at the end of a frayed cuff.

"A Scotch," said the old white man, reaching for a pretzel
with thin fingers.

"That's the tariff," said the bartender, pointing to a sign.

"Too high for this lousy Hong Kong beer," said the old
Negro.

The barman did not deign to answer.

"But reckon it's as good as some we got back home," the elderly colored man went on as he counted out the money.

"I'll bet you wouldn't mind bein' back there, George," spoke
up the old white man from the other end of the bar, "in the
good old U.S.A."

"Don't *George* me," said the Negro, " 'cause I don't know you
from Adam."

"Well, don't get sore," said the old white man, coming nearer,
sliding his glass along the bar. "I'm from down home, too."

"Well, I ain't from no *down home*," answered the Negro wiping beer foam from his mouth. "I'm from the North."

"Where?"

"North of Mississippi," said the black man. "I mean Missouri."

"I'm from Kentucky," vouched the old white fellow, swallow-
ing his whisky. "Gimme another one," to the bartender.

"Half a dollar," said the bartender.

"Mex, you mean?"

"Yeah, mex," growled the bartender picking up the glass.

"All right, I'll pay you," said the white man testily. "Gimme
another one."

"They're tough in this here bar," said the old Negro sarcastically. "Looks like they don't know a Kentucky colonel when they see one."

"No manners in these damned foreign joints," said the white man seriously. "How long you been in Hong Kong?"

"Too long," said the old Negro.

"Where'd you come from here?"

"Manila," said the Negro.

"What'd you do there?"

"Now what else do you want to know?" asked the Negro.

"I'm askin' you a civil question," said the old white man.

"Don't ask so many then," said the Negro, "and don't start out by callin' me *George*. My name ain't George."

"What is your name, might I ask?" taking another pretzel.

"Samuel Johnson. And your'n?"

"Colonel McBride."

"Of Kentucky?" grinned the Negro, impudently toothless.

"Yes, sir, of Kentucky," said the white man seriously.

"Howdy, Colonel," said the Negro. "Have a pretzel."

"Have a drink, boy," said the white man, beckoning the bartender.

"Don't call me *boy*," said the Negro. "I'm as old as you, if not older."

"Don't care," said the white man, "have a drink."

"Gin," said the Negro.

"Make it two," said the white man. "Gin's somethin' we both got in common."

"I love gin," said the Negro.

"Me, too," said the white man.

"Gin's a sweet drink," mused the Negro, "especially when you're around women."

"Gimme one white woman," said the old white man, "and you can take all these Chinee gals over here."

"Gimme one yellow gal," said the old Negro, "and you can take all your white women anywhere."

"Hong Kong's full of yellow gals," said the white man.

"I mean *high-yellow* gals," said the Negro, "like we have in Missouri."

"Or in Kentucky," said the white man, "where half of 'em has white pappys."

"Here! Don't talk 'bout my women," said the old Negro. "I don't allow no white man to talk 'bout my women."

"Who's talkin' about your women? Have a drink, George."

"I told you, don't *George* me. My name is Samuel Johnson. White man, you ain't in Kentucky now. You in the Far East."

"I know it. If I was in Kentucky, I wouldn't be standin' at this bar with you. Have a drink."

"Gin."

"Make it two."

"Who's payin'?" said the bartender.

"Not me," said the Negro. "Not *me*."

"Don't worry," said the old white man grandly.

"Well, I am worryin'," growled the bartender. "Cough up."

"Here," said the white man, pulling out a few shillings. "Here, even if it is my last penny, here!"

The bartender took it without a word. He picked up the glasses and wiped the bar.

"I can't seem to get ahead in this damn town," said the old white man, "and I been here since Coolidge."

"Neither do I," said the Negro, "and I come before the war."

"Where is your home, George?" asked the white man.

"You must think it's Georgia," said the Negro. "Truth is, I ain't got no home—no more home than a dog."

"Neither have I," said the white man, "but sometimes I wish I was back in the States."

"Well, I don't," said the Negro. "A black man ain't got a break in the States."

"What?" said the old white man, drawing up proudly.

"States is no good," said the Negro. "No damned good."

"Shut up," yelled the old white man waving a pretzel.

"What do you mean, shut up?" said the Negro.

"I won't listen to nobody runnin' down the United States," said the white man. "You better stop insultin' America, you big black ingrate."

"You better stop insultin' me, you poor-white trash," bristled the aged Negro. Both of them reeled indignantly.

"Why, you black bastard!" quavered the old white man.

"You white cracker!" trembled the elderly Negro.

These final insults caused the two old men to square off like roosters, rocking a little from age and gin, but glaring fiercely at one another, their gnarled fists doubled up, arms at boxing angles.

"Here! Here!" barked the bartender. "Hey! Stop it now!"

"I'll bat you one," said the white man to the Negro.

"I'll fix you so you can't leave, neither can you stay," said the Negro to the white.

"Yuh will, will yuh?" sneered the bartender to both of them. "I'll see about batting—and fixing, too."

He came around the end of the bar in three long strides. He grabbed the two old men unceremoniously by the scruff of their necks, cracked their heads together twice, and threw them both calmly into the street. Then he wiped his hands.

The white and yellow world of Hong Kong moved by, ricksha runners pushed and panted, motor horns blared, pedestrians crowded the narrow sidewalks. The two old men picked themselves up from the dust and dangers of a careless traffic. They looked at one another, dazed for a moment and considerably shaken.

"Well, I'll be damned!" sputtered the old white man. "Are we gonna stand for this—from a Limey bartender?"

"Hell, no," said the old Negro. "Let's go back in there and clean up that joint."

"He's got no rights to put his Cockney hands on Americans," said the old white man.

"Sure ain't," agreed the old Negro.

Arm in arm, they staggered back into the bar, united to protect their honor against the British—or anybody else who might at the moment come between them.

3007